Alcatraz
The Lost Pearl

A.R. ROBINSON

ALCATRAZ THE LOST PEARL

Published by Authenticity Print

Copyright ©2011 by A.R. Robinson

Cover Illustration by Go Bold Designs by Cory Clubb
Interior design and layout by A.R. Robinson
Edited by Ginger Schmaus, Lisa Lickel and Rachel McDermott

ISBN-13: 978-1508798804
ISBN-10: 150879880X

www.lovegodandtattoos.com

Printed in the U.S.A via Createspace

DEDICATION

Thank you God for trusting me with Alcatraz. I pray your sheep hear your voice.

LOVE, GOD & TATTOOS SERIES

Alcatraz The Lost Pearl
Alcatraz The Righteous Pearl
Kuriko The Damaged Pearl: A Novella
Alcatraz The Prodigal Pearl
Alcatraz The Found Pearl
Ebony The Backslidden Pearl: A Novella
Alcatraz The Restored Pearl

1

My first art class was simple: stick figures, plain white paper, water colors, crayons, and colored pencils. The first thing I drew wasn't perfect, but it awakened something within me. At six years old, I discovered my line of communication in a colored pencil as I drew a blue jay soaring over the pond in my backyard. I had found my reason for survival. Since that day, I have spent every waking moment drawing. My tools were a green one-subject Mead notebook, a number two pencil, Crayola colored pencils and coloring books. I covered the notebook with butterfly drawings and it soon became my best friend. I drew everything from flowers and birds to family portraits, Hollywood pinup girls, and beautiful strangers I noticed in the marketplace.

Mom noticed my passion with art and as I progressed she started to buy me expensive materials:

Utrecht acrylic paint, Loew Cornell American Painter paintbrushes, Strathmore 400 series drawing paper and Tombow pencils. I begged her to buy magazines with picture-perfect celebrities so I could hone my craft. I also forced my family to pose in different positions for freestyle portraits. They hated holding one position for a long time, but the finished product was worth the wait. When I had a break at school, I was drawing. When I hung out with my family or friends, I was drawing. Before I slept at night, I retouched a frame I was working on. The art obsession of my childhood eventually developed me into the tattoo artist I am today.

My art sparked a curiosity about God even though my parents weren't religious. As my inner artist awakened, I deeply believed there was an invisible force behind the scenes. The more time I spent drawing, the more I felt connected to an organic, internal flow. I couldn't put my finger on who or what it was, but I knew God existed. Even now, when I sit down to draw I feel like I am flying with someone above all the trials and tribulations of this world.

I believe whatever goes on in the unseen world is more real than what I can see. I liken this theory to the process of getting a tattoo. When customers come into my shop and describe the tattoo they want, I envision the image in my mind's eye before it becomes tangible. Most art begins this way. Musicians hear tunes before they play. Chefs taste dishes before they cook. Architects conceptualize buildings prior to sketching them. Humankind follows the same process. Life is formed inside a woman's belly before she knows she is pregnant, and after nine months of development a child is birthed into the world. Everything that is seen comes into being from the unseen. It is a natural way of life.

When I was in the fourth grade I painted a delicate blue angel holding a purple Earth in the palm of her hand. The angel had striking facial features, innocent eyes and long, flowing green hair. Her face showed a deep, underlying wisdom.

My art teacher walked over and asked, "What is that, Katherine?"

"God!" I exclaimed without hesitation.

"You believe God is a woman?"

"I guess so."

"I see," she replied. "And what does God represent to you?"

"I don't know yet, but I guess life, in a sense. I mean, how else could I breathe? My parents don't breathe for me."

"Well, I hate to be the bearer of bad news, honey. Your parents might not breathe for you, but they'll probably do more for you in life than God ever will." She paused. "Well, I'll let you get back to your work, dear."

What? If God never helped me in life, where did my art come from? I left class furious and hurt because I thought my angel was beautiful. That afternoon when Mom picked me and my sister up from school, I whipped out my picture.

"Cool!" Natalie said.

"Oh my goodness, Katherine!" Mom agreed. "This is a masterpiece. You painted this all by yourself?"

"Yeah, in art class."

"Oh wow, baby, this is gorgeous!"

"What is it? An angel?" Nat asked.

"Nothing, really," I said, not wanting to talk about the incident.

"What do you mean, 'nothing, really'? This looks like something special to me," Mom said.

"It doesn't matter."

"Why would you say that?" Mom asked.

"'Cause the teacher said so."

"What?" Mom yelled.

"Since when do you care what your teacher said?" Nat asked.

"What did that witch say?"

"This is my version of God, Mom. But my teacher said you guys will help me more than God ever would," I said.

"She said that to you?" Nat said.

"Yeah."

"Well, guess what? I think your version of God is valid," Mom said. "If that is what you believe, then that is your truth. If you don't stand for something you'll fall for anything. Don't let that old hag get in the way of your search. This is your life, honey, and you have to live it your way."

"You think so?" I asked.

"Yeah, what does she know anyway? She's just a fat, ugly, miserable art teacher," Natalie said.

"Natalie!" Mom scolded.

"Sorry, Mom, but it's true. She puts down everybody in class."

"Really? I'm going to have a meeting with her as soon as possible because I won't allow that!"

"That's right, Mom. Get her!" Natalie joked.

"You guys really like my painting?" I asked, needing some assurance.

"Yes, I do," Mom said. "And to prove it, I'm going to Home Depot right now to find the perfect frame for this masterpiece. I'll hang it over the fireplace in the den."

"Really? You're gonna put it up?"

"Well of course I am, darling. I love you and all the work you do. Your interpretation is your interpretation. Don't let my life or your father's mold yours. You find out the answers for yourself. You hear me?"

"I hear you."

"You hear me, Nat?"

"Heard."

"Great. Let's go pick up your brother and head to Home Depot," Mom said.

Both of my parents were raised in religious homes, yet religion was not a staple in our home. Dad was raised a Jew in Chicago, and Mom a Baptist in North Carolina. I knew we were Jewish because Dad occasionally talked about his Jewish upbringing, but we never visited the synagogue three minutes from our house. There were no Torah readings, prayer or holiday observances. Judaism was just a badge we wore, along with our entire neighborhood. I think Dad was ashamed of his beliefs, though. He talked about how Jews were persecuted heavily way back in the day and weren't allowed in San Diego. Jews were looked upon as property, not human beings.

Dad said his family had been serious about Judaism. On Saturdays he and his brother could do absolutely nothing but keep the Sabbath. To my grandparents, the Sabbath represented a restful celebration. To my dad and his brother, Saturdays were torture. They couldn't study, play, accept phone calls or watch television. They couldn't even touch money. Dad's father made them sit in the house and listen to the stories of Abraham, Isaac, and Jacob. They repeated the books of Moses and the Psalms of David. After reading the Scriptures they went to the synagogue for more teaching. Dad said Rabbi Schneider "had to be the most boring teacher ever to walk the earth." Dad often fell asleep during service and his brother would kick him in the shin. The only things Dad liked about being a Jew were the many festivals, which included lots of food, wine, music and dancing. His favorite festival was Purim.

"Oh, I loved Purim," Dad exclaimed one time as he tucked me and Nat into bed. "It was known as the Jewish Mardi Gras, celebrating the deliverance of the Jews from the Persian Empire. The story is about an ill-willed man named Haman who planned to kill all us Jews in the Babylonian Empire, but he was stopped by a woman named Esther. Rabbi Schneider read the entire book of Esther every night of Purim in remembrance of her great deed. I didn't really care about the reasons for the celebration, I just cared about fun. Like every time Rabbi said the name Haman, we all made a lot of noise."

"Really?" I asked.

"Yeah. We would start hissing and stomping and rattling stuff. This holiday was the only time they allowed noise in the synagogue."

"Why would you guys make so much noise?" Natalie asked.

"Well, Haman was trying to kill the Jews back then out of sheer hatred. He was prejudiced to the max," I could tell my dad believed this story because his voice choked up and his face reddened. "Anyway, when the king appointed him to the royal court, he just went crazy and used his powers to hurt us. But God favored the Jews by exalting Esther as Queen of the Empire. And even though women didn't have any authority back then she stood up against Haman, her husband the king and the Persian council to set her people free!

"So, to disrespect Haman we wrote his name on the soles of our shoes and stomped our feet on the ground when Rabbi mentioned his name. I didn't understand it at the time, but now, looking back, it symbolized our victory over the enemy. After Rabbi finished, it was tradition to send two baskets of food to a friend and give money and food to two poor people. The gifts to friends were called *mischloach manot* and the gifts to the poor were called *Tzedakah*...wow! It's amazing I can remember the names after all these years."

"Sounds like you guys had a lot of fun, Dad," I said.

"Yeah, seriously," Natalie added.

"Oh, we did, and I haven't even told you my favorite part. Purim was like our Halloween, so we used to dress up in different costumes. I used to love dressing up like King David because he was my favorite character in the Bible, but other people used to go all out displaying all kinds of fun masks and Old Testament costumes. The kids played games, partied, and got drunk from wine. It was really a festive time. And the food?" Dad smiled and continued, "I mean this meal was beyond anything you'd ever experience. We ate these pastries called hamantaschen. They're like cookie dough filled with prunes and poppy seeds. And Kreplach was my absolute favorite dish!"

"Why don't we celebrate any of that stuff now?" I asked. I wanted to be a part of this festive time that brought my dad so much pleasure.

"Well, honey." He sighed. "That was fun and great as a kid, but as I grew older I noticed those traditions and stories really weren't useful for everyday life. I mean, Moses was a great character in the Bible, but I didn't see how he was helping me pay bills or get a job or raise a family. You know? I think as far as morals and character are concerned, Judaism instilled a lot in me, but your mother and I instill those same principles in you without all the hoopla. I mean, the Torah, as interesting as it is to read--" Dad hesitated. "It's is just not practical, baby. Maybe the Psalms and Proverbs, but all that other stuff is history. My dad forced our family to keep the Sabbath, yet he divorced my mom and ran off with his secretary from his job. If religion was so strong then why couldn't this man keep his family together?" His voice saddened. "Anyway, when I turned eighteen, I said goodbye to religion altogether and never looked back."

He paused a bit then asked, "Do you believe in God?"

"Yeah, I do," I said.

"Me, too," Natalie said. "I believe there is a God."

"Well, that's wonderful. I'm proud of you two. We all have to find the truth on our own, and if God is your truth then I'd be happy to learn more about him with you."

"Thanks, Daddy," I said.

"You're welcome, baby. Goodnight." He kissed us both on the forehead.

Mom didn't openly talk about her family or the Baptist Church. She had a traumatic experience with one of the elders in the church, then fell out with her parents because they didn't believe her. All she would ever say was "You can't have relationships with people you don't trust." I never heard another word about it.

* * * *

Monday, November 17, 2003

I remember this day vividly because an internal void crept into my heart during Mrs. Reed's second period art class. I was 13 and had begun to sharpen my drawing skills. I'd drawn a beautiful portrait of my entire family in class: Henry, Natalie, Mom, Dad and me. I was coloring in Nat's eyes when Mrs. Reed came over to my desk.

"That's a lovely portrait," she said.

"It's my family: me, Mom, Dad, my brother and sister," I said, proudly pointing to each individual. "This is our fireplace in the den."

"Why don't you ever draw your real family?" asked Mrs. Reed.

"What do you mean, my real family? This is my real family!"

She looked at me strangely, then raised her eyebrows. "Oh, sweetheart, the Boydsteins never told you?"

"Told me what?"

Mrs. Reed must have realized she had opened a can of worms because she said, "Maybe I ought to wait and let them explain it to you."

"Explain what?" I screamed, wanting an answer

immediately. By now the entire art class was staring in bewilderment.

Mrs. Reed hesitated. "Well, you were adopted when you were a baby, sweetheart. A Spanish lady gave birth to you, not Mrs. Boydstein."

When she said those words it felt like she had stuck a knife into my stomach, slit it up to my chest and twisted it around. All the air was sucked out of my lungs. I sat there too shocked to retaliate, too petrified to cry. Mrs. Reed observed her damage and quickly added, "They adopted you because they loved you, Katherine. You ought to feel lucky. There are a lot of orphans in the world who haven't a single soul to care for them, but you are very special. You have a wonderful, fine family."

I had always been satisfied with my life. I had no yearnings or cravings because I experienced a contentment, a fullness with my family and my art. This news had struck a nerve, and within seconds I felt like an illegitimate child, unloved, unwanted and unworthy. Now that I knew my own flesh and blood had rejected me, my heart bled. An insatiable desire to learn my roots surfaced and became a priority as my identity splattered out onto Mrs. Reed's floor.

When Mom picked me up that afternoon she sensed trouble quicker than a K-9 dog senses drugs. There was absolutely no way I could hide my emotions, especially from the woman who had lied to me all my life. When I got into the front seat, I slammed the door shut and turned directly to Mom. I stared her deep in her eyes and asked her flat out, "Am I adopted?"

She had been eating Ben and Jerry's ice cream, but now she paused. "What?" she asked around the spoon in her mouth.

"Am I adopted? Mrs. Reed told me that you and Dad aren't my real parents. Is that true?"

"She said what?" Mom screamed.

"She told me that you and Dad aren't my real parents. That some Spanish lady was."

Mom sat in the driver's seat looking stunned. I have seen Mom mad before, but this was the frosting on the cake. Without saying another word, she threw down her ice cream, turned the car off and stormed into Stevenson Prep, locking the car behind her. With the fire I saw in her eyes I prayed to God she didn't light a match to the school when she saw Mrs. Reed. I mean, she was furious. At the time I didn't understand, but looking back I can definitely understand. Adoption was a conversation my parents and I were supposed to have privately, not me, my schoolteacher, and the entire art class.

Thump, thump, thump, thump. I turned around to see Natalie outside knocking on the car window. I unlocked the car. "Where's Mom?" she asked as she got situated in the backseat.

"She's talking with Mrs. Reed."

"About what?"

I turned around to face her. "Natalie, did you know I was adopted?"

"What? Adopted? Nuh huh. Who told you that?"

"Mrs. Reed. She told me you guys aren't my real family."

"What is up with these art teachers of yours? First one teacher tells you there's no God, now another tells you you're adopted? Are they letting off a little steam before they retire, or what?" She paused. "Do you believe her?"

"Well, at first no, but after Mom's reaction I'm starting to wonder. She was furious, Nat, and stormed into the school like a raging bull."

"Wow. Mrs. Reed is probably getting cussed out as we speak. What an awful thing to say to somebody. I mean, even if it's true, you don't tell a student she's adopted in the middle of class. How tacky!"

"What if she's right, though?" I lowered my head, contemplating the reality that the Boydstein's could very well not be my family. They were the only family I'd ever known. "What if another family did give me away? I wouldn't know who they were if I stood next to them at Vons. Oh my God!" I cried, starting to get frustrated. "What if we were sitting next to my parents at the Cheesecake Factory? How would I know?"

"Katherine, calm down. I'm sure Mom and Dad will explain everything to you if it's true. Don't get all worked up without knowing the whole story."

"Mrs. Reed said my mom was Spanish. I guess that explains why I look so different than you guys."

"Well, yeah, that's true. You do look a lot different than me and Henry," Nat admitted. "But I just thought you took after Grandma. She was dark." Natalie was referring to Mom's mom who had a Native American background.

"Yeah, I guess that's true. I do resemble her quite a bit."

"That's what I'm saying, Kat. Don't get all worked up over what could be nothing. Let's just wait and-"

Just then the car door swung open. Mom flopped into the driver's seat and slammed the door shut. Natalie and I didn't utter a word. Mom's face was beet red, painted with black eye-liner tears, and her eyes were bloodshot. Without a sound she turned on the car, fastened her seatbelt, and raced home.

Natalie and I were told to go to our room when we arrived. As soon as we closed the door to our bedroom I whipped around and pleaded, "Are you sure you don't know anything about my adoption?"

"No. I've known you as long as I can remember."

That was true. Natalie was only a year older than me.

"I wonder if Henry knows anything," I said.

"Let's go ask."

We pounded on Henry's door a few seconds before stampeding into his room.

"What did I do? Hey, what's going?" Henry shouted as I pushed him onto the bed.

"Did you know I was adopted?" I asked him, not wanting to waste any time.

"What?"

"Did you know I was adopted? Don't lie to me, Henry! Tell me everything you know. Now."

"Well ..." he started. "I do remember Mom bringing a baby home without having a big belly."

"What?" Natalie asked.

"When Mom was pregnant with Nat she had a big belly. She looked pregnant. Even though I was only three, I still remember Mom walking around looking really fat and throwing up all over the place."

"Eww, Henry! Gross," I exclaimed.

"Well, you told me to tell the story, didn't you?"

"You can leave the sick parts out."

"Anyway." He ignored my comment. "I was playing with my Transformer in the kitchen while Mom baked cookies. Next thing I remember was standing in a pool of water."

"Water?" Nat gasped.

"Yeah, her water broke. You know? The baby lives in water until birth," he said. "You did pass Mr. Ervin's biology class, didn't you?" he added sarcastically. After Nat punched him in the arm he continued his story. "Dad ran into the kitchen after she dropped her baking pan on the floor and he rushed her off to the hospital. A short time later you were born, Natalie, vampire fangs and all."

"Oh shut up, Henry, and just tell the story!" Natalie screamed while punching him in the arm again. By this time I was positive poor Henry had multiple bruises.

"How do you expect me to tell the story with all this abuse?"

"Get to the point and finish the story!" I hollered.

"The point is I remember Mom being pregnant, going to the hospital, and giving birth to Nat. But with you it was different. I remember driving somewhere."

I was sure my heart stopped beating at that moment.

"I think it was an office or something," he said. "I don't remember where, but I sat beside Mom and Dad while they signed a thousand papers. I remember Mom pushing Nat back and forth in a stroller to keep her quiet."

"Are you being serious, Henry? Now is not the time for jokes," Natalie said.

"No, I'm not joking. A fat red-headed woman walked into the room with the thousand or so papers and said, 'Okay, now, Mrs. Boydstein, I will need your signature right here please.' I asked Mom what she was doing, and she said, 'Getting you another sister.' And I remember saying, 'I don't need another sister, Mom. I already don't like the one I have!"

"Oh, shut up, Henry. I know you didn't say that," Nat said as she punched Henry in the ribs.

"I remember the day we picked Kat up at the hospital 'cause Mom and Dad talked to me in the waiting room. They explained to me that I was gonna be a big brother to another younger sister named Katherine. They expected me to protect my two baby sisters, but it looks like I'm the one who needs the protection around here."

Natalie swung a pillow at his head. I was too stunned to react to Henry's crack. He continued, "I remember Mom crying. She was really happy when the nurse came in the room with you wrapped in a pink blanket, and as soon as Mom held you, she burst into tears. So did Dad. Mom bent down and whispered, 'Henry, this is your little sister, Katherine. Katherine, this is your older brother, Henry.' Then she leaned over and did the same thing with Nat, but she started screaming just like the spoiled, annoying brat she is."

Natalie punched Henry on the arm and followed it with a blow to the chest and stomach.

"Hey, I'm just recalling the story the way I remember it," he said.

"I don't need all your smart comments. Just finish the story," Nat said.

"How am I supposed to talk while you're attacking me?"

"Attacking you? I haven't attacked you yet." Natalie pushed him off the bed and began choking him on the ground.

While they were fighting I felt a sense of relief. Wow, Mom and Dad were happy I was in their arms. They wanted me! Even though I wanted to know my blood family, I didn't feel half as bad as I did when I left the school. Just then, Mom opened the door.

"All right you two, don't make me break a switch. Nat, go get your kitchen chores done. Henry, you get back to your homework."

"Thank you. That's what I wanted to be doing anyway before I was so rudely interrupted," Henry said. He smirked, looking over at Natalie.

She gave him one more good punch in the biceps then left the room.

"Kat, your father and I want to speak to you. Come downstairs, please," Mom said.

Tension filled the air as I went downstairs. My stomach knotted up into little balls and I could hardly swallow. A million and one things were going through my mind. What was I about to hear? Dad was sitting in the den by the window staring into our front yard. I will never forget the look on his face. He had definitely been crying because his eyes were watery and his face was red.

"Come over here, honey, and sit down," he said in his sweet, loving voice. I walked over to him and sat on his lap. He gave me the most intense hug I think I ever experienced with him. "You know me and your mama love you, right?" he asked.

"Yeah," I said.

"You know that we do everything we can for you? We do what we feel is best for you and your well-being."

"Yeah, Dad. I know." I looked over at Mom. She

was crying and nodding in agreement.

"Well, we understand that you found out some disturbing news today at school, and you might have some questions, so we wanted to answer them for you."

Just as he finished speaking, Nat popped into the room. "Hey, Dad," she said, giving him a hug and a kiss. She was obviously trying to eavesdrop.

"Hi, darling, how are you?" he asked.

"Fine."

"How was your day at school?" It seemed like he was trying to sound cheerful and upbeat.

"It was okay. We got a book report assignment. I have to read The Adventures of Huckleberry Finn and write a report on it."

"When is it due?" Mom asked. She always asked that when we had big assignments to turn in.

"In two weeks."

"Two weeks! And she is just giving it to you today?" Mom asked, exasperated.

"No. She kinda told us about it at the beginning of the school year. I just checked the book out from the library today."

"Natalie Cindy Boydstein. Now, you know better than that," Mom scolded. "You better hurry up and finish your chores so you can get to reading. No friends for the next two weeks."

"Mom!" Nat shrieked.

"Don't argue with your mother, Natalie. You know that's not allowed," Dad interjected. He always took Mom's side. "Now, do what she says. Finish up and get upstairs to start reading that book. Slackers get no sympathy around here. Now go on."

Natalie pouted and left the room.

Dad continued with me, "Now, where were we?"

"You were telling me that I maybe had questions."

"That's right."

"Am I adopted?"

"Well." Dad hesitated and looked over at Mom. "When your mother and I first got married, our initial plan was to have three healthy children. While your mother was pregnant with Natalie the doctor found some tumors growing in her fallopian tubes. It's a miracle that Natalie was born as healthy as she was with no complications because these tumors started to grow the size of grapefruits during her third trimester. The doctor wanted to take the fallopian tubes out in order not to spread the cancer all over her reproductive organs. So your mother had to go through a hysterectomy after giving birth to Natalie and that ended our chances of having our third baby naturally. But our hearts were set on three kids, so we agreed to adopt another girl."

"Is that why I'm so much darker than the rest of you?"

"The doctor said that your mother was Hispanic, Colombian I think, but I'm not quite certain. They didn't know much about your father."

"It was really important for us to adopt you very soon because I wanted you and Natalie to have each other to play with," Mom chimed in. "I really wanted Natalie to have a companion, a best friend to be with while growing up. All girls need that. Boys, not so much. But girls are relational creatures. We need someone to talk to at all times, and I wanted to give that to my daughter and to another girl in the world who would be an only child. So we adopted you."

"That's right," Dad said, picking up where Mom left off. "We wanted to provide a home for someone to grow up in and realize her full potential. Someone who would be an orphan otherwise and someone we wanted to love. And that was you, sweetheart. We loved you from the moment we saw you, and we wanted you. That's why you're here."

"What happened to my real parents? Do you know?"

"Well," Dad said, sounding careful, "your mother died while giving birth to you. Your father, well, nobody really knows his whereabouts. So you didn't really have any parents and from what we understood you didn't have any immediate family in the States. We're not quite sure where your dad was born, but your mom was illegal so there was a chance you'd be shipped off to Colombia. There was no one to claim you so the State of California put you in its custody, lucky for us. But we love you, Katherine, and we don't want this new information to make you feel any less a part of our family than our biological children."

"Right," Mom said, jumping in quickly. "We don't love you any different than Henry or Natalie. As far as I am concerned, I gave birth to you myself. You are just as much my child as the other two. So don't let this make you feel unwanted or unloved, because you are not! You are loved-very much." Her eyes welled up with tears again, and mine did, too.

I felt their sincerity in my heart, and I knew they loved me unconditionally. Knowing my biological mother passed put me at some ease, but knowing my father and relatives were alive in South America somewhere birthed a curiosity to meet my family one day. My blood family.

"Why didn't you tell me this earlier?" I sobbed.

"Honey, it's like I said at the beginning. We thought it was in your best interest right now for you not to know. We were eventually going to sit you down and tell you, but the time wasn't right and the age wasn't right. I don't know if you could have understood adoption any earlier than now. We didn't want to dump this on a young child, but we would have definitely told you later, like in college years, so you could fully grasp it. Your comprehension about life is just better as you get older. It gets too confusing when you're young."

I nodded my head, but inside I felt like an emotional wreck. Even though they were probably right to wait, I still felt deceived.

"Wh-what were my parents' names?" I stammered out.

"Your mother was named Rosario. The hospital said she was born in Bogota, Colombia. We don't know anything about your father," Mom said. "We also waited because we didn't think you were ready to deal with death at such a young age. I should say, we didn't want you to have to deal with death so young. But we were in no way trying to deceive you or manipulate you. In no way. Not telling you was for your own good. We would not hide information from you unless we thought it was absolutely necessary. I just wanted you to know that. I don't know what all your teacher said to you, but our intentions were pure. We did everything for you out of love. Do you believe that?" Mom asked. She started sobbing. "Do you believe that we love you, and we want only the best for you?"

"Yeah. I believe it," I said. And I did!

The next morning we woke up to Mom's buttermilk biscuits, red country ham, maple brown syrup bacon, sweet corn grits, poached eggs, and fresh fruit. Although they'd seen my lunches, the kids at my school had no idea what kind of food Mom prepared. Most parents in Diego weren't born and raised in the Deep South. Southern cuisine was often frowned upon when we talked food in the cafeteria. Most of the kids at school ate very healthy breakfasts consisting of granola, Greek yogurt, fresh fruit, or old fashioned oatmeal with a scoop of Whey protein powder, raisins, walnuts and berries. Many parents in the area lived organic, green, yogic lifestyles, and their children reflected it. Healthy food was not common in the Boydstein house, and though Mom did incorporate some health-conscious snacks with our lunches and dinner, her Southern roots took priority.

This particular morning stands out in my mind because we didn't have to go to school. None of us. We ate breakfast as a family and we just laughed and cracked silly jokes. Much of the adoption tension dissipated after my night's sleep. I still desired to learn more about my biological family but for now the Boydsteins were my family, and I was fine with that.

After breakfast, Dad informed us we were going to Sea World! We were so excited. Sea World was my favorite place to visit, mainly because I loved the water. We had a blast riding all the rides, sailing on the dolphins and killing each other on the go-carts. Mom always packed our lunch on day trips because she said food at those venues was too expensive. When she prepared breakfast she had also fried some chicken, tossed a beautiful green salad, and baked homemade chocolate chip cookies. She was truly

Supermom.

When I finished eating breakfast I flew upstairs to change into my bathing suit and slather on sunscreen. I stuffed my bag with asphalt paper, pencils, art magazines, and my iPod. Mom threw all the food, water, and sodas in the cooler and loaded up the Yukon. Along our way we stopped at the gas station to get a big bag of ice and fill up on gas, then we pulled onto I-5 South. Dad was in the driver's seat, Mom in the passenger seat, Henry behind the driver's seat, and Nat directly behind Mom. I sat all the way in the back with the cooler and backpacks. Henry played one of his video games while Natalie read Huckleberry Finn. I drew a picture of the Pacific Ocean's crystal clear blue water with colorful fish swarming around a coral reef.

Dad started to yell something over the radio, then he turned it down. "Hey, how would you guys like to go to Hi Life after Sea World?"

We all shouted in agreement within a matter of seconds. Our family absolutely loved Hi Life! It was a fancy American-style restaurant known for the best homemade food in Diego. We only dined there when we drove to Sea World because it was a considerable distance from our house in La Jolla, but the food was worth the trip. My favorites were the Apple Arugula Salad and Lobster Ravioli. Natalie liked the Fish Tacos. Henry always ordered the Steak Pizza. Mom usually got the Sea Bass, and Dad always ordered the filet with béarnaise sauce. We typically began our feast with an order of the Black Calamari, Crab and Lobster Dip.

We used to order just one dessert for the whole table, but Mom and Dad learned quickly that if they wanted a bite or two they'd be better off ordering their own. Although it would be hours before we were even in the restaurant parking lot, Henry, Nat and I immediately started to argue on which dessert we would split.

"I want the Chocolate Molten Cake!" Henry announced. I was not surprised.

"Well, I want the Key Lime Pie," Nat shot back. "And if my memory serves me correctly, it's my turn to choose the dessert."

"I want the Apple Cinnamon Tart," I jumped in, knowing if I didn't say anything now the chance would never come. "And it is my turn to order, Nat. You ordered the Tiramisu at the Olive Garden the other night remember?"

"That wasn't the last night we dined out. Henry ordered the Peanut Butter Chocolate Crunch at the Cheesecake Factory. And what about Boston Market? You ordered the Pecan Pie. It's my turn!"

"Boston Market doesn't count. That's not considered a restaurant!" I argued, fighting for my Apple Cinnamon Tart.

"It doesn't matter if it's a restaurant, Kat. We sat down and ate there and you chose the dessert. It's my turn!" Natalie said. Neither one of us backed down.

"Why don't we flip for it?" Henry suggested. He reached into his pocket and pulled out a nickel. "If it's heads we get the Apple Tart. Tails we get the Key Lime Pie."

"That sounds like a fair deal to me," Dad said.

"No, I don't want to do heads or tails with you, Henry, 'cause you know how to manipulate the coin to do what you want. Let's do rock, paper, scissors," I said.

"That's fine. Rock, paper, scissors it is," Natalie said. She put her book down and turned around to face me.

"Well, if you guys are doing rock, paper, scissors then I want in." Henry said. He threw down his video game and turned to us.

"That's not fair. You shouldn't have a say." Natalie whipped around to face the front. "Dad, Henry is trying to order dessert when he knows it's not his turn."

"Henry, let this be between your sisters, now. Play fair," Dad said.

"All right, fine. I'll let the losers decide, but if I don't like your choice then I get to choose the next two times we go out to eat."

"Whatever," Natalie said. She ignored Henry and turned to face me again. The stage was set for rock, paper, scissors, and I was the undisputed champion. I usually won with scissors, and I knew Nat was aware of my strategy. I planned to start with paper because I knew she would start with rock.

"Are you ready?" Henry said, umpiring the round.

"Yep, I am," I said confidently, knowing Nat was about to go down.

"Me too," Nat replied.

"All right, losers. Get your hands ready."

"Henry," Mom snapped sharply. "Stop calling your sisters losers. Now you apologize."

"What?" Henry shrieked. "Seriously, I'd rather give up my Steak Pizza at Hi Life than apologize to these two annoying brats."

Mom started to turn her whole body around but Dad's laughter stopped her halfway.

"Hey, that's not a bad idea, honey. We could stand to save an extra thirty dollars," Dad said.

"Thomas Allen Boydstein! I know you are not laughing at your son!"

"What?" He shrugged, still chuckling. "Cindy, the boy can eat. I say we invest his food money in an emerging growth fund and pay off his college tuition."

"Oh my goodness, Tommy." Mom broke out into laughter. "I don't know what I am gon-"

BANG! was all I heard before our Yukon swerved around to the right. Something blew out the front passenger tire and my dad lost control of the vehicle. As he mercilessly tried to jam on the brakes and avoid moving traffic, a U-Haul entering the expressway slammed into the passenger door by Natalie and caused us to flip over several times down Interstate 5. I don't quite remember all the details, but I do recall screaming, crying, and flying. Both Natalie and Henry had unfastened their seatbelts in order to turn around. As the truck flipped down the freeway, they flew from the ceiling to the floor along with the ice chest, food, video games, book bags and my sketchbook. We flipped over the side rail and our car finally came to a halt, upside down.

I wasn't knocked unconscious, but I wasn't fully present, either. My eyes opened long enough to see shattered glass. Smoke and fire billowed from under the hood. Nobody moved. Natalie lay face down with her upper body outside the window and her legs inside the vehicle, pigeon-toed. Henry had landed in the fetal position to my right. I strained my neck to look for my parents but couldn't see them from where I lay. I was stuck. After a few minutes a stranger popped his head inside the broken window and yelled, "Are you all okay? Oh my God! Can anybody hear me? Jessica, call 911, now! Can anybody hear me?"

With all the strength I could muster I grunted as loud as I could. I didn't think the noise was loud enough, but apparently it was because he ran to the back of the truck and quickly yet gently removed the remaining glass from the window. He was very careful not to flick any remnants into my eyes or his.

"Hey, can you hear me?" he asked again.

I slowly rolled my head to the left to get a good look at him. He had piercing, deep sea green eyes and dirty brown hair. Something about his eyes made me feel like everything was going to be okay. I attempted to move towards him but a sudden awareness of pain in my body halted the movement.

"Hey, someone is alive. Tell 911 to hurry up!" he yelled at someone. "Don't worry," he said to me. "I'm gonna get you out of here." He crawled inside the truck and unbuckled my seatbelt, then grabbed me under both my armpits and slid me out of the car head first. My body ached even more when he picked me up in his arms and carried me away from the car. It was a slow, dull pain shooting from the base of my neck down to my legs. Surprisingly enough, I didn't have a headache. He carefully placed me on the ground next to a blond lady panicking on the phone. "Are you okay, honey? Can you hear me?" she asked me. I nodded. "Yes, operator, she seems to be okay," the lady said while squeezing my hand. "I don't know...I don't know...He hasn't removed anyone else yet. I don't know. Just hurry up before the whole truck explodes!" I turned my head slowly toward the truck to see the man running back toward us. Why was he running? I thought to myself. I looked behind him in time to see the white Yukon burst into flames. With that vision seared into my mind, I shut my eyes and fell into a deep sleep.

2

A pale-skinned redhead with freckles was my first sight upon opening my eyes. Two machines stood next to my bed on the left and a night dresser with a floral arrangement and telephone to my right. A flat screen television was mounted on the wall and a thin narrow desk was in front of my bed. I realized I was in a hospital.

"Hello, Katherine. How are you feeling?" the nurse asked.

I looked down at the badge pinned to her white uniform top. Her name was Anne.

"Can you hear me?" She spoke in a sweet voice. "Squeeze my hand if you can hear me." She gently put her hand in mine. I squeezed it as tightly as I could. "Good." She smiled. "You are so lucky, Katherine. With the exception of a few minor bruises and scrapes you are doing fine. Just fine. I am changing your IV here and putting some more liquids into your system. We don't want you hungry and losing weight now, do we?" She smiled again.

Her eyes were sincere, and her voice nurtured my inner child. I felt a warm safety in her presence but I didn't have any energy for dialogue. I smiled faintly and fell back into another deep sleep.

Upon waking the next time, I had more strength and energy to move around. The tubes attached to me limited my movements, but I did manage to lift my head. A sharp pain down my spine made me lie back down. I tried to look around the room as much as possible from that position. It looked pretty much the same as how I saw it last time. Then I noticed something: I was alone. Where were Mom and Dad? Nat and Henry? How come they weren't beside my bed? I pressed the button for Anne, hoping she'd be able to go get them. To my delight she came quickly, but not with the response I expected.

"Good afternoon, dear. I see you're up again. How are you feeling?"

"Where is my mom?" I whispered.

"Oh well, dear…don't worry about your family right now. You just focus on getting your strength up and standing on your own two feet again. That's all that needs to be going through your pretty little head right now."

"I want to see my dad. Where are Nat and Henry? Tell them to come here."

Anne looked nervous. She seemed to be hesitating to come up with an answer, which meant the truth wasn't good! Before I realized it I was leaning up on my elbows, oblivious to the pain.

"Where is my family?" I demanded. "I want my dad. I want my mom. I want to see Nat and Henry. Where are they?" Anne was holding something back from me. It was obviously tearing her apart, and she finally headed out the door.

Good. She's finally going to get my family. Wonder what her problem was? I lay back down on the bed and smiled at the thought of Henry teasing me. I just knew he was going to say something smart, and Natalie and I would beat him up like we so enjoyed. Torturing my big brother was my favorite pastime.

I looked over at the door and saw Anne speaking with an African American woman in the hall. Who is she? I thought, and why is Anne talking to her and not my family? The lady entered the room and walked toward me. Her expression was somber, but her fashionable style caught my attention. She was extremely overweight, yet rocked a chic black and white tailored suit with pinstriped pumps and no stockings. Red hoop earrings, a red choker and a matching bracelet accessorized her look. She stood about five feet four inches with the high heels, had mocha chocolate skin, short black hair, and a beauty mole on her upper lip.

"Hello, Katherine. How do you feel today?" she asked.

"Fine, I guess," I said.

"My name is Mary Jett. I'm a social worker for Child Protective Services."

"What's that?"

"CPS is a government-affiliated organization that helps children from broken or unhealthy backgrounds find a stable home in a healthy environment."

"I already live in a healthy environment, so why are you here?"

"Well, Katherine ..." She looked at Anne uncomfortably. "You"-she paused-"were the only survivor in the accident. The others didn't make it."

"What do you mean?"

"I hate to be the bearer of bad news, but your mother, father, sister, and brother all died in the accident. Your brother and sister died in the fire before the arrival of the ambulance, and your parents died on the way to the hospital. You are the only survivor." She paused again. "But I promise you that the State of California will find you a healthy family to live with. I know they won't replace the Boydsteins, but you will have a loving mother and father in no time."

I saw her mouth moving but couldn't process her words. Dead? Fire? Only survivor? State of California? New mother and father in no time? Someone could have dropped me on my head at that moment and I wouldn't have felt it. My entire body numbed and the room spun around me. It felt like all the blood in my body rushed to my feet and I passed out.

* * * *

I was pretty much a zombie during my fourteen-day stay in the hospital. I was in and out of consciousness most of the time and I don't remember going to the bathroom, taking a shower, eating or drinking. I couldn't even tell you if I had visitors during that time or not. I found out later that my family's funeral took place a week after the accident, but I was too weak to attend at the time. I was okay with not going to the funeral since I probably would have crawled into one of the caskets and buried myself alive. Life was just not worth living anymore.

Everything I loved was gone. All I wanted to do was sleep and never wake up.

Around day twelve I finally stayed conscious. That was the day I met Willie Jones, the hospital chaplain. He waltzed right into my room, unannounced. And unwanted, I might add. He was a black man in a gray suit, a short haircut and he carried a thick book underneath his arm.

"Hello, Katherine," he said. "We've never met, but my name is Willie. Willie Jones. I am here to pray with you."

"For what?"

"For whatever you need. I know you're going through a traumatic time in your life right now, and I just wanted to help you cast your cares on the Lord."

"Cast my what?"

"Casting your cares upon the Lord' means talking to God like you would talk to a friend. Tell him your situation, worries, fears, or anything in your heart that you need peace about. I guess another way you can say it is prayer. Do you need prayer over anything?"

"Why would I want to pray to God? He took my family away from me. He got us into a car accident and killed the only people alive who loved me. Who needs a God like that?"

"Well, now, hold on there," Willie said sitting down on the edge of my bed, again uninvited. "There are other people in this world who love you, and Jesus is one of them. His sole purpose of bringing you into this earth was to shower you with his unconditional love. Don't be confusing his work with the work of the enemy. God is good. The devil is a liar. You remember that, now."

"Whatever, man. There is no God, and if there is,

I don't need him. Why would a supposedly good God take the only family I have away from me? I was so happy." Tears staggered down my face. "I had the best mom, dad, brother and sister in the world. There is no way killing them is for my good. That doesn't even make sense. Why talk to a God that kills people you love?"

A look of concern crossed Willie's face. He opened the book he carried and flipped through never-ending pages. The words Holy Bible were engraved on the brown leather cover.

"I know what you mean, Katherine," he said. "It does seem like God's sovereignty controls all of what goes on down here, the good, the bad and the ugly. But that is just not the truth. Sin is a huge reason for a lot of bad going on down here-sin and just plain consequences. Many times it is our own actions that cause a lot of bad stuff to happen. But let's look at the situation, okay? The front tire blows out on the passenger side of the car causing the driver to swerve, get hit by another car and flip over several times. Right?"

"How did you know what happened?"

"Ms. Anne filled me in before I arrived."

"How many other people has she told my story to?"

"Oh, not many, darling. She just told me because I want to help you. That's all. She's not gossiping about you. Anne filled me in just in case you didn't feel up to it. The nurses up here always do that for me." He paused and seemed to study my facial expression, then continued. "But let's get back to my point. You think God caused the accident? Well, one can say the tire caused the wreck, seeing as that started the whole thing. Was there enough air in the tire? When was the last time the tires were rotated? Was there a nail in the middle of the road? I mean, all kinds of different elements could have taken place for this to occur. Now, was that all God's fault? Was it human negligence, or was it the fall of Adam?"

"The fall of Adam? What are you talking about? I'm not in the mood for this right now."

"I know, baby, I know. I just want to plant these seeds of truth in your spirit now while you're still processing. I don't want you growing up believing lies about this event in your life. That's all."

I saw the sincerity in his eyes, so I decided to listen to him.

"Without going into great detail," he continued, "we live in a fallen world, but it didn't start like that. In the beginning God made man in his image and gave us authority over the earth. But when Adam and Eve ate the apple in the Garden of Eden they gave our authority over to Satan, and he became the prince of this world. Since then he roars around like a lion trying to destroy all he can and stop people from fulfilling their journey. So a lot of bad things that happen in the world are caused by the devil, yet people blame God. This is your case here, Katherine. The devil tried to kill you in that crash, not God. This is NOT God's work. I want to read to you a passage of Scripture from the Bible. Have you ever read the Bible before?"

"No."

"In the tenth chapter in John, in the tenth verse, Jesus described his ways and the devil's ways. It says, 'The thief comes only to steal and kill and destroy; I came that they may have life, and have it abundantly.'

You see, Katherine, anything that kills, steals, and destroys comes from Satan. Jesus is the author of abundant life, including forgiveness, health, money, relationships. Your family dying is the manifestation of evil, and he is trying to destroy you too, Katherine. You have a huge calling on your life."

"I do?"

"Yes, my child. Never have I sensed the calling of a prophet as I do in you. You will spread the gospel of Jesus Christ, manifesting his gifts mightily. The devil is trying to knock you off course and confuse you with his deception, but I was sent here to tell you that you are loved by God. Jesus loves you."

"Why didn't God love my family?"

"He did love your family, darling. It's just that ..." Willie sighed, turning his head away from me. I could tell his mind was racing for an answer. "God did love your family, dear. I can't explain to you why you're the only survivor, but I do know that this accident was not God's will. I don't know why the enemy got his way, but I do know that God loves you, Katherine. He loves you very much."

"So if God wants all this good for me, isn't family a good thing? Wouldn't my family help me prepare for this calling you say I have? Why couldn't he overcome this devil guy and keep them alive? Why did the devil win?"

"Now that I can't answer for you. Yes, it is in the will of God for you to have a blessed, healthy, and stable family life. I don't know why the devil got his way, but I know he doesn't have to continue to get his way if you put your trust in Jesus."

"Who is Jesus?"

"Jesus is the Lord. He is the only one who has

power over Satan. And Jesus wants to have a relationship with you, Katherine."

"All-powerful? Well if he is so damn powerful why didn't he stop the tire from blowing out? Why didn't he know there was no air in the tire? Or if there was a nail in the middle of the road? Wouldn't he have known that my family would die in the car accident and prevent it? What is the point of him knowing all this stuff if he's not gonna do anything about it? No, I don't want a relationship with him! The dude is a loser!"

"Katherine. Listen."

"No, I'm done listening to this crap. This God of yours is nowhere in my situation."

"He is in your life right now, Katherine. He sent me in here to help you start a relationship with him. Jesus is the only one who can get you to heaven, Katherine, and not only to heaven when you die, but heaven here on Earth as well.

"I know it looks bad. Trust me. There are many unexplained events that have happened to me during my life, but Jesus has kept me like he kept you! Your life was nearly untouched in fire and smoke, have you realized that? You were the only one saved from a burning car that flipped upside down, and you barely have a scratch on your body. Now I know that might not mean much to you now, but you have to see that it is a miracle you are even here speaking with me. God was with you in the car, and he is with you now."

"Well, you can go now. I want nothing to do with your God. Thank you, but no thank you. I'll take my chances on my own."

Willie sighed, closed his Bible, got up from the

edge of my bed and walked toward the door. Before leaving he whipped around and said, "Regardless of your resentment toward him, Katherine, he will always love you whether you love him or not. And with that love comes people He puts in your path to love you. It might be hard to believe right now, but there are people in this world who love you and want the best for you. And Jesus will make sure to connect you to those people. He will never forsake you. Just know that when you need him, he will be right there for you with open arms."

"Get out of here!" I yelled, throwing my pillow at him as he sprinted out the door.

I was an emotional mess after Willie left. I was already upset about my family dying, then I hear about a God who claimed to love me? Really? Who would want to serve a bipolar God? One day he wants what's best for you, and the next day he takes your family away? I can do without that kind of love. Life has enough problems of its own.

A couple of days later I encountered my last visitors. Mary, the social worker, came into my room with an older man and woman.

"Hello, Katherine. Do you remember me? I'm your social worker, Mary Jett," said Mary.

"How could I forget you?" I said to myself. You are the best-dressed overweight lady I have ever seen. Today she rocked a black sheer blouse with bell-bottom sleeves, matching Capri pants and black high heels. Her accessories included diamond studs and a matching choker.

"Katherine, I would like you to meet your aunt and uncle! Eddie is your father's brother and this is his wife, Maria. They will be taking care of you from now on."

I could tell she prided herself in finding a caretaker for me so quickly. Eddie resembled my dad, but with more facial hair. He stood about six foot one with a big beer belly, greasy hair and waxy ears. He wore khaki pants, a plaid shirt and a brown suede jacket. I instantly detested him; he gave me the creeps. Maria looked like she belonged in a mental institution. Her disturbed demeanor reminded me of the religious mother from the 1976 movie Carrie.

"Hello, Katherine. It is so nice to finally meet you," she said as she gave me a hug. "I heard so much about you over the years. It's good to match a face to all the stories."

All what stories? I thought to myself. How have you heard so much about me yet I have never heard anything about you?

Eddie stood there looking me up and down for a few minutes. "Hello, Katherine. I'm your Uncle Eddie. Good to meet you." He hesitantly reached out his hand to shake mine. These people were definitely not from California. Their accents were gritty, cold and harsh, totally unlike the friendly voices in San Diego. "You ever been to the Windy City?"

"The Windy City? Where's that?" I asked.

"Chicago!" Maria said, grinning.

"No."

"Well." Eddie paused. "Hopefully you'll like it."

"Katherine, you will be moving to Chicago with your uncle and aunt," Mary said. "They also have a son and daughter around your age so you should fit right in. You will enroll in school and resume your old hobbies. You might even make some new friends, if you feel up to it. Your life will be back in shape in no time."

"What if I don't want to go?" I asked Mary.

"Well, sweetheart, you have to give it a chance first. This is temporary for now, but you never know. After you move there and start meeting new people, you might learn to enjoy it. You just have to give it time." Mary glanced up at Eddie and Maria and motioned them to head toward the hallway.

"We are so happy you will join our family, Katherine. I think you're really going to like Chicago. There are a lot of fun things to do and good food to eat. It's quite different from California, but once you get adjusted, you'll fit right in," Maria assured me.

They walked out in the hall to talk, but I could still hear them.

"How long will she be like this?" Maria asked.

"She has a very acute case of trauma right now," Mary said. "She could very well stay like this for the next six months or six years. It just depends on her and how well she processes what happened. The priority is that she comes to grips with what's going on inside of her. That's where the problem lies. Most kids internalize emotions and manifest them in unhealthy ways. It's our job to make sure she expresses her emotions and thoughts verbally or artistically, but in a healthy communicative manner. It is vital she doesn't miss any doctor's appointments. She is not emotionally stable right now, so don't be surprised if she's not very friendly at first. She is going through a very severe time in her life, and how she processes this information will shape the health of her future. Some kids undergo trauma and it makes them stronger, motivated and highly successful. Then you have kids who become suicidal or sexually active. You just never know. Each case is different.

"It's imperative you keep an eye on her at all times, so don't let her spend too much time by herself. Girls who lose families at young ages are prone to be suicidal. She will need to talk to a doctor twice a week for the first three months, then they'll reevaluate her case after the trial period. Just try to stay positive and be patient. It will be a long recovery to get her back to her normal self, but nothing is impossible."

When I woke up the next day, I saw Anne arranging a pair of jeans, red sweater, white socks and a pair of red and white Converse shoes at the foot of the bed.

"Well, good morning," Anne said gleefully. "Today is your lucky day. You're being released into your new life. You uncle is on the way to pick you up." She touched up the red sweater with a lint brush. "Oh, I am so jealous. I love Chicago! Have you ever been?"

"No. I haven't," I said, depressed.

"Oh, it is the most exciting city. Different breed of people. They aren't as nice as we are here in Cali, but they are honest and pure at heart. So many wonderful adventures await you, Katherine. Chicago has the best food ever! Do you like pizza?"

"I guess."

"Well, then, you'll love Chicago. The best deep dish pizza is at Giordano's. The best hamburgers are at Portillo's. The best gyros are at Chiggy's. The best Indian food is on Pulaski. There are tons of fun activities to do: Navy Pier, Sears Tower, art galleries, small theaters, ice skating rings, outdoor concerts, Michigan Avenue. I mean, you name it, Chicago's got

40

it! The city really is a mini New York City. You're going to love it! I just know it."

She sounded like an overenthusiastic travel agent.

"I don't see the point, Anne," I said.

"What do you mean?"

"What's the point of getting excited about life just to have it stolen?"

Anne's face dropped instantly. She seemed to recognize the pain and looked like she had been there herself. "Oh, sweetheart," she said. She stopped fixing my clothes and walked over to my bed. "I know life just doesn't make sense right now. It does seem like a big waste of time, sometimes. We are all here just taking up space until the universe calls us home."

"The universe? Oh my God, don't tell me you believe in God too?"

"Well, in a way. I believe the universe is God and God is the universe."

"How disappointing."

"We live in a world full of cause and effect. We are our own biggest problem, most of the time." She laughed while I sat there, not amused. "To make a long story short, my life has not always run so smoothly, you know? My dad was an alcoholic and my mom abused my sister and me, partly 'cause Daddy abused her. So I was raised in a house full of deception, lies, and mistrust. My parents ruined me for a while there. I started drinking and smoking and just, you know, doing what naughty girls do.

"It wasn't until a friend invited me to a Kabbalah meeting where my heart began to heal and understanding sprouted forth. The truth of the Zohar, or God's word, was hard to believe because my mind was so brainwashed with lies. But eventually

God's light conquered, and he literally changed my life! Like, I didn't even think about nursing school as a child. I was always interested in science and health, but my mom called me stupid and dumb, and she said that I'd never amount to anything, that I'd turn out just like my father. Same with school. I didn't have any encouraging teachers so the low self-esteem deepened. People proclaimed degrading affirmations over me for a long time and I believed them until I studied the ten attributes of God. My thinking changed then and I believed I could go to college and do something great."

"What are the ten attributes of God?"

"Oh dear, that gets confusing if one is not a student. Basically the Sephirot, or enumerations, of EinSof, the Infinite, illuminates the divine plan as it unfolds itself in creation. It is a step by step process that we humans endure to reach the highest form of self, which in turn is a reflection of the God of Creation. I'll start from lowest level to highest. The tenth level is Mulkath or Kingship. Nine is foundation. Eight is splendor. Seven is Netzach or eternity. Six is beauty. Five is Seventy. Four is kindness. These are all the primary emotions better known as the conscious emotions. Then one graduates to conscious intellect which is understanding and wisdom. The highest form is above consciousness, Keter, or crown.

"Each quality represents a different side of the Infinite, in turn, representing us human beings. We are all created in the image of the Infinite or God or Creation, whatever you want to tag it. Whomever created this Earth created us in its exact image. The more revelation I received of God's true nature and my identity, the more peace entered in my hectic situations and flattened all my ruffles."

I chewed on her words a moment. Something about that last statement rang true within me: understanding God's true nature and my identity would bring peace into my situation. My heart was in total agreement with Anne, but my brain couldn't figure out why I was even taking advice from her. Nonetheless, a picture was formed in my heart that day in the hospital. I needed to learn the character of God, and when I unravel that he or she will reveal the true me.

Anne had stopped talking and I could tell she was about to cry. After a moment she continued, "Well, anyway, I finished my GED, enrolled in a community college, and here I am today. I would not have the courage to do this if it weren't for EinSof edifying me in a way that man simply couldn't."

"Kabbalah did all that?"

"And more. My thoughts are calmer after chanting. My actions are more deliberate since I started interpreting scriptures, and overall I make better choices. A lot of wisdom has been instilled in me since that first invite."

The expression on my face must have given away my unbelief. She backed up.

"It's okay if you don't agree with this right now. You've been through a lot these past few weeks," she said.

"I don't know what to believe anymore. It's not like I had faith in the first place."

"Oh, it will start to make sense as you grow older. My words will reappear in your mind when you least expect them. It's okay, you don't have to believe anything right now. Just be free and live life. You'll find your way as you move forward on your journey. Just worry about right here and right now. And all you need to focus on is some water and soap because you stink!" she winked, displaying a grin that was surprisingly contagious. "Now get up and into the shower, missy. They'll be here any minute."

As I stood there in the shower, a dark presence invaded the bathroom and despair instantly jumped on me. What is this? I asked myself. Who are you? Silence. Heaviness, hopelessness and fear cloaked my heart. I intuitively knew that my life was about to change for the worse in Chicago, but what choice did I have? The Boydstein family was all I knew. I didn't have a clue as to my biological family's whereabouts, and I didn't even know where to begin searching for them. I stood in the shower wishing I could flow down the drain with the water and soap suds.

3

9104 Lincoln Drive, Des Plaines, IL 60016 was my new address. Nearby were many apartment buildings, town homes and condos surrounded by brown, slushy snow and lifeless trees. There was no body of water, no sun, no trees with green leaves, no flowers, but there was lots of wind! I understood why Dad moved to Cali. In San Diego, I lived in a huge five-bedroom home surrounded by an iron gate, a rose garden, pine trees and an outdoor pool overlooking the Pacific Ocean and Laguna Mountains.

My new house was a three-story, three-bedroom, one-and-a-half bathroom town home lodged between a Hindu and Hispanic family. I'd never seen so many cultures living in one neighborhood in my life. I mean, San Diego had its share of nationalities, yet in my neighborhood there were only whites and Jews. Chicago showcased all kinds of people living together on one block. When I got out of the car I heard Hindi, Spanish and what sounded like Russian all before I walked into the house. The driveways on this street were filled with Toyotas, Hondas and Nissans. I had seen mostly Mercedes, BMWs and Jags in San Diego.

People didn't speak to or smile at strangers here. They seemed to walk a lot faster and mind their own business. The attire was jeans, boots and down coats with matching scarves, gloves and hats—unlike the surfer shorts, tank tops and flip-flops I was used to. I had never owned a down coat in all of my existence. It was never needed in sunny California.

The entire interior of the house couldn't have been bigger than my old living room and dining room combined. I walked into a kitchen cluttered with loads of dirty dishes. Pots and pans were sitting on the stove. Cereal boxes, milk, bowls and spoons were still on the table from breakfast that morning. There was a half bathroom to my left in front of a door leading to the basement. The living room had gray carpet, a brown furniture set and an old television. A stereo system sat behind the couch. All the walls in the house were white, which gave it an insane-asylum feel. There was a small, narrow hall upstairs with three bedrooms right next to each other and one full bathroom.

This was a far cry from my San Diego house, which had four-and-a-half bathrooms. I had shared one large bathroom with Natalie, and it had a Jacuzzi tub with a separate shower. The Jack and Jill sinks had granite counter top with twelve drawers underneath to store our toiletries. Henry had his own bathroom. Here, everybody used one small, nasty, soap-scummed bathroom.

Uncle Eddie was born and raised in Skokie, just

outside of Chicago, and his wife, Maria, was from Puerto Rico. They met on his college spring break in Puerto Rico. Maria was a waitress at the hotel Eddie and his friends lodged. They married a year and a half later and had two kids, James and Joan. James was seventeen, Joan, fifteen. I was thirteen at the time, so I didn't vibe with those two from day one. They each had their own room in which I was never invited. I barely saw inside their rooms because the doors were always closed.

My bedroom was in the spacious basement. They had a living room set down there with a nice-sized television. The laundry room in the corner kept me up at all times of the night, along with heavy footsteps overhead.

I assumed my bedroom had been a storage room because of the boxes and containers pushed up against the wall. The room was tiny. Really *tiny*. I could take three steps across the entire space. They had thrown a twin-sized mattress on the floor between an old wooden dresser with a chipped mirror attached and a white nightstand with a green lamp sitting on top of it. Nothing in the room matched, including the sheets on the bed. There was no window, no closet, no bathroom. I guessed I should be grateful I had a home and family right out of the hospital, but I wasn't. I missed San Diego.

To make matters worse, Maria was a die-hard Catholic. She was born and raised Catholic in Puerto Rico, and she carried the tradition into this house. Catholic relics hung all over the place: Virgin Mary candles, rosary beads, crosses and pictures of different saints and angels. There was a huge archaic-looking Bible on the living room table that remained untouched. Down in a corner of the basement she had placed a huge five-foot-tall statute of Mary that lit up at night. There was a picture on the wall right next to my room. The picture was of a tan man with long, flowing brown hair, blue eyes and an angelic face. His focus was upward and his hands were in a prayer position.

Unlike the Boydstein house, Maria required all the kids to attend weekly mass. "Church will help you make everything better, Katherine. Just go and listen to the priest and what God is saying through him. I promise you will be happy afterward."

"How many people are gonna shove this God thing down my throat?" I yelled. "I don't believe in God! I don't believe in Jesus! I don't believe in the universe! God took my family away from me and put me here with you. I don't want to go and listen to what he has to tell me. What could he possibly say to me to bring my family back? I'm not going!"

"Ay," she said in her Puerto Rican accent. "You will not talk like that in this house, Katherine. Maybe it was okay in your other home but not here. You will go to church, and you will listen to whatever the priest has to say. You have no choice in this house. If you want to eat my food then you will go to my church."

I was stunned! I couldn't believe this complete stranger is telling me what I had to do to eat. No matter how much I argued with Maria she wouldn't give an inch, so on that cold Saturday morning in December I got into in the Honda CRV with my sketchbook, James and Joan to attend my very first church service.

St. Peter Cathedral was nestled on the corner of

Dempster and Crawford. When we first pulled into the parking lot I thought the place was a museum. It had to be the most beautiful piece of architecture I had ever laid my eyes on: 111 meters long, 46 meters wide with two flanking towers 92 meters tall. Constructed in Neo-Gothic style, St. Peters boasted a beige exterior with a blind arcade, several huge connecting pillars, vaulted doorways and stained glass windows. 27 steps led up towards the front door and one big waterfall was mounted in front of the building. It didn't look like a house of worship but a place where tourists would take pictures for a scrapbook. It was simply breathtaking.

As I walked through the doors I just knew the Queen of England dwelt in this majestic palace with stone walls, huge windows ornamented with stone tracery and stained glass, multiple columns and marble floors. The Virgin Mary was everywhere, and I do mean everywhere. Statues, paintings, candles, altars and books all had Mary on them in some form or fashion.

The sanctuary seemed to be the size of a football field and had high ribbed, vaulted ceilings, several Corinthian-styled columns and 3 wide aisles interspersed with hundreds of stone benches leading up to a highly elaborate, custom-made pulpit. I'm not quite sure what I expected church to be, but it sure wasn't this.

The service itself didn't have the same impact as the architecture and decorating. The people seemed to be robotic. Everyone walked into the room, bowed, put their finger in water and touched three places on their bodies. What was all that about? Nothing seemed to happen afterward. There was no life in the priest's eyes, no energy in his voice. Luckily, the service wasn't long; thirty-five minutes to be exact. The priest talked about the Immaculate Conception. Something about how the Son of God came into the womb of a virgin to take away the sins of the world. Whatever. Inspired by the scenery around me, I pretty much focused on drawing the sanctuary.

The stained glass paintings on the wall stood out the most. There were twelve in all surrounding the sanctuary. After church I walked around to unravel the story. The pictures followed in this order:

1. A tanned man with shoulder length hair stood next to a king in front of an angry crowd pointing their fingers at him.

2. One person in the crowd punched him while another spat on him. A woman had a rock in her hand about to throw it at him, yet he appeared unaffected by the people and their assaults.

3. A soldier handed the man a wooden cross while someone else placed a crown of pins into his head. Blood covered his face.

4. The bloody man walked through the angry crowd with a wooden cross on his back. It looked heavy. People continued to punch, spit, and kick him.

5. He lay on the cross with his arms and legs stretched out. A soldier hammered a nail into his left wrist while another soldier pulled his right arm out of its socket.

6. The man hung on the cross between two other men. Everyone was staring at him, including the two men next to him.

That was the end of the pictures on one side of the sanctuary. Something about this story moved me to tears, and I ran to the other side of the building to finish the story.

7. The man looked up to the sky while a soldier pierced him in the side with a spear; another soldier used a hammer to break the legs of the man next to him.

8. The man looked dead, limply hanging on the cross between the two men.

9. Some woman wrapped his bloody body in a white cloth.

10. There was a war between angels and demons. The angels wore white and they crushed the demons in red.

The next picture was odd:

11. The same woman stood in shock inside a cave. It looked like she was talking to an angel dressed in white, face unseen. A very bright, white light hovered over the cave.

12. There was of an empty cave with the white cloth folded at the head of the rock couch inside.

After I viewed the series of pictures, a rush of energy surged through me and I sobbed. Something about these pictures spoke to me. I couldn't quite figure it out, but there was something more to this than met the eye. Who was this man? How was he able to maintain such peace with all of the aggravated assault? As I stood looking into his eyes, rest came upon me. At first I couldn't describe why I felt so at peace.

I walked around to take another look at the pictures and I noticed his eyes. There was so much love beaming from his eyes. In every picture, no matter what the event, his eyes never changed. That man loved those people, even the ones who spat on him and punched him! He looked at them with so much mercy and understanding in the midst of humiliation and degradation. He was not angry at his persecutors. He didn't defend himself. He just allowed these people to torture him and never lifted a finger. When I realized this, I started bawling again.

Maria startled me. "What is wrong with you?"

"Do you see this? Have you ever looked at these pictures?" I asked, wiping snot from my nose. "They are just torturing him, kicking him, spitting on him, punching him, yet he is not fighting back."

Maria turned to look at the picture as if she never paid any attention to it before today.

"Who does this?" I continued. "Who just beats up someone who cares for them so much? That's like me beating up my parents if they were still around. What kind of people are these?"

"I know, mi hija, I know. It's sad, but that's why we worship him, because he endured all this for us."

"Who *is* he?"

"Aye, mi amor. This is who the priest talked about today during the service. His name is Jesus."

I paused for a moment, remembering the chaplain in the hospital. "This is Jesus?"

"Yes, mi amor, it is. Why?"

I stared at the pictures, unable to move. "What is he doing?"

"He is going to the cross to die for the sins of his people."

"Why is everybody so mad at him?"

"I don't know why they are so mad at him. I don't think he did anything to anybody. I think they just killed him because that was his plan from the beginning of creation. Why are you crying?" Maria asked.

"Look into his eyes. Do you see how he looks at the people hurting him? He is so patient. His eyes are so kind and loving. There is not one ounce of hatred or anger."

Maria looked at the pictures intensely then said, "I don't see that. He looks like he is in pain to me. I really don't see the big deal. Come on, we need to go. Your uncle is hungry. He is at home waiting for me to feed him."

Seeing this conversation wasn't heading the same direction, I sighed, rolled my eyes and mumbled, "I'll be there in a minute,"" under my breath.

I took my time walking out of the church and my eyes stayed on Jesus in the pictures. Call me crazy, but as I walked by each picture it looked as if this Jesus character was following me with his eyes. The pupils of his eyes shifted from right to left in each picture I passed. I moved around to make sure I wasn't losing my mind. I stopped. Ran forward. Backward. Squatted down to the floor. Jumped up in the air. He stared straight through me.

Stopping dead in my tracks, I stared deep into his eyes and heard, "Come to me, Katherine, and I will give you rest." I quickly spun around to see if Maria, James or Joan was talking to me. All three of them had already walked out the front door toward the car. I turned to the strangers in the middle aisle, but no one even noticed me. Everyone seemed to be off in their own world, completely unaware I was even standing there. So I looked at the picture of Jesus again.

"Katherine, come to Me, and I will give you rest. The life you are looking for is only found in Me. The answers you want can only be answered by Me. The pain you have can only be healed by Me. Come to Me, Katherine. I am what you are looking for!"

I spun around in a 360 degree circle to see where the voice was coming from. On my third or fourth spin my body stopped, facing the picture of Jesus hanging on the cross. Surely this guy wasn't talking to me from a picture? Nervously looking to the right and left to see if anyone was seeing what I was seeing, I glanced back at the picture. I was not hallucinating. Our eyes connected! I slowly walked closer. *This couldn't possibly be real. Pictures can't talk,* I thought.

As I approached the picture, I heard, "Katherine, come to Me, and I will give you rest."

My voice trembled. "Who are You?"

"I am the Truth your heart longs for, my child. I AM."

"Katherine! Katherine!" Maria shouted from the front door. "Come on right now! We have to go!"

I snapped out of my trance and ran out of the church.

* * * *

The next few months of my life were pure hell on earth. Eddie and Maria had totally changed after I moved into their home. Appearances were very important to this couple. Maria acted one way in public, yet went out of her way to humiliate me in her house. Her kids played Anastasia and Drusilla while I was Cinderella. Maria often cooked Spanish feasts and invited her husband and kids to eat at the dining room table while having me clean the kitchen during dinner. While the family laughed and ate together as a family, I washed the dirty pots and pans, reorganized the refrigerator to make room for leftovers and swept and mopped the floor. After everyone cleared their plates and lunches were made for the next day, I was allowed to eat leftovers, followed by washing all their new dirty dishes and tidying up the kitchen again. I *never* sat around the table and ate breakfast, lunch or dinner with the family, a tradition I was used to having with my own family. I either ate in the basement or I sat at the kitchen table by myself.

I also did all the other household chores, including everyone's laundry. While James and Joan were involved in after school extracurricular activities I was at home cleaning house—without an allowance, I might add.

Joan was a total snob. She would invite friends over and hang out without ever asking me to join them. I heard them laughing hysterically through the walls, blasting music and showing off the latest dances. I never experienced envy before because I always had friends and family. Natalie always let me tag along with her friends and vice versa. We never rejected or isolated each other. That was never the case in this house. Even my birthday came and went without notice. I turned fourteen on February 25 and nobody said a word.

I never felt accepted or wanted by anyone, including my so-called uncle. If I ever tried to watch television in the living room, James would walk into the room, take the remote out of my hand and change the channel. If I showered longer than three minutes I would hear frantic pounding on the door, but Maria and Joan enjoyed thirty-minute showers or hour-long baths. If Maria bought my favorite sweets like honey-glazed donuts or pecan swirls she hid them from me so I couldn't eat them, but I would see her kids walking around the house eating them.

My uncle didn't treat me in this fashion, but he never said a word. He chose to sit in his lounge chair with a beer in his right hand and remote control in his left. He tuned out the world with the news. I understand now that with awareness comes responsibility, and with responsibility comes action. My uncle was too much of a coward to bring fairness into his home. All he thought about was his own comfort. As long as Maria exalted him, he had no problems. I began to wonder if they adopted me to earn some extra cash. Whatever their reason, they made it very loud and clear they didn't want me around.

Kenilworth Middle School enrolled kids sixth through eighth grade. Even though I left San Diego in December as a seventh grader, I somehow tested into the eighth grade in January. All the kids had been friends for at least four months by the time I arrived. Most of them had been best friends since elementary school and didn't want anyone new involved in their little cliques. No one picked on me per se, so I don't have any horror stories about being bullied at school. I just didn't have any friends.

The one thing I loved about school was the distraction-free art therapy. I would love to say my teachers really cared about my education enough to stop me from drawing and pay attention in class, but the fact is, in the public school system teachers didn't want to be there any more than I did. Nobody bothered me during class. I sat in the back with my decoupaged composition book and pencil and got lost to the point where I missed the bell. I had to indulge myself at school because as soon as I got home I lived in absolute bondage.

I hated life at this point. I hated my new room, my new house, my new family, my new neighborhood, my new clothes. I hated everything about my life in the eighth grade and needed a place to escape. My only outlet was art, and I immersed myself into drawing all the time. I drew *all the time*. There was not one waking moment I didn't spend in my sketchbook expressing my internal frustration. In fact, the only time I exhaled was while I created art. Art soon became my number one priority in life.

Up until then I had focused on realism, perfecting my portraits, lines and shadows, yet as my life got darker my art grew complex and abstract. I drew nature displaying the paranormal turmoil and rage I felt on the inside. I lived in a new city with unloving strangers. I moved away from home and classmates I'd known since kindergarten. My attire changed from sundresses, barrettes and flip-flops to down coats, rubber bands and snow boots. Psychologists say children who undergo trauma in their lives usually fuel their pain into something or someone. My art became a conduit for my pain.

Part of the agreement of my moving to Chicago was therapist visits twice a week. As much as Maria complained about driving me to the city I was never late. Mrs. Mary back in California hooked my family up with her network of doctors at the DePaul Psychiatric Center in Chicago.

I simply loved Chicago! It vibrated a different energy than Des Plaines or San Diego: elevated trains, narrow streets, funky shops, cultural eateries, creative youth and a variety of nationalities. My appointments were in Lincoln Park, an eclectic yuppie neighborhood on the north side right off of Fullerton and Clark Street, across the street from DePaul's main campus. Elizabeth Dodd was my first counselor, Tuesdays and Saturdays were our appointment dates and Zoloft was my first medication.

I hated talking to a complete stranger. Our sessions never progressed through anything although I wasn't the most compliant patient. She asked me the same redundant questions, yet was never able to get to the root of my problems. Our sessions sounded like this:

"So how are you adjusting to life in Chicago?" she asked.

"Fine, I guess," I replied.

"How do you like it?"

"I don't."

"Why not?"

"'Cause."

"Because what?"

"'Cause I just don't."

"Well there has to be a reason as to why you are not enjoying yourself here. How different is it from California?"

"Like night and day!"

"Why is that?"

"Well, let me see," I said. "In California I had a mother, father, sister, brother. I had my own room and shared an elaborate bathroom with my sister. I ate breakfast at the kitchen table with my family and a maid cleaned our house. I went to the movies with my family. The sun shone all year long. I had friends. I had laughter. Beach, mountains, skateboards, sunscreen. I didn't have to bare my soul to a complete stranger or get put on crazy medication. You know? Differences like that."

"I see. And how are you coping with those differences here?"

"Look, I don't want to talk right now."

"Well, we have to talk about something, Katherine. That is why you are here, to express your feelings and possibly start afresh. I am here to help you do that. So...would you like to tell me more about California?"

The conversation usually ended there.

* * * *

The only time I drew at home was right before I went to bed. I hid my favorite sketchbook in my school locker and kept a small, pocket-sized spiral notebook underneath the mattress in my room. Living in the basement meant no privacy for me, so I begged my uncle to add a lock on my door. To my surprise, he actually listened. That is when the nightmare started.

I did my usual routine: finish my slave work, take a shower, get dressed in the bathroom and walk down three flights of stairs to my bedroom. I closed my door, locked it, pulled out my sketchbook and got to drawing. I suddenly heard the creaking noises outside my room, meaning someone was coming down the stairs.

At first I thought it was Maria finishing up her laundry since she favored to put a load in the washer and dryer at night right before she went to sleep. I learned to sleep through the noise so it wasn't a big deal. I ignored the noise and continued drawing. The footsteps moved off the stairwell onto the concrete floor, walking the opposing direction of the laundry room. They were heading my way! Then they stopped. All of a sudden I heard a key slide into the lock. Somebody was unlocking my bedroom door! Who had a key? I didn't. I didn't even realize there was a key when my uncle installed the lock.

My door slowly crept open, and my heart felt like it leaped out of my chest when I realized it wasn't Maria. As the door closed behind James I jumped up and ran to the corner.

I started screaming, "Oh my God! What are you doing? Why are you in my room? What do you want? Who gave you a key to my door?"

James stole my innocence around midnight on February 28, 2004, three days after my fourteenth birthday. All of it was gone in an instant while my uncle, aunt, and cousin slept peacefully on the third floor. Any idea of saving my virginity until marriage faded into the background before I even had a chance to consider the fairytale.

I felt powerless. Dirty. Violated. Worthless. I jumped in the shower to wash away the blood, sweat, and guilt and removed the sheets from my mattress for fear of someone finding out and accusing me of willingly sleeping with their precious jewel. He was smart enough to throw me on the floor so the mattress wouldn't get stained. After my shower I bleached blood and other bodily fluids off the floor and placed the soiled clothes, sheets and towels in a garbage bag. I threw the evidence in the outside trash can where I knew Maria wouldn't look, then I grabbed some clean clothes from my drawer and jumped back in the shower.

I blamed myself. That night changed my self-perception forever and skewed my view of men. I trusted no one. The experience shaped the person I would later become: a girl I hated and didn't want to be around, a girl who escaped life by inking images on bodily canvases while immersing myself in sex, drugs and rock and roll. I felt so helpless in that house, a complete victim with no sense of peace or safety. This was the first night of what began to take place several times a week.

No one protected me from this degrading, embarrassing act. It's not like anyone truly cared for me. For all I knew, James was hired to torture me by Maria. *Well, maybe if I hadn't asked for the lock on the door, then he wouldn't have been stupid enough to walk in my room. Maybe if I hadn't worn that tight gray shirt in front of him, I wouldn't have tempted him. Or, maybe if I would have kept a weapon in my room, then I could have fought back better.* I equated myself with a prostitute, a hooker, a cheap thrill. I didn't tell a soul because I had no one to confide in.

* * * *

It was now spring in Chicago. April 18, to be exact. The slushy brown snow and layers of thick ice disappeared as the sun emerged. The lifeless, bare trees bloomed white and pink magnolias. The brown grass changed into vibrant green after a few days of April showers. The dead stumps in the ground grew into bee-yellow daylilies, carnation-pink peonies, and purple knockout roses. Even though the temperature was around fifty degrees outside, the air was cool, clean and crisp. It wasn't the 70 degree weather I was used to in San Diego, but it was better than the bone-chilling wind and slushy mess I endured since December.

This particular Tuesday I anxiously desired to see my counselor, Elizabeth. I wasn't going to share what happened between me and James, but she was the only person I knew that didn't live in this house. When she asked me how family life was going my body locked up. I wanted to tell her about the hell on earth I experienced in that house, but the shame I felt was too great. My throat was completely locked shut!

"You know, Katherine," Elizabeth lectured, "it's cathartic to express your emotions. Talking cleanses the soul and unclutters the mind. It releases the heaviness in your heart. You begin to take back control of your life if you harness your emotions you hand over your power. It is impossible to grow and change as a woman if you're not in full control of your mind, soul and body. Acceptance and self-responsibility is the first step to take back your life and live healthy. I know this is very difficult for you. You have made so many adjustments within the past few months, and I am proud of you, but I want to help you go deeper. I want you to experience true healing at a heart level."

"Are your parents still alive?" I stuttered. My body began to shake.

"As a matter of fact, they are still alive. They both turn eighty-five this year." She beamed with joy but then stopped when she realized I wasn't smiling with her.

"Then how are you gonna help me process my feelings when you don't know what I'm feeling? A textbook can't talk you through this."

"I haven't experienced the loss of a parent, Katherine. I did, however, lose a brother in a DUI accident when I was twelve years old, so I can relate. He was only two years older than me and we were the very best of friends. When he was killed in that accident my entire world fell apart, especially since I was somewhat of an awkward child. My brother defended me against the world. He was my shield. My protector. So I can relate to your situation a lot more than you realize." She looked at me like she knew something I didn't. "I have been where you are on many different levels. I know it's hard, and I know it hurts. But I also know that it does help to talk with someone. Talking can position you in the driver's seat."

Everything in me wanted to tell Elizabeth about James and those nights, but I couldn't bring myself to do it. I sat there hoping she could read my mind.

"Well, okay. There is no need for us to continue this session in silence. We will pick up again on Saturday, okay?"

"Whatever," I said as I got up and walked out. As the door closed behind me I heard, "See you later, Katherine." In that moment I realized how much I loathed the name Katherine and I disconnected from it. I don't even know who called me Katherine, my birth mom or adopted mom. Both of them were six feet under now, so why should I keep it alive? I was on the hunt for a new name. Katherine seemed so sweet and so pure, and at that moment I was neither.

I longed for something darker and more depressing to mirror the internal turmoil I felt. My mind ran through a list of names while walking to the car from Elizabeth's office. I stopped for a minute to tie my shoe and glanced up at my surroundings.

There was so much activity going on in this neighborhood. Students scurried to class with books in their hands. Bicyclists rode in the street. Joggers ran their dogs. Professionals hurried up the stairs to catch the train. Actors rehearsed their lines in front of the local theater. Patrons sat on the café patio enjoying the scenery. I really liked this city. It was a different vibe than Cali, but a whole different world compared to suburban Des Plaines. There was a refreshing creative yet grounded spirit in the air. All I wanted to do was sit at the corner café, order a hazelnut mocha and freestyle the life around me. I loved this atmosphere. Everyone seemed comfortable in their own skin.

"I want to live here," I said to myself out loud. "I want to find a job, get a studio, and move to the city. To hell with school. I'm not learning anything anyway. I want to live on my own and maybe find something to do with my designs. Work in an art gallery or maybe the Chicago Sun Times comic section. Surely someone would hire me."

I knew those were not normal thoughts for a fourteen-year-old girl in the eighth grade, but the thought of staying in that prison made me want to commit suicide. I hated everything about that house and I wanted out.

"Katherine! Venga, chica! Come on! Tenemos que ir ahora!" Maria shouted from the car.
I snapped out of my trance and immediately planned my escape.

4

The next day I strolled through the art history section of the school library. I saw a book on a cart waiting to be re-shelved: *Inside the Walls of Alcatraz.* For some reason the title caught my eye and I picked up the book. The cover had a picture of a guard standing attentive with a rifle inside of a prison encircled by water. I flipped through the 127-page book and learned that Alcatraz was a lighthouse, military fortification, a military prison and a federal prison. Alcatraz housed notorious criminals such as Al Capone, Machine Gun Kelly, Alvin Karpis, and Robert Stroud. Many escape attempts were made, yet few succeeded alive.

As I stood there reading about this unique island off the coast of San Francisco a connection emerged. *A prison...an island...a place of no return...Alcatraz. Yeah, that's it! Alcatraz! That's my new name!*

This place described exactly how I felt at that point in time in my life. I felt alone, isolated with no one to trust. I felt like there was no love left in the world. Everyone that meant something to me was gone. I was stuck living in that prison of a house as a domestic slave with an aunt and uncle who treated me like a dog, one cousin who ignored me and another who had free access into my room whenever the mood suited him. I felt trapped with absolutely no way out. I couldn't run away if I wanted to and if I did, I'd probably get caught and thrown back in the basement. Yeah. Alcatraz. That name fit me like a glove. Katherine was long gone.

Back in San Diego I had taken a lot of pride in my appearance. Mom, Nat, and I spent hours prepping in the mornings making sure mascara was neat, lips were glossy, skin sun-kissed, hair perfectly in place. Burnt orange had been my signature color, I liked a lot of floral material and carried a hot pink handbag. I usually wore butterfly earrings, sundresses and sandals. Now black became my signature color and I wore faded jeans with Docker boots. My makeup included dark, smoky eyes, black eyeliner, deep purple lipstick and nail polish. Skulls dangled from my ears and a long black leather trench coat finished off the look. Alcatraz was the perfect new name to match my new look.

Needless to say, my research on Alcatraz inspired me to concentrate on blacks and grays in my art. I studied the prison details intensely and replicated the famous A, B, C, and D Blocks with grim gray walls, hard cold floors and iron bars. I investigated some of the prison's famous inhabitants like Robert Stroud and drew him isolated in D block. I captured Big Al gambling behind bars wearing his fedora and smoking his cigar. I did an oil painting of three men trying to escape. One was shot in the head by a guard on the lighthouse, one was ensnared on a hook and the other was attacked by a sea lion.

I even went so far as to look up the meaning of Alcatraz, which came from the Spanish word pelican. I free-handed a brown Peruvian pelican with a white strip from the top of the bill up to the crown and down the side of the neck.

"Katherine…Katherine…Katherine…" I heard faintly. "Hey, didn't you hear me? I said turn over!" James ordered as he slapped my right cheek. I saw no use in putting up a fight anymore; it just led to more bruises I'd conceal and lie about later. I willingly turned over onto my stomach, escaping into my fantasy world of art until he was done.

When I woke up the next morning I was so sore I could hardly walk up the stairs.

"Katherine, what's taking you so long, girl? Move your behind up them steps and get ready for school!" Maria shouted at me. She seemed not to notice my bruises or limp. "Hurry up!" she screamed, grabbing my shoulder and shoving me toward the other flight of stairs. My legs were so weak I fell to the living room floor. "What's wrong with you, girl? Get up and get in the bathroom! You're making everybody else late for school!"

I couldn't do anything but cry. She obviously didn't care so I didn't try to explain. I finally crawled my way up the stairs to the bathroom. I was done. I wanted out. Out of this house. Out of this life. Out of my misery.

I locked the bathroom door and leaned against the wall. Tears rushed down my face as I contemplated ways I could leave this god-awful place and be done with the pain altogether. I saw no reason to live. I wobbled over to the medicine cabinet above the sink and opened it. Colgate. Listerine. Neutrogena. Dental floss. Sun block. I closed the door and opened up the small drawer on the left-hand side of the counter. I picked up my uncle's black toiletry bag. Deodorant. Vaseline. Carmex. Old Spice. Gillette shaving gel and razors. I pulled a razor out of its packaging and returned his stuff the way I found it.

To this day I remember my last thought before my first attempt at suicide. *Life can't get any worse than this, and if it can I don't want to be around to experience it.*

I started with the left wrist. I positioned the tip of the razor on the side of my wrist bone and slashed as deeply and rapidly as I could. I wanted to get it over with so I wouldn't chicken out at the last minute. As I watched the blood flow from my arm into the sink I cut the right wrist. I leaned over the sink to make three more big cuts on my left arm, trying not to make a mess on the floor. The last incision must have passed through a major vein because blood gushed out so fast it spread all over the mirror, walls, toilet and eventually the floor. I dropped the razor. I placed my right hand over my mouth and fell to my knees. Feeling weak, dizzy and useless I lay on the floor in a pool of blood, ready to reconnect with my family. A bright white light suddenly appeared and I felt myself smile.

I whispered, "Thank you, God." and slipped into unconsciousness.

* * * *

My eyes opened to a blank white ceiling resembling the hospital I stayed in for weeks after the crash, only this was worse. I turned my head to the left. Three angry faces met my gaze: Maria, Eddie, and James. I rolled my head to the right to see Joan's folded arms. She had an annoyed look on her face. I realized that every joint ached terribly and it hurt to move. It felt like I'd been dumped into ice cold water. My surroundings looked familiar. Was I in a hospital?

I couldn't quite decipher my location until Joan unfolded her arms and huffed, "Can I go to my room now? She's alive."

"Go ahead," Maria said, "but don't use the bathroom until she feels better enough to clean it." She pointed her finger at me. "Do you realize what you've done?" Maria asked me. "You spilled blood all over my floors. Do you know how much it's going to cost me to thoroughly clean blood-stained tiles, if it's even repairable?"

"What happened?" I completely forgot how I got in this situation.

"Oh, well, let me be the one to remind you," Joan snapped. "I needed to use the bathroom but couldn't because the door was locked for like eternity. After pounding for forever, I had to get James to kick it open and found you lying dead on the floor in a pool of blood. I mean, there's blood everywhere! The sink, the floors, the tub, the hamper. Even the toilet reeked of splattered blood. I yelled for Mom and Dad while I had to walk all the way downstairs just to pee. We have spent the last hour tying towels around your wrists to stop the bleeding. Then on top of that Dad made me help carry you back to the basement.

"Look, I don't know what you're used to with all those meth labs in California but cutting yourself with razors is not cool in Chicago. We're not spoiled brats here. We live normal lives."

"Enough, Joan," Eddie interrupted. "Go upstairs and find something to do until we take you to school."

"Ugh! Dad, this isn't fair! I'm gonna miss my math exam I studied so hard for."

"Vete arriba ahora, mi hija!" Maria shouted.

"But, Mom!" Joan complained.

Uncle Eddy came alive. "Quit your bitching and get up those stairs, now! You too, James. I'm not in the mood for this shit! Upstairs!"

"But, Dad, I want to stay and make sure she's okay," James whined.

Oh my God. If only the Academy were here to present the Oscar for Best Actor in a Drama. Pathetic. I saw every bit of perversion in James' eyes. He pretended to look concerned, yet I know deep down the emotions were all remorse and guilt.

As James and Joan walked out my room and up the stairs, Eddie turned toward me and said, "We bandaged you up pretty good so the bleeding should have stopped by now. You wasted a lot of good towels we use for bathing. There are still some bloodstains in the bathroom, so I want it spic and span in there when you are well. Right now I want you to think about what you've done and how you could have affected this family. This was a pretty selfish act of you, Katherine. We have done everything we know how to do for you. We took you into our home after your parents died. We put you in school. You have a roof over your head, food on the table, and clothes on your back. You have a lot to be grateful for. You could have it a lot worse off than you do. A lot worse."

Is he serious? Did he really think he was doing me a favor by treating me like Cinderella? Having his son treat me like I worked in the back alley of Motel 6?

Just as I began to cry he put his face closer to mine and whispered, "I don't want to hear any more of this, Katherine. You lay here and count your blessings. Afterward, you make your way upstairs to finish cleaning up your mess. You didn't win. You're still here."

I wondered if he was aware of the happenings in this house or was he truly oblivious to the truth. From the looks of it, he sincerely believed his words. He stood back up, turned to Maria and motioned for her to walk out the door. She turned around with what looked like a glimpse of concern in her eyes then closed the door behind them.

When the door closed, I managed to lift my head enough to see my body. I could immediately tell that I hadn't been to the hospital. I was wrapped like a mummy: brown tape held towels around my arms and bound my arms to my thighs. I was back in my bed, the place I had tried to run away from. My mind wandered to my blood family. Dad had said my biological mother was Colombian. I wondered if I had any brothers, sisters, nieces, nephews, cousins or grandparents in Colombia, or anywhere else in the world. Any place except this place.

My next therapy session with Elizabeth took place three days after my "little ordeal," as the family called it.

Elizabeth immediately took notice of the bandages around my wrists. "What happened to your wrists?"

"I fell on the soccer field at school," I lied.

71

"When did you take up soccer?" She sounded excited, probably because she finally got an answer out of me.

"Oh, I don't play soccer. I was just walking on the field and my foot got caught in one of those little holes they never fix in the ground," I responded convincingly. Or so I thought.

"I see." She clearly wasn't convinced. She looked me over and said, "Is everything okay with you, Katherine? How are things going in your uncle's house?"

"Fine. Things are fine," I answered quickly. I lowering my face to avoid eye contact.

"What is that?" she asked. She reached and grabbed my sketchbook out of my book bag on the floor. Before I could stop her, she was already thumbing through the pictures. "What are these?" she asked, glancing up with a concerned look on her face. I didn't bother to explain anything to her. She wouldn't understand. "You are an extraordinary artist, Katherine. Where did you learn?"

"Alcatraz," I said.

"I beg your pardon?"

"My name is Alcatraz."

"Alcatraz? After the prison?" She raised her eyebrows.

"Right."

"Oh. That's nice. Suitable, I would even say. When did you change it?"

"Few days ago."

"Do you know the meaning of Alcatraz?" she asked.

"I know it was a prison where no one hardly ever escaped alive."

"And that's how you feel right now? Like you'll never escape the pain you're in?"

I sat silent. She had hit the nail right on the head.

"Kath…Alcatraz, if I can say something."

"Not that it matters if I wanted to hear it or not," I said.

"Well, you're right. I want you to hear this. I don't believe this is the end for you. Your future is bright, loaded with potential waiting to be ignited. It will just take time to materialize. That's all. I know that's not what you want to hear right now, but be patient. You are going to be okay." Her words sank deep into my heart. "Have you ever researched the name Katherine?"

"No. Why would I do that?" I asked.

"Why did you study the name Alcatraz and not look up Katherine to see the meaning of it? Your parents gave you that name for a reason. Don't you think you at least owe it to them to see why they called you that?"

She was right. Why did the Boydsteins name me Katherine? I didn't vocalize my curiosity, but I definitely wanted to go to the library after our session.

Elizabeth continued looking at my pictures. "Did you study art in California, Kath…? I mean, Alcatraz?" She stopped at one picture and began to study it intensely. "What does this mean?" she asked, showing me the picture.

It was my rendition of the night James raped me the first time, except I recreated it as an angel and a demon. The angel dressed in white lay on her back with her legs wide open in mid- air and the demon dressed in red lay on top of her. The angel was screaming in anguish with one hand on the bedpost and the other one pinned down by the demon. His face demonstrated pride, conquest and power. There was blood on the bed, floor and splattered across the walls.

"Alcatraz!" Elizabeth said sternly. "What does this mean? Has this happened to you?"

I quivered. "It's just a sketch. It means nothing."

"The hell it's just a sketch," she said in a tone I never heard her use before. "Is this happening to you in your new house?" I couldn't retain the tears. "Why are your wrists bandaged? Was this an attempt at suicide?" Elizabeth pointed to my wrist.

"What?" I tried to act stupid.

"On your wrist. What is that?" She put down her notebook and pen.

"I don't know what you're talking about."

"Give me your arm," she demanded.

"What?"

"Give me your arm!" Elizabeth grabbed my right arm and lifted the bandage. She stared at the razor marks, then switched her focus to my left arm. "Did someone do this to you? Or did you do this to yourself?" she demanded. She looked like she was on the verge of tears.

Was she aggressive with everyone? I thought. "Look, it doesn't matter." I snatched my notebook out of her hands. "Can I go now?"

"Is everything all right at home?"

"Why do you care? Nobody even asked me if I wanted to move to Chicago. Why would it matter what happens to me while I'm here?"

"It does matter!" she retorted. "We placed you with family to love you, not hurt you. You do have other options."

"What are you talking about, Elizabeth? I didn't even have an option to come here!"

"Alcatraz, listen. I am on staff at an incredible home for girls. You do not have to live with your uncle. This was just a temporary situation, unless it worked out. But the way it's looking..." She stopped.

"What? The way it's looking, what?" I was dying to know what she was thinking.

"The way it's looking, you won't be there much longer," she announced, opening the door for me to leave. "I'll be seeing you soon, Alcatraz. Very soon."

* * * *

I was downstairs folding clothes when I heard the doorbell ring. I paid no attention to the company and continued folding; no one ever visited me. I sorted the laundry into piles by owner: Joan, James, Maria. As I reached the top of the stairwell with the big basket I overheard my uncle say, "Now, what's this all about?" I peeked around the door to eavesdrop. Two police officers stood on the threshold between the kitchen and living room, and my uncle was in the living room talking to two ladies.

I recognized one of the voices. "I'm concerned about her safety here. I saw some pictures she drew, and we just want to be sure she is in a safe environment while we investigate." It was my counselor, Elizabeth! Wow! I was completely shocked. I didn't realize "very soon" meant two days later!

"Investigate what? Some pictures?" My uncle asked. His tone was full of sarcasm.

"Mr. Boydstein, we need you calm down sir,"

one of the cops said.

"My main concern is that Katherine is safe," an unfamiliar voice stated. "We sent her here to live with you because you were the next living relative, and thankfully you were gracious enough to allow her into your home. But I am afraid we are going to have to remove her for now until we get some clarification of the situation."

At that, I walked right into the kitchen. Several people now sat on the living room sofa and the two police officers stood by the door.

"What?" Maria sounded irate. "How can you take her without any evidence of anything?"

I gasped. Before I could compose myself, I dropped the laundry basket. Everyone in the room turned and looked at me.

My uncle attempted to get up. "Katherine, what have you been telling these people?"

One of the police officers leaped in front of him. "Have a seat, sir."

"Katherine, this is my immediate supervisor, Ari Chesterfield," Elizabeth announced quickly.

"Hello, Katherine," Ari said, standing up to shake my hand. "I'm the Director of Psychiatric Counseling Services at DePaul University. How are you this evening?"

"Fine, I guess," I stuttered while shaking her hand.

"Katherine," Elizabeth said, "go pack your bags, honey. We're taking you with us."

"Katherine, don't listen to her!" my uncle shouted at me. "You guys have some nerve coming into my house this way. Who do you think you are?"

If I hadn't known any better I would have

thought my uncle cared about me for a split second. But I knew better.

"We are protectors of children, Mr. Boydstein," Ari snapped. "When a child is in our care and we feel she is in an unsafe environment it is our job to rectify the situation with or without your cooperation. Now we can do this the easy way, or we can do this the hard way, Mr. Boydstein. The easy way is to let us leave with Katherine quietly."

Just as Ari finished her statement, Elizabeth moved in front of me and said, "Take me to your room, honey, so we can pack your things and get you out of here."

Was I dreaming? Surely this moment couldn't be real. Before anyone could wake me up, I dashed downstairs to the basement to pack my things, leaving the angry adults in the living room to duke it out. Elizabeth followed me. Her lips looked thin and white when she saw where they had graciously let me stay.

After my bags were packed I headed straight out the front door without turning back to say goodbye to anyone. As I hopped inside the backseat of Elizabeth's black Nissan Sentra, Willie's words came to mind: "And with that love comes people He puts in your path to love you. It might be hard to believe right now, but there are people in this world who love you and want the best for you. And Jesus will make sure to connect you to those people."

As we pulled away from 9104 Lincoln Drive, never to return again, I was starting to believe that maybe he was right.

5

The second the Nissan stopped in the driveway of the beautiful campus I felt a strong sense of peace and safety. I broke down crying.

"What's wrong?" Elizabeth asked.

"I don't know. I really don't know," I said, wiping the tears from my eyes. "I guess I just feel..." I sniffed, "Like things will be okay here."

"Great!" Elizabeth smiled. "I think you're feeling the presence of the Spirit."

"Huh?"

"Don't worry about it. You'll see what I mean soon enough."

"What kind of school is this?" I asked. I didn't even know where she was dropping me off.

"This is a privately-owned Catholic school and a home for girls. The campus looks big, but the school itself is relatively small. There are only eighty-eight girls on campus, but they all come from different backgrounds. This school is a pioneer in helping young ladies heal from past trauma and move on with their lives. I believe you have peace right now because you are going to love it here."

"Am I staying here for good?" I asked.

"I'm not going to say for sure yet. We will just have to see how it works out. But you will be here through the school year, at least."

Our first stop was the outpatient clinic because Elizabeth and Ari had ordered a physical. I've never been poked, prodded, squeezed or humiliated so much by a doctor before. I'm not quite sure what she was looking for, but the doctor mashed down my breasts, bent me over, laid me on my back and opened my legs, spread my arms apart to look at my spine and performed all these crazy walking exercises.

As I got dressed again, I overheard Elizabeth talking to Ari and the doctor. "That's what I thought. That's exactly what I thought. We need to press charges immediately while her signs are still visible." Elizabeth and Ari entered my room while I was on the bed tying my shoes.

"Katherine," Ari said very gently. "We got your test results back from the doctor. Um…" She looked at Elizabeth. "Did anybody hurt you during your stay in that house? Did anyone do something physically bad to you?"

Silence. Goose bumps appeared from nowhere.

"It's okay. It's okay," Elizabeth said with so much compassion I thought she was going to cry. "You won't ever have to return to that house again. Okay? You don't ever have to see those people again if you don't want to."

"I don't want to. I'd rather be anywhere than in that hell hole," I said.

Ari walked toward me with a somber look on her

face. She placed her hand on my shoulder. "We need to ask you a few questions, Katherine. We need to know precisely what happened to you in that house. Who did what, when, where and how many times? We'd like to notify the police and press charges to..."

"Police? For what? No, I don't want to talk to the police! Not now, not ever!" I shouted. I didn't want to share my shame with anyone. Even though Ari and Elizabeth knew the truth, I couldn't bring myself to describe in words what James did to me in that basement. I couldn't let anyone in on the feelings of worthlessness, guilt, and pain indwelling my heart. Those were incidents I planned to keep buried inside even if it meant letting James off the hook.

The two ladies glanced at each other, then Elizabeth looked at me and said, "It's okay, Alcatraz. You don't have to talk if you don't want to. It was just a thought." Her eyes met Ari's again briefly. "Let's just get you to your new room now. Okay?"

I agreed and they left the room. I caught my reflection in a small mirror on the wall and I stopped to look at myself for the first time since my suicide attempt. I looked tired, defeated and weak. The bones protruding from my face revealed how much weight I had lost the past four months. My eyes were bloodshot and lined with dark, sagging bags. My skin was pale and my stringy hair had no body or bounce. I had often received compliments about my natural curls back in San Diego, but now the curls were gone.

I hated what life did to me these last 4 months, yet being here at the doctor and listening to women willing to press charges against the family who hurt me offered a glimpse of hope. I didn't know what this school had in store for me, but I knew it could only get better.

* * * *

Valeo was the last stop for help before the State of Illinois gained custody of a girl. The breathtaking campus had a 24-hour counseling center, a psychiatric ward, a rehab center, on-call nurses and hospital facilities for emergencies, a pharmacy and a religious sanctuary. Valeo Academy educated sixth through twelfth grade girls. The Family Center offered counseling for mothers desiring change, and the Life Empowerment Center helped adults heal past hurts and foster life skills.

Valeo's architecture resembled the Catholic church I visited with Maria. There were hiking trails, tennis courts, waterfalls, Olympic-sized swimming pools, basketball courts, a bowling alley, game rooms, art galleries, fully furnished workout facilities, a yoga/Pilates dance studio, a theater which staged plays, dance performances and symphonies, a botanical garden and my favorite room on campus: a fully furnished art studio.

There was no need to leave the campus for anything; an on-site convenience store provided toiletries and feminine items. Valeo went out of their way to make sure we were comfortable at every hour of the day. As much as I missed my parents and California, living at Valeo Academy eased my loss. Looking back, it was the best thing for me at that time.

There were six residential dormitories around the campus. Guadalupe House was for pregnant women and teen mothers with their children. Mary Magdalena

House was for girls with mental illnesses and intellectual disabilities. Verona House was an emergency shelter for girls forced into prostitution and stripping. Ruth House treated girls with substance abuse disorders. Jude House for Women helped eighteen-to-thirty-five year olds transition from a life of chaos to normalcy. And finally, there was Teresa House. The other houses focused on helping girls heal and cope, and those girls returned to their families after treatment. The Teresa House girls remained on campus until age eighteen. I was assigned to Teresa House.

When I arrived at Teresa House A with Ari, she introduced me to the residential hall advisor. "Katherine, this is your residential hall advisor, Mandy Burton."

"Hello, Katherine. It's nice to meet you," Mandy said.

"Alcatraz. Call me Alcatraz," I stated authoritatively, shaking Mandy's hand.

Mandy was a Norwegian beauty in her mid twenties. Her amazingly sculpted body stood about five foot three inches. She had green eyes and chin-length brown hair cut into a bob with bangs. "Oh, okay." She glanced at Ari and Elizabeth, then winked at me. "Alcatraz it is, then."

"Jessica Law and Dana Shroud work this shift as well," Elizabeth explained to me. "All three ladies oversee the day-to-day activities on this floor from three p.m. to eleven. You will see new faces on the night shift between the hours of eleven p.m. to seven a.m., and again in the morning at seven a.m. to three p.m. There are a total of nine workers in this house, and each are here to care for you. Don't be afraid to ask them for anything."

I nodded in agreement.

"We are one big family," Mandy said. "I'm sorry I'm the only one here right now. Dana is preparing snacks and Jessica is handling a situation with a girl, but you have plenty of time to meet them later. I hear you'll be here with us for awhile, yes?"

"This will be her home for now," Ari confirmed. "We believe this will be a great fit for her." Elizabeth nodded in agreement.

"Well, if Valeo does anything for you like it did for me, you will transform into your best self here," Mandy confessed. "We'll do our best to make sure you have an easy transition to our way of life. There are rules, but they are only for your protection and safety. Once you make some friends and get involved in activities you won't sweat the small stuff."

"Yeah I'm sure my life will sail just peachy," I said. "I'll forget I ever had a mom, dad, brother or sister. You guys will wash all my pain away. Is that right?"

Ari and Elizabeth exchanged uncomfortable looks.

"Well, let's show you to your new room," Elizabeth offered. I sensed a bit of apprehension in her voice.

"Actually, I have to get back to the office," Ari stated. "But it was a pleasure meeting you, Alcatraz, and I look forward to hearing good reports about you in the future."

"Okay. Thank you," I said.

Ari looked me up and down once more. She had a sad look in her eyes like this would be our last meeting. "I'm really happy you are in our custody,

Katherine. It may seem foreign to you right now but later you'll see we have your best interest at heart."

My new room was Room 217. That sounded like music to my ears after sleeping in the basement frequently wakened by the harsh noises of the spin cycle.

My first impression of the room was that it was *tiny*. It was smaller than my room in the basement, but it had an adjoining bathroom I had only to share with a roommate. Both sides of the room were identical and none of the furniture could move. Every piece of furniture was nailed to the floor, wall or each other. A mini-sized coat closet for my clothes sat off to the right. Panning left, a mirror was attached to the wall over an adjoining dresser, which was also attached to the wall. A twin-sized bed with a shelf was next to the dresser and the shelf was attached to the wall. A mini refrigerator was tucked away in the corner off to the left. Right next to the fridge was a chair with a tiny desk facing a ceiling-to-floor window overlooking the campus.

The view from the window was amazing. Bikers, joggers and roller bladders worked the mini park's forest trails and students studied on the sprawling green landscape. Girls engaged in conversation by the man-made lake in the middle of the campus while soccer players ran up and down the field to my right. This place bustled with life. *Positive* life. I just stood there, mesmerized by the beauty of the campus. This is where I was going to live?

"How do you like it? Not exactly Des Plaines is it?" Elizabeth strutted towards the window. It only took three medium-sized steps from the door.

I smiled sadly and said, "I like it. I really like it a

lot."

"Good. Have no worries of being hurt here. I have sent many girls like you through this program and they turn out fine just like Mandy. You get a personalized program tailored directly to your needs and the undivided attention crucial for your growth as a woman. Valeo can reach you on a deeper, more intimate level than a weekly visit. Plus, you'll have access to a world only the filthy rich can afford, and you'll meet some incredible girlfriends."

"Starting with your new roommate Nicole Le Ray," Mandy added. "She's a great person to have as a roommate. We get no problems out of her whatsoever. She'll be moving to another house next year because of age, but I believe there will be an instant connection."

"Exactly," Elizabeth agreed.

"Let's take a tour of the facility, shall we?" Mandy invited.

"Can we do it later?" I asked. "I just want to stay in my room for now."

"Sure," Elizabeth said. "Get unpacked and settle in. Mandy can show you around a little later."

"Yeah, that's no problem," Mandy agreed. "You've had a long day so get some rest. Dinner is from seven to eight downstairs in the kitchen, but I can show you that when you're ready. Or maybe Nikki will return before then and she can show you. If you need anything, just know my office is down the hallway here to your right." Mandy stepped in the hallway pointing in the direction of her office.

"Thanks," I said.

"I'll see you next Tuesday then. Our Saturdays have been canceled," Elizabeth said as she walked toward the door.

"Next Tuesday?" I asked.

"Yeah, you forgot our appointments already?"

"How are we gonna meet next Tuesday now that I live here?"

"Remember, I told you? I am a resident therapist here. I counsel on Tuesdays and Thursdays. Instead of you coming out to Chicago we will meet in the counseling center here."

Joy welled up in my heart and I couldn't contain the tears. I dove into Elizabeth's waist and gave her the biggest hug I had given anyone since my parents died. I was *so* grateful for all she had done for me.

"I'll see you next week, okay?" she said, returning the hug. "And don't forget your assignment."

"My assignment?" I asked before I stopped to think about it. "Oh yeah, my name. I won't forget. See you next week." I let go of her, leaving a huge wet spot on her blouse.

"See you at dinner, Alcatraz," Mandy said.

"Okay. See you in a few," I said. Mandy closed the door behind Elizabeth.

I spent the next few hours lying on my bed and soaking up the moment. I felt safe for the first time in months. I didn't have much stuff with me, just two suitcases and a box full of past sketches—the only true valuables in my life. I just lay there staring at the ceiling, so happy to be out of the fear and violation of that house. I wondered what life would unfold next.

Although I was only fourteen years old, I felt like I'd lived on earth for thirty years. My life had shifted one hundred eighty degrees in the last four months from a life of security, purity and joy to uttermost pain, darkness and uncertainty. A hopeful child in me craved the feeling of security again, but the only thing I could count on was myself. Right there in my room I made a conscious decision that affected my future life choices: I vowed to trust no one except myself. Anything and everything external sat on quicksand. Nothing in this world was for sure.

The only trustworthy cause I believed in was enhancing, edifying and improving the world around me. I wanted to leaving the world a better place than the way I found it, yet I did not want to be attached to the results because nothing in life is rock-solid. I could spend the next twenty years drawing to my heart's desire and build a gallery as a world-renowned artist, only for it to be destroyed in a fire a five year old child accidentally started by playing with his mom's lighter he snagged out of her purse.

Nothing in this world could be trusted except for me, and even that could pass away as quickly as a tire that blows out on the highway. There was no peace or security in this world that I could see.

After meditating on those thoughts, I fell asleep.

* * * *

I jumped up from my nap, completely disoriented. I realized I'd heard the door slam.

"Hi, I'm Nicole. You must be my new roommate." I looked up to see a very pretty black girl staring down at me. I rolled over to my left side to sit up, wipe the drool off my face and get a better look at her. I wondered how long I had been asleep. "You must be Katherine," she continued.

"Alcatraz," I said.

"What?"

"My name is Alcatraz." I was annoyed that I had to repeat myself.

"Oh, Dana told me your name was Katherine. Sorry."

"Yeah, well Dana doesn't know me yet. I haven't met her. Just Mandy."

"You haven't missed anything," Nicole said. "Dana has the least personality out of the bunch. She's very by-the-book so don't get offended if she calls you Katherine after you tell her your name is Alcatraz."

"Okay. Thanks for the heads up."

"How long you here?"

"I think forever," I replied.

Nicole started laughing. "Yeah, they tell everybody that until they find you a foster family. Don't get too comfortable 'cause you never know."

"How long have you been here?"

"This will be going on my second year. Next year I'm moving to House B since I'll be turning sixteen. How old are you?"

"Fourteen."

"Oh, wow. You're the exact age I was when I entered, minus the pregnancy," Nicole said.

"Pregnant?" I shouted in horror. "You were pregnant at fourteen?"

"Yeah, unfortunately." She paused. "Long story." She looked away and shrugged. "I guess my life could be a lot worse."

"Where is the baby?" I asked, still stunned.

"She's with an adopted family somewhere. After I gave birth some doctors told me to sign these papers in the hospital to give her away to a family that could provide a better life for her. I didn't know what

I was signing at the time or else I would have …" She wavered, like she was trying to figure out why she was being so open with a complete stranger. She redirected the conversation. "Why are you in here?"

"My parents got killed in a car accident, so Elizabeth thought it would be good to move me here."

"Elizabeth Dodd?"

"Yeah, you know her?"

"Oh my God, yes. She's the most unorthodox counselor here. She breaks a lot of codes of conduct, but she does care."

"What do you mean, she breaks codes of conduct?" I asked.

"Well, for example, how long did she counsel you before you ended up here?"

"I started talking to her in January of this year."

"And when did she find out you were being abused?"

"How did you know I was being abused?"

"'Cause you wouldn't be here if you weren't. We're all damaged goods here. Everyone pretty much has the same plot, just different characters and scenes. No one is here because they came from the Brady family."

"Yeah, I guess that makes sense." I was baffled by her ease of talking about the subject that was still so painful to me.

"So when did she find out?"

"Um. I guess two days ago in our counseling session. She saw some pictures I drew. I didn't explain them to her but she guessed accurately."

"Two days ago? Are you kidding me?" she shouted.

"What's the big deal with that?"

"That is not standard protocol, girl. Most counselors who find out their patient is being abused don't move *that* quickly. They investigate the situation while the girl still gets slapped around. They do interviews with the family first before they just walk in the house and abduct the child. They don't hear your story at nine and have you in a home by four. It is a lengthy process. At least it was for me and most girls here."

What she said rang true to me. "Yeah, I guess you're right. She did move kinda quickly. But she said she was on staff here in our meeting, so I just thought she had pull."

"Still girl, pull or no pull, that was fast!. There are plenty of counselors on staff here who work all over the city of Chicago and they don't pull like that. You are lucky, girl. I never heard of that!"

Now that Nicole mentioned it, I did realize that my life had moved quickly. I mean, the accident was only four months ago. I stayed in the hospital for three weeks and moved to Chicago with my uncle. Now here I was at Valeo Academy.

"How many families did you live with before you were placed here?" Nicole asked.

"What do you mean?"

"I mean foster families? How many foster families have you lived with?"

"Well…none, I guess. Unless you count my uncle as a foster family. But I don't think they considered him one. He was actual family."

"Yeah, girl. You are definitely special. Most girls live in at least three foster families before they get moved in here. This place is a last resort for the state, not a first. You must have angels looking out for you or something."

"I guess so," I said. I didn't know where this conversation was going. "Elizabeth thought this place would be better for me. I just thought she was doing her job."

"Don't you think it's funny how all these people make decisions based on what *they* think is best for us?" Nicole asked.

I had never really thought about it like that, but my mind was disoriented from the whirlwind I experienced in the past four months so I didn't mind someone else thinking for me.

"Are you from here?" I asked, trying to change the subject.

"No. I'm from Houston, Texas. I lived with my crackhead mom, but after I got pregnant my grandparents sent for me to move here with them. But then my grandma died from kidney failure, and my grandpa died three months later of natural causes. I believe he died 'cause he missed his wife. You know how they say if a couple is married for a long time and one of them dies then shortly after the other spouse dies? They were married fifty-six years, and I think he just got wife sick.

"My mom pretty much turned me to the wolves after the funeral, and to make a long story short, I ended up in foster care for about a year or two, then here at the good 'ole Valeo Academy." She paused. "Well anyway, tonight is Sloppy Joe night down at the cafeteria. They have pool tables, pinball machines and a bunch of crazy chicks. Do you want to come? I can introduce you to some of my people."

"Uh, sure. Can I shower first?" I asked.

"I would hope so." She laughed. "You do want these people to be your friends?"

"Yeah. I just didn't know how soon you were leaving."

"Oh, I can leave whenever you're ready unless you're a prima donna. Dinner ends at eight, so you don't have all damn night."

"No, I don't take all day. I'll be out in a few minutes."

"Okay, let me use the toilet first then you can take your shower." Nicole jumped off the bed and went into the bathroom.

"Sounds good to me," I answered. I started to unpack my things. I placed my few articles of clothing into the dresser on my side of the room, laid my toiletries on the desk and slid my sketchbooks underneath the bed. I threw my suitcase in the closet, closed the closet door and looked around the room. My heart was full of gratitude and my mind was completely still. I inhaled slowly then exhaled. I realized for the first time since my accident that I felt at peace.

6

There were about thirty girls downstairs, each doing their own thing. Some girls sat on the floor with a book, others watched *I Love Lucy* reruns on the seventy-two inch television in the foyer, a few played pool on one of the five pool tables and the rest were in the kitchen preparing the meal.

Every race was represented: White, Black, Asian, Hispanic, mixed. The girls were tall, short, thin, overweight. Some of them had pink hair, black hair, one earring or five earrings. There were all kinds of girls here. Some were loud, class clowns while others quietly observed from the corners of the room. All of them had suffered from some kind of past traumatic experience, and they all lived under one roof. Even though we all had different stories, there was a connection between us: we each identified with pain.

"Hey, hey, hey," Nicole said, making her way toward the pool table. "This is my new roomie, Alcatraz. Alcatraz, this is Leinani and Rosa."

"Hello," I said faintly with a shy wave.

"Hey. Alcatraz, is it?" Rosa asked

"Yeah," I said.

"What kind of name is that?"

"Mine."

"Did your parents name you after the prison or something?" Rosa continued.

"No, they didn't. I named me that. And yeah, you could say I named myself after the prison."

"Very nice. I like it." Leinani smiled. "I'm Leinani Cabe," she walked toward me with a pool stick in one hand. She extended her other hand to shake mine.

Her name sounded foreign to me. "What kind of name is Leinani?"

"Hawaiian. My family is from the island of Lanai. Where are you from?" Leinani asked.

"Originally from California, but I've been here since December."

"Oh, what brought you here?" Rosa asked, continuing their game of pool.

"I moved in with my uncle after my parents died," I said.

"How'd your parents die?" Rosa asked.

"Dang, girl, you nosy! What'd I tell you about butting into grown folks business?" Nicole shot at Rosa.

"Hey, I'm just trying to start a conversation here. Trying to build a relationship."

"Well, give the girl some breathing room for now. She just got here today. You got all year to document her life story," Nicole cracked.

"Ha, ha, ha," Rosa responded sarcastically. All three of these girls were very pretty. It made me wonder why in the world their parents gave them away.

"Come and get it!" a blond girl yelled from the kitchen. When I turned around I saw a buffet line set up. It featured a house salad with a choice of ranch, blue cheese, honey mustard, Italian and French dressings. There was also fruit salad with mango, strawberries, blueberries, and pineapple, Cesar salad, Sloppy Joe meat, toasted hamburger buns, sliced lettuce and tomatoes, fried potato fries, vanilla and chocolate pudding, water, ice tea and fruit punch.

"Hope you're not a vegetarian," Leinani said, putting down her stick and walking toward the buffet line. "'Cause you don't get much of a choice here."

"She could eat the fruit and salad," Rosa offered.

"Oh yeah, that's true, but that can't be too filling, huh?" Leinani answered.

"Who said the girl was even a vegetarian?" Nicole asked. She apparently did not like jumping to conclusions.

"Actually, I'm not really hungry," I said, noticing I had knots in my stomach. "I'm, uh, gonna go back to the room and lay down. I'll see you guys later okay?"

"Hon, we just got here," Nicole said. "Don't you want to hang out just a little while? You don't have to eat if you don't want, but you can sit and chat with us."

"No, I don't feel like chatting right now. I'll talk to you later," I said. I waved good-bye and headed toward the stairs.

"Do you remember how to get back to the room?" Nicole asked.

"Yeah, I'll figure it out. Thanks, though."

"All right. Nice meeting you. We'll hang some

other time," Leinani said.

"Yeah, see you tomorrow," Rosa followed.

"See you guys tomorrow," I said.

As I walked up the stairs another blond-haired lady with blue eyes walked down. She stopped to speak to me. "Oh, hello. You must be the new girl, Katherine. I'm Dana Shroud, one of your resident advisors. I'm sorry I couldn't greet you earlier."

"It's okay. Good to meet you," I said.

"Are you not eating with us?"

"No, I'm not really hungry right now. I just want to go back to my room and rest a bit."

"Oh, okay. Would you like me to make a plate you can put in your refrigerator? You might get hungry later in the night and the kitchen will be locked after dinner."

"It's okay. Thanks anyway."

"Did someone tell you your schedule for tomorrow?"

"No, not yet. I have a schedule?" I asked.

"Oh yes, we all do. You will need to go take some tests tomorrow to place you in your classes. What grade are you in?"

"I was in seventh grade in Cali but tested in eighth here."

"Okay. Well, hopefully you will test out of English, reading, math, and sciences. Then maybe you can ride out the rest of this semester with electives."

"But what if I fail the tests? Do I have to start all over?"

"Not necessarily. Depending on the results you probably can take summer classes to catch up. Then you can start on time in September. The school year ends in about eight weeks so you might have to take some classes this summer, but let's see what the tests say first. Your day will start at nine tomorrow morning. Breakfast is from seven to eight, then you'll go on a school tour, meet your counselors, take tests, and select your classes. You have a busy day ahead of you so it's wise to turn in early."

"Alrighty then. See you tomorrow," I said.

"Do you remember your way back to your room?"

"Yeah, I got it. See you tomorrow."

When I returned to my room I plopped down on my bed and stared at the ceiling. I was happy to be out of my uncle's house and in a new place, but I really missed my family in San Diego. I wished I could just call them right now and tell them to come pick me up.

None of this would be happening to me if they were still alive. If there had been no crash, if I hadn't wanted to go to Hi Life, then maybe they would still be here with me right now. Mom would be in the kitchen fixing us a delicious Burgundy Beef Stew and warmed butter croissants with her famous Peach Tea. Dad would probably be with Henry in the garage building the six foot tall Empire State building out of Legos. I would definitely be in Nat's room drawing a portrait of something while she worked on a science project. The house would be a peaceful whirlwind. The conversation would be wholesome and the air would smell like love. The nostalgia of my life in San Diego returned and my heart filled up with emotion. I started bawling. I couldn't control myself as the bottled up emotions released themselves onto my pillow.

Why was I the only survivor? Why couldn't I

have died along with them? Or at least, why couldn't I have died when I slit my wrists? I wouldn't be moving from pillar to post, rooming up with strangers, eating Sloppy Joes for dinner and talking to a therapist every week. All of this could have been avoided if I had just died in the crash. A deep sense of remorse suffocated me and I cried myself to sleep.

* * * *

My schedule at Valeo Academy kept me busy: two elective classes, seventy-two hours of fitness training, thirty hours of life skills, one hundred twenty hours of community service and ninety hours of spiritual formation were mandatory. I also had the individual therapy sessions with Elizabeth on Tuesdays and group therapy on Thursdays. Since there were only eight weeks left in the semester, the school enrolled me in seventh grade electives: Art History and Art Therapy. For my fitness training, I chose soccer. For my community service, I picked up trash around campus. For my life training, I chose cooking. Religious Studies 101 fulfilled my spiritual formation requirement.

I couldn't wait to dive into the art classes and study the passion that had captured my heart. After I registered for classes I headed straight to the library to work on the assignment Elizabeth had given me.

"Do you have any books on the meaning of names?" I asked the librarian.

"Well sure, sweetheart. Are you looking for a rare cultural name or a common everyday name?"

"I need to look up the name Katherine."

"Oh, well, that's easy. Follow me, sweetie," the

librarian said, walking from behind the desk toward the bookshelves. "Is this for a class you're taking now?"

"Yeah, I guess you can say that."

"Okay. I think we need to go down this aisle. My name is Josephine, by the way."

"Hi. I'm Alcatraz."

"Oh, Alcatraz. Now that's an unusual name," she said, looking at the titles on the shelf. "*Meaning of Names.* Here we go. This book should have the definition you need in great detail." She handed me the book. "I think this is a great assignment for you."

"Why? You don't even know me," I said.

"That's true, but the meaning of your name says a lot about you. For example, Josephine is a feminine form of the name Joseph, which is Hebrew for 'the Lord increases.'"

"The Lord increases?"

"Yes, ma'am. That is the root definition of my name, and it truly represents the decisions I have made. I am a librarian by day and a successful realtor by night and weekend. I sell multi-million dollar homes in my spare time!"

"And you think your name controlled that decision?" I asked.

"Yes, of course I do. I believe my parents ignorantly named me Josephine, but the stars knew exactly who was forming. My life has always prospered no matter what position I found myself in. The stars always increased me."

"So, you praise the stars?"

"Yes. The universe definitely kept her promise to my name, that's for sure."

I considered her rationale.

"This could be an eye-opening experience for you, Alcatraz," she continued. "This could explain your past, present, and future."

"All that?"

"Yes, all that," she said, laughing. "Be open to receive something new today."

She sounded more like a Bohemian psychic than a librarian, but I took her advice to heart. I even got excited to learn the origin of my birth name. I sat down at a table in the middle aisle and flipped straight to the names beginning with the letter K.

Katherine is of Greek origin, and it means pure, to purge or to cleanse. Many prominent women were named Katherine, yet the one woman spotlighted in the book was Saint Catherine of Alexandria. I discovered that my birth name was popular in Christian countries after this saint.

Saint Catherine is noted as one of the fourteen holy helpers in the Catholic Church. She was the daughter of a pagan governor who announced to her parents at a young age that she would only marry someone who surpassed her in beauty, intelligence, wealth and social status. This statement foreshadowed Catherine's relationship with Jesus Christ. She was raised a pagan but became a Christian in her late teens. Her influence in the church converted a lot of pagans including the empress, the wife of Roman emperor Maximinus.

Saint Catherine was thrown into prison for spreading the message of Jesus, and all who visited her in prison converted to Christianity. After the emperor saw prison couldn't stop this lady from talking about Jesus, he condemned her to death. Legend has it she was ordered to die on the breaking wheel, yet when she touched the wheel it broke into pieces. Feeling completely powerless against this woman's authority, the emperor beheaded her publicly.

I slammed the book shut and sat silently at the table. A rush of anger flowed through my body. I most certainly wasn't pure anymore, nor was I some intercessor praying for people's salvation. I didn't believe in this Jesus guy and I definitely wasn't about to die for him. This assignment only amplified my desire to rename myself Alcatraz. There was nothing in the name Katherine I identified with. I gathered my belongings, placed the book back on the shelf and darted out of the library.

When I returned to my room Nicole was sitting on her bed next to Leinani and Rosa sat on top of the desk.

"Hey, roomie!" Nicole chirped. "Hope you don't mind the company."

"Well if I did, would it matter?" I asked sarcastically. I was not in a good mood.

"What? Oh, I'm not trying to deal with this attitude!" Rosa snapped. "We'll hang some other time, Nikki."

"No, we shouldn't have to leave," Leinani interrupted. "This is Nicole's room, too, and besides, we need another person."

My snit cleared up instantly, replaced by curiosity. "Another person for what?"

"Light as a feather, stiff as a board." She smiled eerily.

"What's that?" I asked.

"A game we used to play back in New Orleans. You connect to spiritual energy and use it to supersede the natural," Leinani clarified. "You want in?"

I wanted to spend time by myself to focus on my drawing, yet I had never played this game before. After hearing the concept of "connecting to spiritual energy" I thought I should check it out. The object of the game was for one person to lie on her back on the floor while three to four people kneel around her with their two peace fingers underneath her body. We were to connect to the cosmic forces of the universe with our combined mental powers and lift this person up. We wouldn't use our muscles; the force of the universe would lift her.

"Okay. So here's the deal," Leinani explained. "We have to agree on one common object to focus on or we have to agree to focus on nothing. One or the other. As we empty ourselves of our thoughts, the power of Aether flows through us."

"Who is Aether?" I questioned.

"He is the creator of everything in existence. Seen and unseen. He is what holds this world together." She paused to see if I comprehended her explanation, then continued, "Who's going in the circle?"

"I'll go," Nicole jumped hastily onto the floor.

This concerned me somewhat seeing that Nicole was six feet tall and one hundred eighty or so pounds. I was hoping Rosa would volunteer since she couldn't be taller than four foot eleven weighing a maximum of ninety pounds. But I guess that just intrigued me all the more.

"Okay, so here we go," said Leinani. "Let's all kneel around her. Rosa, you kneel around Nikki's waist. Traz, you by her legs. I got her shoulders. So,

Nikki, just get comfortable, okay? Cross your arms in front of your chest. Close your eyes and relax your body into the ground." Leinani's voice got very soothing like she was conducting a meditation class. "Now, you three imagine that you are on a beach in Fiji."

"What is Fiji?" Rosa asked, opening her eyes.

"The most beautiful island off the Pacific Coast of New Zealand. It's got turquoise water, white sandy beaches, and vibrant, green vegetation."

"Where's New Zealand?" I asked.

"New Zealand is by Australia, near the Polynesian Islands."

"Where's the Polynesian Islands?" Nicole asked.

"Okay, you guys, seriously." Leinani was getting frustrated. "This is messing up the mental connection with Aether's energy!"

"Well, you're the one naming all these exotic foreign places no one even heard of! Why can't we be somewhere like Jamaica or something?" Nicole retorted.

"Oh, Jamaica! I've seen pictures of that place. My ex-foster family used to visit there a lot," Rosa contributed.

"I can imagine Jamaica. My family was planning a trip there. They had Jamaican travel guides around the house," I inserted solemnly.

"Fine. Jamaica it is then, you narrow-minded dogs," said Leinani.

"Why we got to be all that?" Nicole laughed.

"Everybody, close your eyes," Leinani said, ignoring Nikki. "Imagine yourself sitting on the white sand listening to the ocean water along the seashore. The sun is hitting your face and the sand is soft and warm underneath your body. Take yourself there. Envision yourself breathing in the salty air. Listen to the waves. Feel the breeze. Exhale. Breathe in the salt water. Listen to the seagulls above you. Breathe out."

Nicole and Rosa both giggled. Trying not to burst into laughter, I stayed tuned.

"Okay, ladies," Leinani continued. "We are on the beach. Now we need to get in sync. Inhale through your nose. Hold. Now exhale. Again. Inhale, hold. Exhale. Clear your mind of all the clutter and connect to the ocean waves." I didn't know what the others were feeling from this little exercise, but I was getting sleepy.

"Now let's try and synchronize our breath," Leinani continued. "Inhale. Hold...two...three. Exhale...two...three. Let's connect our mental energies. Inhale. Hold...two...three. Exhale...two...three." Leinani repeated this three more times until I could no longer distinguish my breath from hers or Rosa's. After a few minutes, Leinani instructed, "Repeat after me. Light as a feather, stiff as a board. Light as a feather, stiff as a board. Light as a feather, stiff as a board."

As I chanted the words a presence entered the room. It was dark and heavy and I recognized it as the same presence in the shower with me back in the hospital. I'm not sure who or what it was, but fear crept into my heart again.

Before long, all three of us were chanting in unison and I couldn't distinguish my voice from Rosa's or Leinani's. We were no longer in the building. All three of us were flying high in the sky. Higher than my drawings take me. I was completely detached from reality and everything in me wanted to live this high forever.

When I opened my eyes what I witnessed challenged every belief about God as I knew it. Nicole was floating in thin air! Her feet were at eye level and nothing visible was holding her up. What astounded me the most was the dark presence in the room. It became heavier, like a fog. Someone or something was in the circle! I felt its presence all over my body as an immobilizing, invisible force. I didn't know much about spirits at that point but I knew this presence was not good.

"Do you guys feel that?" I asked, looking at Rosa and Leinani for a response.

"Oh, yeah." Leinani beamed, eyes still closed. "I feel his presence often."

Rosa finally opened her eyes and gave a shriek. "Oh my gosh. Oh my gosh. It worked! We made it happen."

"Of course we did," said Leinani, looking over at her. "Aether is always there. We just have to tap into him."

I needed clarification. "Who is this Aether again?"

"Spirit. The fifth element of the universe. Earth, wind, air, and fire are the physical elements people connect with because they are connected to the five physical senses of smell, taste, touch, sight, and sound. We can smell, taste, and touch dinner when it's ready, and our communication is a combination of hearing and sight. Air can't be seen but inhaled. Wind is the air we feel. Earth is the terrain we walk on, and fire can grab anyone's attention when touched. But spirit cannot be realized with our five senses or with the four elements. We have to turn off our five senses to connect to this sixth sense. It is within all of us, but we don't know it. Spirit is always there, always ready to bend at your will to do whatever you wish. Spirit is there to help you create the life you want."

I know I had to be drooling as she explained this as I realized my mouth was wide open.

"How do we get her down?" Rosa asked, still stunned at the floating body.

"You use the same connection to spirit. Watch," Leinani said. She closed her eyes and motioned with her hands. Nicole's body lowered to the ground gracefully. Leinani obviously didn't need our help for results.

This supposedly harmless game changed the way I saw the spiritual world from that moment forward. It was a turning point in my life where I had a deeper desire to learn the truth about the unseen world. I had always been intrigued but I brushed it off after the death of my parents.

Leinani's magical powers revived my innate curiosity of the Creator. She was really into different types of spirituality. Members of her family were spiritual doctors in Hawaii, so when they moved to New Orleans they felt right at home with their practice. She demonstrated supernatural powers unlike any I had ever seen in someone who claimed they love God. This incident whet my appetite to learn more about Leinani's beliefs.

7

"So, what did you discover?" Elizabeth asked, pen and notebook in hand.

"Discover?" I repeated, pretending like I forgot about the assignment.

"Your name? Did you have a chance to look into the original meaning?"

"I haven't really had time," I lied.

"What else have you been doing since you've been here?"

"My schedule is super jammed. I have school, therapy, art classes, friends—"

"Friends?" Elizabeth perked up. "You're making friends here?"

"Yeah, I guess. My roommate and her friends are pretty cool. We've been hanging out a lot."

"I see," she said. She seemed to be studying me intensely. "What have you been doing together?"

"Pretty much just hanging in each others' rooms or in the cafeteria. We don't do a whole lot but talk and play games and stuff."

"So you like them?"

"Yeah, they're okay."

"Alcatraz, I'm really proud of you. This is a big step for you since you moved here. While you lived with your uncle I remember it was really difficult to make friends. What do you think changed?"

"I don't know. I haven't really analyzed it."

"Would you like to try?"

Ugh. I so hated when she made me think deeply into my situations. Why couldn't "I made new friends" be enough for her? "I don't know. They are easy to get along with, I guess. I am not the oddball out here. Back in Des Plaines, I was the new girl with all the problems. Here everyone has problems, so I guess it just works."

"But you are the new girl here, too. It has only been a week and you have a few new friends. That's more progress than you made in the four months living with your uncle. You didn't get along with anyone there."

"I think it was that house. I hated living in that house, but I don't know. I...I don't hate living here. I mean, don't get me wrong, it's not like living with my family back in San Diego, but it's also not like living with my family in Des Plaines."

"I understand. It's easy to grow to your fullest potential when you're dwelling in a harm-free environment. You feel like you belong here."

"I don't know about all that. I just know it's not that bad."

"And you didn't have time to look up your name?" she asked.

Seriously! This chick doesn't forget anything. "Well," I hesitated, "I didn't completely forget. I just didn't like what I found."

"What did you find?" Elizabeth leaned toward me with an eager look.

"Katherine is Greek for pure, to purge, or to cleanse."

"There's nothing wrong with that. Did you look up the definition of pure?"

"No, 'cause I know I ain't it," I snapped. "Look, are we almost done?"

"Alcatraz, we need to talk about what happened to you in your uncle's house. You might not want to deal with it with me, but sooner or later you will have to face your pain. It will be a lot easier to walk through it with someone who can help you deal with it in a healthy way rather than opening up to someone who is going to use that as bait..." She paused. "Why don't you like the word *pure?*"

"'Cause I just don't."

Elizabeth rose and walked over to her library of books on the wall. She pulled out the Merriam-Webster dictionary.

"Well, let's see what the word means, shall we?" She flipped through the thick book.

"Pure. Here it is," she said, pointing to the word as if I could see in her lap. "Would you like to read me the definition?"

"Why can't you read it?"

"I think it will be more beneficial if you read it, Alcatraz. Here you go."

She handed the dictionary over to me. I snatched it out of her hand and rolled my eyes. "Fine, I'll read." I looked at the page. "Pure. Number one says 'unmixed with any other matter. Spotless or stainless.' Definition number two says 'being thus and no other, sheer, unmitigated.' Definition three…"

As I continued to read the definition my voice shook. I could feel my chest tightening, and my throat got really dry. Tears began to form in the corners of my eyes, but I used every force in my body not to let them fall.

"What's wrong?" Elizabeth spoke compassionately.

"Nothing, I'm just really tired," I lied again.

"At ten o'clock in the morning you're already tired?"

"Look, I really want to go now. I appreciate you bringing me here, but I don't want to talk to you."

The exasperation on her face was so obvious: she wanted a confession. "Okay. We don't have to go there if you don't like. What else did you discover about Katherine?"

"Well," I wiped my eyes and closed the dictionary, "many successful ladies were named Katherine including a saint who influenced a lot of people in her day. She moved Christianity forward and died for her beliefs."

"That's interesting! How do you connect to that? Being a positive influence on the people around you?"

"I don't have anything to give the people around me, Elizabeth! Look at where I am! I'm in a home for girls. What could *I* possibly have to give to anyone? Plus, she gave her faith to people, not material things. It sounded like she was a preacher, and I definitely don't relate to that 'cause I don't believe in Jesus. So I think Alcatraz suits me just fine. Can I go now?"

"Yes, you can leave now if you wish. I will see you back here next Tuesday at the same time. We'll pick up where we left off. Okay?"

"I don't really have a choice so it has to be okay."
I left and closed the door behind me.

* * * *

My favorite class at Valeo Academy was Art
Therapy. It attracted all the eclectic people on campus
and the instructor gave us fun projects. We studied
the elements of design, including lines, shapes, forms,
spaces, colors, values and textures. My instructor,
Mrs. Tan, propelled me into my work and made me
think about my craft as more than a hobby.

"I want you to connect to a piece of art," she
instructed, pacing back and forth in front of the
classroom. "I want you to go to the library and delve
into magazines, books or paintings on the wall and
find a piece of work that resonates with you on some
level, be it superficial or profound. Then I want you
to freestyle using one of the five modes of design.
Remember what they are? Who can tell me?" She
looked around the class. "Billy, tell me one."

"Stylized," she said.

"Good! Stylized. How would you describe it?"

"It means to simplify the details. Not get so
bogged down with all the nooks and crannies of a
picture, but just keep it simple."

"To just keep it simple. Great!" Mrs. Tan smiled.
"Stylized art follows rules. It's art nouveau. It's a
Superman comic strip with exaggerated muscles,
sharp lines, and shadows. Stylized art is very iconic
like Tony the Tiger on the Frosted Flakes cereal box.
Pictorial simplification is the point here, people. What
else? Betty, give me another one."

"Abstraction is to distort the picture—to overlap

work and create new shapes and designs," she said.

"Yes! Good. Abstract art is ethereal art departing from reality using totally unrecognizable objects. Think Malevich, van Gogh, Leger. You really don't know what you're looking at but you like it. It's vague. It's disorder. It's like a Rorschach test. No one really knows the true interpretation except the artist, yet its madness appeals to inner turmoil of the soul. That's why people like it. Yes, Amanda."

"Non-objective," Amanda said. "It's similar to abstraction in that there's no recognizable objects. The different facets of the design produces its own design."

"Fabulous, Amanda!" Mrs. Tan shouted passionately. She was such a drama queen. "Abstract art has a distorted version of some recognizable object while non-objective art doesn't. The work itself does not represent anything but colors and forms composing an image. The results are similar but the initial intention isn't. The lyrical abstraction painters from the sixties are a classic example. What else? There're two more."

"Naturalism," someone blurted out.

"Excellent, who was that?" Mrs. Tan asked, twirling toward the right side of the room.

"Dora."

"Dora. Tell me about naturalism."

"It's photo-realism. It looks like the real thing," Dora said.

"Exactamundo. Pays attention to exact details. Precise. Accurate. Portrays things as they truly are. Think Renaissance period. That's the origin of this genre. William Bliss Baker's landscape paintings are a classic example. Now that leaves one more. Who knows it?" she asked, looking around the room. "Katherine Boydstein, tell me the last mode of design."

"Um," I stuttered, "I don't know it."

"Come on. Yes, you do. It's your specialty."

What? My specialty? I didn't realize I had a specialty. Uh…I looked over at my neighbor, trying to pry an answer out of her with a sorry look on my face.

"Ah, no you don't. Don't help her. She knows it." To me, she said, "Think about it. What do you like to draw?"

"Well, I like my work to be real—oh, Realism!" I shouted.

Everybody laughed, including Mrs. Tan.

"See. I knew you knew it. Now what is it about realism that makes it realistic?" Mrs. Tan asked.

"The work is representational of the real thing."

"And what's the different between realism and naturalism?"

"Realism is more about truth and accuracy?"

"You're on the right path. Naturalism desires to depict things accurately and objectively in a nature setting while realism doesn't try to be pretty or ideal. It prefers a more down to earth approach of how life is actually lived. It's unembellished. It's raw. While naturalism depicts the beauty of a butterfly on a red rose, realism prefers to show a caterpillar squirming in the dirt. Edgar Degas, John Singleton Copley and Gustave Courbet are examples of realism. Why do you like this genre, Ms. Boydstein?"

"I don't know. I guess 'cause it's harder to master. It's easy to make an abstract photo where you are the only person who knows the design. Then you can hide behind your interpretation when asked to describe it, but with realistic art there's no hiding. You are judged more harshly 'cause everybody knows what the real thing looks like. So to draw it requires more skill, in my opinion."

"I see that you're a girl of risk-taking and chance. You like a challenge. That's rare. You're going to go far in this field if you choose. Just keep drawing."

Every eye in the room was on me, and I sincerely wished I could twitch my nose and vanish into thin air.

After class I immediately immersed myself in our new assignment by heading straight to the second floor of Valeo's library. I meandered along the aisle browsing through the hundreds of different subjects resting in alphabetical order, just waiting to be read. For whatever reason an astronomy book grabbed my attention and I flipped through the many pages of our solar system. I stood in awe as I scrutinized the vastness of the universe, wondering about life on other planets.

How was all this created? I thought to myself, observing the deep, endless black void embedded with starlight. *How big is this universe and what else is out there? How is all this held together?*

As my mind traveled through the origin of creation I pondered on the order and variety of nature. I heard yesterday that scientists were still discovering new life and plants on the ocean's floor. I thought about all the sorts of produce in the grocery store and how each food was ingrained with natural vitamins and minerals our bodies needed to digest. I thought about the development of a baby in its mother's womb for nine months and how men have yet to give birth to children. I concluded there was an enormous amount of orderly conduct in the earth! *How did this come to be?*

As I continued to flip through the book a photo of Saturn absolutely stunned me! I got lost in its rainbow of deep gold, vibrant oranges and burnt reds. I admired the natural beauty of Saturn and noticed the ball of gas no longer reflected a planet but a human eye! Someone was looking at me! It caught me so by surprise that I closed the book on my finger to hold the page and dangled the book down in front of my legs. I *had* to be dreaming this. There was no way I was looking into the iris of a human eye inside an astronomy book.

I wanted to use this book for my art project so I reopened the book. I expected to find normalcy on the page but the eye still stared back at me, looking deep into my soul. And then, as if we met before, I realized a familiarity I'd seen in previously experiences!

Praying no one heard me, I quietly asked, "Who are you? And how did you get inside of this book?" I rolled my eyes at myself, disbelieving my capacity to converse with a piece of paper.

I heard a male voice say, "I hear your heart, Katherine. I created the heavens and the earth and the fullness thereof. I hold this world in the palm of My hand and I know how big this universe is. I spoke it into being!"

I couldn't utter one syllable as I listened to the compassionate yet authoritative voice answering my thoughts. As his words melted in my heart a presence surrounded me, loving and full of peace. This presence was totally unlike the presence of Leinani's god, Aether. Where had I felt this presence before, and where had I seen these eyes before?

"Who are you? Who's doing all of this?" I asked.

"I AM!" he responded.

"What is 'I am'?"

"I AM all things good. I AM the Prince of Peace. I AM the lover of your soul. I AM your healer. I AM your provider. I AM your protector. I AM the One who sees. I AM your husband. I AM wisdom. I could continue with all that I AM, but I want you to grab hold of the part of Me you have a hard time receiving."

"What is that?"

"Love, Katherine. I AM love. I AM unconditional, infinite, non-condemning love. I do not judge you. I do not reject you. I do not condemn you. I do not put bad things in your life to teach you a lesson. I AM your father who loves you endlessly no matter what you think, speak, or do. You can't earn this love. You can't work for this love. You can't perform for this love. All you can do is receive this love. Receive!"

"Love? Like, God or something?" I asked.

"Yes, My daughter. I AM the Father of the universe. The One that separated the light from the darkness. That separated the sky from the expanse of the water. That sprouted forth vegetation on the dry land. The One that created every living creature that lives in the sea, in the sky, and on the land. I AM the One who created you in My image so you could rule and reign over the fish in the sea, the birds in the air, over the livestock and over every living thing on the earth. Yes, My child. I created this earth for your enjoyment. For your pleasure. For your indulgence.

All because of My love for you."

My heart skipped about ten beats at his words. This eye penetrated the very crust of my soul and hit me in places I never felt before, even with the Boydsteins. I noticed the book pages were getting wet from the tears falling from my face. *Where had I seen this eye before?* The familiarity started to really bother me.

"You are trying to remember where we have met before?" the voice asked. "You have met Me in quite a few places. The first time we met was in your home in San Diego. I revealed Myself to you through Tom and Cindy Boydstein. Even though they didn't know Me personally, my love still flowed through them toward you. I then became acquainted with you in the car crash. I sent a man to rescue you from the flaming fire. At the hospital I sent Willie across your path, and again through Elizabeth Dodd."

"Elizabeth Dodd!" I shouted, not paying attention to how far my voice traveled through the library.

"Oh, yes. She is one of my laborers."

"Laborers?"

"Laborers, yes. And you have met others."

"Oh my God. I totally remember!" I blurted out, now unashamed about how stupid I sounded to others in the library. "You were the dude I was looking at in the paintings in the Catholic Church Maria dragged me to. You were the eyes I saw in the twelve pictures mounted on the wall." And then it hit me.

"Yes, My beloved. You saw Me in the paintings manifested as the Son."

"So you mean, you're...you're..."

"I AM Jesus!" he said.

My body quivered so profusely I dropped the book on the floor. I glanced down the aisle to see if anyone overheard my conversation then picked up my backpack and ran out of the library. A flutter of thoughts ran through my mind on my way back to the room. Was I going crazy or was I really encountering the Spirit of God? Was I the only one who could hear his voice like that? Why was he talking to me, anyway? What is so special about me? Or better yet, what does he want from me?

All I could see in my mind were his eyes. I remembered his eyes back in the Catholic church. The same eye stared back at me from the astronomy book. My eyes watered at the thought of someone looking straight inside of my wounds.

I don't think I've encountered that kind of love with any other human being. I mean, I thought the Boydsteins were a perfect family. I felt accepted, secure and respected in their house. I even felt respected by my big brother, Henry, though he had he teased me a lot. None of that compared to the favor I felt from the eyes of Jesus. His look penetrated the deepest parts of my being, all the pain, all the hurt, the flaws and the weaknesses. He looked past the junk in my soul and saw someone of worth and value. That's it! He saw the junk, yet still made me feel valuable, like a lost pearl.

I remember five years ago when Dad made reservations to eat at the Ivy, a famous restaurant in Beverly Hills. Mom planned to wear this very beautiful red St. John dress with the pearl earrings and necklace set Dad bought her when they first married. When it came time for her to put on her earrings there was only one pearl. She flipped out so bad! She removed drawers, turned down her bed, searched among shoes in the closet, cleaned the bathroom and combed the entire house. She even looked in the dishwasher. She searched for that pearl to the point where Dad canceled the reservation at the Ivy.

Mom refused to leave the house until the pearl was recovered. For about four hours she inspected all eight thousand square feet of our home in tears.

Just when she'd about given up, Henry ran from the basement screaming, "I found it! I found it!"

"What? Where was it?" Mom jumped up and retrieved the slimy pearl from Henry's hand.

"In the downstairs bathroom trash can."

"In the trash can!" Mom exclaimed. "How did it get in there?"

Henry lifted his hands, palms up. "I dunno."

"Maybe it fell in when you leaned over to sit on the toilet, sweetheart," Dad concluded. "You know the back on that thing isn't very secure. Maybe we need to take it to a jeweler…"

"First thing in the morning!" Mom commanded, before Dad finished his sentence. And so it was. That pearl meant the world to her not because of the price, for my Dad could have bought her another pair much nicer, but because those were the first set of pearls her husband bought her over fifteen years ago. They were priceless to her, something irreplaceable and special.

That was how I felt when I looked into Jesus' eyes. I felt like he valued me so much that he would tear apart the house and miss an important dinner date just to love me. I seemed precious to him and irreplaceable. And, honestly, those feelings scared me.

I didn't feel valuable and precious but powerless, weak and broken. I couldn't understand why anyone would want to love such a mess. I wasn't ready for that kind of love. I couldn't submit to that type of relationship. After all, I didn't deserve it. I figured sooner or later Jesus would realize this fact and desert me.

When I got back to my room, Leinani was there with Nicole. Rosa was at track practice.

"Are you alright?" Nicole asked.

I never shared my spiritual experiences with anyone but today I was in desperate need of communication. I couldn't make sense of anything right now and appreciated the offer to share my heart. I sighed and explained my encounters with the man who claimed he was God. I told them about the man who pulled me out of the burning truck. I told them about Willie and the Kabbalah nurse in the San Diego hospital. I told them about the twelve pictures in the church. I told them about the eye in the astronomy book.

Upon finishing my story I expected laughter and criticism for being such a freak, but to my surprise Leinani spoke up boldly.

"You have a special calling on your life, Alcatraz," she said. "You are a priestess of some sort and the gods are trying desperately to lead you in that direction."

"Or you could be called into ministry," Nicole contended. "It sounds to me like Jesus is chasing after your spirit to bring you into the kingdom of God and preach the gospel. There's a war going on in the spiritual world for your soul."

"Huh?" I said.

Leinani, who was sitting Indian style on Nikki's bed, uncrossed her legs and turned toward me. A somber look crossed her face. "When my mother was a child back in Hawaii she had a special connection with the spiritual world and displayed supernatural powers from age three. Her first manifestation was when she telepathically moved my grandma's cookie jar from the middle of the table from where she couldn't reach it to the edge of the table right in front of her."

"No way!" I exclaimed.

"Way," she answered. "My grandma told me she dropped the laundry basked when she walked in the room. 'How did you get the cookie jar to the edge of the table?' 'I moved it.' 'How did you move it, Kiki? You are too short.' At three, my mom couldn't explain in words how she'd moved it, but grandma soon figured it out. When Mom was five she let go of a pencil while writing the alphabet. The pencil stood up vertically and twirled in midair, unattended. When my grandma walked in the room and asked her what she was doing she lost focus and the pencil fell to the table."

"Wow. You're on some witchcraft bull. That's crazy," Nicole belted out.

"It's not different than light as a feather, stiff as a board," Leinani fired back.

"Yeah, and that was crazy too!" Nicole said.

"Well, nobody asked you!" Leinani shouted.

Those two had the weirdest relationship. They always argued, yet they hung out at every spare moment.

Leinani continued, "Mom's kinetic spiritual powers were so great that by the age of eight my

121

grandma introduced her to a high priest. As soon as the two walked through the door, the high priest declared, 'This child is a natural witch. She is to stand in the gap between the natural and supernatural and be the voice of our ancestors.' From that day forward my mom literally slept by the side of the high priest and became one of the youngest high priestesses in Oahu. Then she moved on to be a healing doctor in New Orleans.

"What I'm saying, Traz, is if you are connecting to the spiritual world without any effort on your part then you have a gift. You could be a natural witch, a shaman, or a healer. But whatever it is, I wouldn't just sit on it. Cultivate it. You never know where it might lead you."

"Well I say you a minister," Nicole budded in.

"I just said that," Leinani claimed.

"No, you didn't. Jesus is speaking to her louder than your god. Didn't you hear her? She said she has peace when Jesus speaks to her, not when the 'gods of the universe' do." Nicole turned from Leinani and faced me. "Listen, Traz, I don't know all the details but I do know about spiritual warfare. When I lived in Texas with my crackhead mom she had the nerve to drag me to church every Sunday, and I used to sit in the pew and watch all these over-emotional Baptists get all full of the Holy Ghost, dance around, fall on the floor and whatnot."

"Are you serious?" Leinani asked.

"Dead serious. It was crazy. If I didn't know any better I would think the church and my mom were smoking the same pipe." We all burst into laughter. "Anyway, every Sunday Pastor Tate would give an altar call and discuss spiritual warfare. Every Sunday!"

"What's an altar call?" I asked.

"It's usually at the end of the service," Nicole said. "It's when the preacher asks people in the audience to get born again and give their lives to Jesus. He would say—"

Nicole jumped off the bed and grabbed a hairbrush for a microphone to imitate Pastor Tate. "I know you out there 'cause I can feel your spirit. Ha. The devil don't want you to walk down this aisle, ha, 'cause he already know, he already know, if you do, your struggling days are over. Ha. The enemy tryin' to play tricks on your mind. Ha. He tryin' to get you to think that living this life with him will get you somewhere fast. Ha. But I'm here to tell you this morning, ha, that Jesus, ha, Jesus, ha, Jesus is the answer to your prayer. Ha. More powerful than any two-edged sword. Ha.

"There's a fight going on in the spirit. Ha. For the possession of your soul between Jesus, ha, and the devil, ha, between light, ha, and darkness, ha, between truth and a lie. Ha. But all you got to do, all you got to do, is walk down this aisle. Ha. Give yo' life to Jesus. Ha. Prince of Peace. Ha. King of Kings. Ha. Lord of Lords. Ha. Give yo' life Jesus and put an end to that warfare and start living a life of victory, love, truth, and most of all, peace. Ha. It's all in Jesus, all in Jesus, all in Jesus! Thank you. Ha. Thank you, Jesus. Thank you."

Nicole dropped the hairbrush to do this hysterical, spasmodic dance screaming, "Thank you, Jesus!"

Leinani's and I doubled over laughing until we got stitches in our sides as we watched Nicole's rendition of her old Baptist preacher.

"They really do that?" I asked after collecting myself.

"Baptists really do that. Well, the church I went to did, anyway. They were very emotional there, or as they called it, 'filled with the Holy Spirit.'"

"Oh my goodness, I don't think I ever laughed so hard in all my life," Leinani said as she rolled around on the floor. "How did you watch this with a straight face?"

"I guess I got used to it after awhile," Nicole said. "Just like with any other childhood experience, you begin to think it's normal and everybody lives like this."

"Yeah, that's true," I agreed. "I thought perpetual sunshine was normal until I moved to Chicago."

"Exactly! But my point of telling that story was to explain spiritual warfare 'cause that's what it sounds like you're going through. Your story reminded me of the people who didn't want to walk down the aisle and submit their lives to Jesus. Pastor would claim an all out war is happening in the unseen realm for who will control your soul."

Leinani blew her nose and switched into a serious mode. "Do you actually believe in that stuff? Jesus, I mean?"

"I don't know if I believe Jesus is Lord or not. There's just too much bad going on in this world to believe in a God, period," Nicole answered.

"I hear you on that," I chimed in, "but then I keep getting these occurrences with him so there must be something he wants me to know."

"Time will tell," Leinani concluded.

"Yeah, I guess so. Why do you believe in

Aether?" I asked her.

"Well, Aether is just the fifth element, the material that fills the universe above the terrestrial sphere where everything is permanent and unchanging. I mainly practice Wicca."

"What's that?"

"It's when a bunch of crazy white people make a circle, sacrifice animals, drink blood, and put spells on people they don't like," Nicole joked. "Or they make someone fall in love with them by writing their name on a popsicle stick, pouring honey on the stick and burying it in a jar of sugar."

"That is not the heart of it, Nikki. Cut it out! I don't make fun of your beliefs, do I?" asked Leinani.

"That's because I don't have any real beliefs. I'm agnostic. I just know about Christ because I was raised in the Baptist Church, but I'm no Holy Roller. But you? You're a pagan fanatic."

"I just believe in what I believe, that's all."

"Will someone please tell me what a pagan fanatic, Holy Roller and Wiccan is please?" I yelled.

"I'll give you the basics," said Leinani. "Wicca is a pagan religion, literally translating 'rustic' or 'from other country.' Some people say it started in Europe, but its roots are prehistoric. Most Wiccans believe in a god and goddess, which can then translate into different gods. Some don't believe in god at all. It just depends on the school."

"Which school are you?" I asked.

"The Looney Tunes School," Nicole cracked.

Leinani gave her a cold glare then turned back toward me. "I'm an eclectic Wiccan."

"An eclectic Wiccan? What the hell is that?" Nicole ranted.

"Well, if you shut up, I can tell you."

Nicole rolled her eyes, but she listened.

"An eclectic witch doesn't follow a single path exclusively. We each interweave our own tapestry, creating the path that works for us individually. It has less to do with the spellbinding and craft associated with Wicca and more to do with a peaceful path utilizing positive energy to achieve goals in life. We take elements of different religions, mostly pagan, and create a belief system that works for us. I love it!"

"So what was all that 'light as a feather' stuff?" I asked. ""How was that creating positive energy?"

"That was more for practice than anything. I just wanted to have some fun using the power of our minds. We are very powerful, spiritual beings. Our ability is infinite with the help of spirit but we limit our circumstances with our minds."

I sat and pondered on this explanation. "So basically, you create your own religion?" I asked her after a moment.

"Well, yeah. All religions intermingle with each other. Sects like to believe they are unique but there is no pure religion. I mean, there are Wiccan texts I follow, but not to a T. I read other texts as well 'cause it's all recycled wisdom anyway. Nothing new is under the sun. Religions pretty much say the same thing just in different ways."

"Not in Christianity. Jesus is Lord, the Bible is the text and love is what we, I mean they, practice. There is no mix and match the way you're talking about," Nicole informed.

"Yes there is, preachers just don't admit it. The notion of a baby born in a manger to a virgin didn't start with Christ. It was a fable originating centuries before Christ was even born. Just like the creation story, Moses and David were all origin myths, not original stories like the teachers of the Bible will have you to believe. Besides, Christianity is not pagan, Nikki. Most Eastern religions differ from Christianity and I don't readily read the Torah, Bible, or Koran. I study ancient Eastern texts predating Western religions."

"How has Wicca helped your life?" I asked.

"It hasn't," Nicole butted in. "I mean, look at her. She's living in the same hellhole we are with the same problems we have."

Leinani ignored Nikki. "It has helped me to cope with the tragedies in my past. Even my counselor says I am becoming more stable."

"Wow, that's good! What do you do every day to make that happen?" I asked.

"A lot," Nicole said on her way to the bathroom.

"Yeah, she's right about that," Leinani said. "I do a lot, but it is paying off. I've adopted many different practices, chanting being the main thing. I chant at least thirty minutes a day."

"What and how do you chant?" I asked.

As Leinani bared her daily spiritual regimen with me, the dark presence once again entered the room and my heart got heavy with fear.

"What are you thinking?" Leinani stopped to ask me.

"Probably that you crazy as hell with no earthly sense. I know that's what I'm thinking," Nicole said re-entering the room.

"I am listening to you, but I don't know," I said. "Your beliefs just aren't sitting well with me. When you began chanting I felt this really dark, heavy presence in the room that wasn't there before. Same as when we played light as a feather. The atmosphere grew thick and heavy and well, evil. The god you serve just feels evil. I don't have a good feeling about him when he enters the room." I awkwardly looked at Nikki expecting a rude comment, but to my surprise she actually looked concerned.

"Oh, that's okay," Leinani encouraged me. "My testimony is just that...*mine*. Your path illuminates in front of you as you travel through life. Just keep walking."

"You may be a minister, Traz. A lot of well-known preachers started off life on the wrong side of the tracks and God miraculously flipped their lives right side up. Now they travel all over the world teaching," Nicole said.

"But I don't know one thing about being a preacher, much less anything about traveling all over the world. I don't even have a passport!" I said.

"This is my opinion, but I think you're a witch that hasn't tapped into your power yet," Leinani said.

"Well, I think you're a minister of Jesus," Nicole said. "You're just not ready to receive. There's a reason he is seeking you the way he is. Many people don't encounter these types of interactions with him, but you are. I think Jesus does send a witness to everyone before they die to give them a chance at salvation, but there is something I believe he wants to do in your life or through your life that's special. You are called to something very unique, a ministry nobody has tapped into yet. A group of people the church may be shunning. But don't feel you have to rush and believe in something until you're ready."

Light flooded my heart at Nicole's prophecy. It

felt like a huge boulder lifted off my chest and shoulders. Even though this conversation hadn't settled anything for me spiritually, I felt more at ease knowing my friends believed in me and didn't think I was crazy. When Leinani left and Nikki retired for the evening, I looked up the word *minister* in the dictionary. It meant to give help in the time of need: a helper; a servant. This boggled me because I thought the word meant to travel the world and preach from the pulpit, and I wanted no part of that.

* * * *

"Hello, class. My name is Greg Lubbock, and I will be substituting for Mrs. Wang for the rest of the semester while she takes maternity leave," the substitute teacher said.

This was music to my ears. Mrs. Wang, my Religious Studies teacher, was born and raised in Thailand so her class veered heavily toward the Eastern beliefs of Thailand, Laos, Malaysia and Cambodia. To hear what this American man had to say about the different belief patterns in the world intrigued me.

"What have you been studying so far?" Mr. Lubbock asked the class.

"Taoism," a student answered. "She just finished Confucianism."

"Okay, so more Eastern Asian religions. That's good. I'll get you more exposed to the other side of the world. I teach more down the middle, venturing into both East and West. Since we only have a few weeks left in this class I'm only going to give you a general idea about the four popular religions of the world. Can anyone tell me what those are?" Silence. "Anyone can answer. Don't be shy." Silence. "Okay. The four main believed religions are"—he turned toward the blackboard and picked up the peach chalk—"Christianity, Islam, Hinduism and, believe it or not, agnosticism."

"Agnosticism?" someone asked.

"Yes, Agnosticism. I know that may shock you because agnostics aren't looked at as religious, but they are."

"How is that?" a girl in the corner asked.

"Someone give me the definition of religion," Mr. Lubbock challenged the class. Silence. "Not everyone at once," he cracked.

"Isn't it someone who believes in God?" Janice asked.

"Well, if you believe in God, it is, but what if you don't believe in God? Are you still religious? Is it considered a religion if the beliefs you *do* have don't include God?"

This was a good question. I had never thought of before and judging from the silence in the room, neither had my classmates.

"Religion is a personal or institutionalized set of beliefs, practices, or attitudes held by a person or group of people," he continued. "Agnostics hold their belief of unbelief pretty dear. In fact, in my life, I have found more agnostics surer of their belief in the unknown than Christians are in their faith in Jesus. It's become a very fast-growing religion that many people fall into." Silence. "Okay, so let's discuss these four religions in this class, then I'll take the next few weeks we do have to delve deeper into each one. Sound like a plan?"

Everyone seemed excited, including me. In five minutes Mr. Lubbock totally captured the attention span of this entire ADHD class. Something was definitely different about this man.

Mr. Lubbock turned back to the board and started writing as he spoke. "So you got humanism, or rather, agnosticism. Atheists, or humanists, don't believe there's a God. They believe in evolution, Darwinism or the survival of the fittest, that we are all just one big accident waiting to happen."

"Is that the big bang theory?" some girl shouted out.

"Yes, that is. Who asked that question?" Mr. Lubbock looked around the classroom.

"Me, Chandra Pebbles."

"Very good, Chandra, that's exactly correct. Agnostics, or humanists, believe that the world came into form by a big explosion, and we humans are a mere product of that explosion. There's no afterlife when we die. Once you're gone, that's it. There are also no sacred texts to live by, unlike many other religions, like Hindus, for instance. Hindus study many different sacred texts such as the Shrutis and the Smritis. Many of their texts fall into one of these two categories. Now, I know a little bit about Hinduism because I taught English in a middle school in Nepal for two years and befriended many Hindus. My friends invited me to their temple, which was overrun with monkeys and rats."

"Monkeys and rats!" a few people yelled.

"Yep, monkeys and rats. But the reason they were in the temple with the people is because Hindus worship animals. They believe in absolute freedom in worship so there is really no right or wrong way to worship the gods. They believe in many gods and they conceive the whole world as one family unit."

"That's not the whole truth. There is more to Hinduism than that," a soft-spoken girl retorted from the back of the class.

"Well, all right. What's your name?" asked Mr. Lubbock.

"Asma."

"Okay, Asma, tell us a little more about Hindu."

"Self-realization is actually the ultimate goal in Hinduism, where god becomes fully actualized in the soul and then manifested in the earth. We focus on materializing the god within us. That is the true point."

"Well said, Asma. Now, do you guys believe in the afterlife?"

"No, we do not. The bodies are cremated unless a child is under five years old. Otherwise, we reincarnate. We believe life is a circle."

"That's strange," somebody remarked. The class agreed in harmony.

"Hey, hey, hey. Now wait a minute," Mr. Lubbock said, trying to calm down the class. "The point of this class is to enlighten you to different cultures and beliefs, not pass judgment on them. Now everybody settle down." Once the class returned to silence, Mr. Lubbock faced Asma and said, "Thank you, Asma, for having the courage to enlighten us about your upbringing. I want as much of your input as possible in this class. Okay?"

Asma nodded her head and smiled faintly.

"And that goes for anyone else in this room," he continued. "If we discuss a set of beliefs you were raised with, I want you to feel free to share your experiences and personal knowledge. Your input is valuable in this class. Got it, ladies?"

Everyone nodded.

"The next religion is Islam, which was born out of Abraham's first son, Ishmael," Mr. Lubbock said. "*Islam* is an Arabic word that means submission, surrender, and obedience. These people do believe in one god, whom they refer to as Allah. As a religion, Islam means complete submission to Allah. They uphold the five pillars and the Islamic law for Allah's approval and acceptance. They read the Quran, which they believe is the verbatim word of God. But before the Quran existed Muslim people believed Allah gave the Torah to Moses, the Psalms to David and the Gospels to Jesus. These people are important prophets in this religion, but the divine message of Allah came directly to Muhammad. According to their beliefs, Muhammad sums up and finalizes the entire word of Allah to the whole world."

"What are the five pillars?" a student asked.

"The five pillars of Islam are profession of faith, prayer, fasting, charity and pilgrimages. Muslims believe the purpose of their existence is to serve God. But even so, many don't have confidence they are going to heaven. A student has to be chosen."

"How do you know if you're chosen?" the girl seated next to me asked.

"They believe when you die an angel comes down and asks you questions. If you answer the questions right then your soul rests in peace until the day of judgment. Then on that day Allah comes down to weigh your sins. If you have more good sins than bad, then you go to heaven and vice versa. Basically they have no idea if they are going to heaven or not."

"So you mean these people submit their whole lives to Allah only for him to tell them their actions weren't good enough and send them to hell?" I asked, a little irately.

"Pretty much. I don't know the gauge they use to judge how many good or wrong deeds are done but there is no security within Islam. Allah determines who gets in and who doesn't on the day of judgment. The practitioners just live the best they can."

Who would want to worship a God like that? *What a waste of time.* I didn't want to spend all my days struggling to be this really good person just for Allah to send me to hell. That was not worth it to me.

Islam was definitely not the religion for me, and neither was Hinduism. I didn't believe animals were gods or even equal to humans. I mean, we have brains that can change the world. Animals don't. How are they gods? I had no intention on worshiping a cow in my sanctuary along with the Creator of the universe. How sick! I believed animals were meant as food and pets, not to be put on a pedestal. So far I wasn't feeling the Hindus or the Muslims.

"Then there are the Christians," Mr. Lubbock continued. "Christianity is the number one religion in the world. Would anyone like to guess why that is?" Silence. "Christianity is the only religion in the world that has a Savior. In all the other religions, being Eastern or Western, people have to earn their way to their final destination through good deeds."

"What's the final destination of Christianity?" another student asked.

"Christians believe in heaven and hell," Mr. Lubbock explained. "They believe the way people arrive in heaven is based solely on their belief in

Jesus."

"Jesus!" I screamed impulsively.

"Whoa, that was a reaction," Mr. Lubbock said. "Yes, in Christianity Jesus is Lord. The only way to go to heaven, to spend eternity with him, is to believe that he died on the cross for your sins and rose from the dead. It's all about belief, unlike other religions which are all about good works."

I raised my hand. "Can you explain that some more?"

"Certainly. Can I have your name, please?"

"Alcatraz."

"Oh, wow. You mean like the prison, Alcatraz?"

"Yes, like the prison." I was getting used to this comparison. And annoyed.

"This is your lucky day, Alcatraz, because I happen to be a minister of Christ," Mr. Lubbock said.

"Oh, no. You are not gonna start preaching, are you?" a biracial girl asked from the middle row.

Mr. Lubbock laughed. "No, no, no. I am here to inform you about different religions, not to preach to you about mine. But I do know quite a bit about this one, so if I overwhelm you, just let me know."

"You're overwhelming me," a girl with spiked blue hair cracked.

The class laughed, including the instructor. "Well, like I stated earlier, the main difference between Christianity and other world religions is that Christians believe in a Savior. Now, what does that mean? Most people believe that doing good things and being a good person gets you to heaven. Muslims believe their prayers and acts of submission get them to heaven. They measure their lives against each other and the laws of the land saying, 'Well, I don't kill, steal, rape or burn down houses. You know I take care of my parents, feed the homeless during special times of Ramadan, attend Bible studies every other Tuesday and give clothes to the Goodwill. Compared to most people, I'm a pretty good person.' And they expect their good decisions to be good enough to be right with God. But they're not."

A girl in a fuchsia sweater raised her hand.

"Yes, ma'am," said Mr. Lubbock.

"Where does that mentality come from? Like, why do people try to be good?" she asked.

"That's an excellent question! Why do people work for their salvation when it's a gift? Well, it wasn't always free. Before Jesus came into this world the only way man could get right with God was by keeping the law."

"What's the law?"

"The law is a set of high standards that man had to keep in order to come into the presence of God, like, 'Do not steal. Do not kill. Do not commit adultery.' There are 613 laws man had to keep in order to commune with God. There are more laws in the Islamic Quran."

"Why did man have to do all these laws?" she asked.

"Because God is holy, flawless and supreme. He will not stand for anyone less than that to enter his presence. It's likened to royalty here. Imagine you had a dinner invitation with the Queen of England. Now, you wouldn't go to dinner in ripped pants, oversized shirt, tangled hair, no deodorant, no socks and sneakers. No. You would go out of your way to look your nicest and act your kindest simply because, in the royal house, you're expected to look and act a certain way. Well, on a grander scale, that was what it was like to enter the presence of God. You were expected to be holy, sinless, and blameless."

"How is that possible?"

"It wasn't—and still isn't. Before, only God's chosen people, the Levites or prophets, were able to talk to Him personally. And they had to prepare themselves before going into his holy place. The only way other people became right with God was through animal sacrifices. But Jesus became the final, ultimate lamb for us. You see, God himself became a man, Jesus. God did not want man to be separated from him so he sent Jesus to be the sacrifice for us. Instead of killing a lamb, now we trust in the blood of Jesus as our sacrifice."

"I'm confused," an Asian girl admitted. A few others agreed.

"It's okay if you don't fully comprehend it," Mr. Lubbock said. "Like I said, this class is a general overview of the major religions of the world. I'm not expecting you to fully comprehend the details of all of them, just the basics to pass the test."

Everyone sighed with relief when the bell rang.

"Can I ask you one more question before we go?" I shouted before the chit-chatting began.

"Sure. What is it, Alcatraz?"

"Why would God send Jesus? Like, what was his motivation for that?"

"Aha, the million dollar question. Why did God send His only Son into the world? Someone want to take a wild guess?"

"'Cause he was bored?" a girl asked.

"No, ma'am," Mr. Lubbock smiled.

"'Cause he was tired of smelling all those nasty

lambs?" someone else asked.

"Wrong again. Anyone else?"

"'Cause he was desperate?" I asked.

"For what?"

"I don't know," I replied.

Mr. Lubbock smiled. "You are on the right path. God was desperate, but not in the way you think he was."

The girl with spiked blue hair spoke up again. "How was he desperate?"

"God was desperately in love with each and every one of you and he sent His Son, Jesus, into the world to have a relationship with you."

Nobody moved. We all sat there in complete silence.

Finally Mr. Lubbock said, "You guys are free to leave now."

Everyone else slowly gathered their belongings and left the classroom, but I stayed behind. As Mr. Lubbock packed up his things from the teacher's desk he glanced up and jerked, surprised that I was still in the classroom.

"Ms. Alcatraz. What can I do for you?" he asked.

"Can I ask you something?"

"Sure. What's going on?"

"You said you're a Christian minister, right?"

"Yes I am. I've been in ministry for twenty-three years now," he said.

"Well, how did you come to your belief?"

Mr. Lubbock smiled and stopped sorting his papers. He leaned at the corner of his desk and said, "I was born again at the age of eighteen after getting drunk at a friend's party."

"Are you serious? You were drunk when you

submitted to God?"

"That's right. My friend Al threw a fish fry at his house and one of his 'holier than thou' cousins stayed with him at the time. He disapproved of the party, the beer, the music, the carpet."

I laughed lightly.

"He pretty much preached about Jesus the entire time we were there, and of course he made everyone uncomfortable and miserable in the process."

"What did he say?"

"He basically said that I didn't have to live life drunk, partying and chasing girls all day long. That there was more to my life than I had realized and that I had a purpose. He said by putting my faith in Christ my life would be transformed."

"So you believed right then?"

"No, I finished partying first. Then a group of us went to the local 7-11 to get some more beer. I stayed in the car. When my friends were inside I sat in the car half-conscious, half-unconscious and prayed a simple prayer like this: 'Jesus I know I'm not in the best shape right now but I really do want to know the purpose You have for my life. Come into my heart.' And he did."

"How do you know for sure he came into your heart?" I asked.

"Because when my friends returned to the car with the cases of beer, I opened one, took a swig and spit it out! The taste disgusted me even though I had spent the past five hours chugging kegs of it."

"Whoa."

"Yeah. My experience was pretty tangible. Ever since then I've had this insatiable fire to learn more about God and who he is."

"How did you quench your thirst?"

"By reading the Bible. Everything you want to learn about God, his ways, his purpose for your life, his creation, can all be found in there."

"I see," I said.

"Here." He reached in his briefcase and took out a thick, leather-bound book. "Here is the complete bible in the King James Version. Just ignore the first half for now and start reading in the Gospels, which starts in the book of Matthew. That will give you a firsthand look at the character of Christ."

"But I'm not sure I really believe in him yet. You know? I just want info."

"Yeah, I get it. Today you learned a little about the main texts of agnostics, Hinduism, and Islam. You could go to the library, check some books out, and read about all of them at the same time."

"How will I know which one is truth?" I asked.

"There is only one truth, Alcatraz. When you hear it, your spirit will let you know. Just don't deny it upon hearing. A lot of people do that. They hear the truth, but then reject the truth out of fear. Just remember the truth is love. It will never condemn you."

"Thanks, Mr. Lubbock."

"All right, Alcatraz, good to have you in my class."

"See you later."

As I walked down the hall with my new Bible in hand I felt a sense of excitement. My life began to come together at Valeo. I missed my family, but I was making some new friends here, developing my inner artist and settling some God issues that had been bothering me for some time now. I believed my life was progressing forward, like I was on the verge of discovering something very good.

8

"What! What do you mean?" I shouted.

"We searched long and hard for a family that could give you a loving, peaceful, environment and we found one in Utah. You should be happy," Elizabeth boasted.

"Utah? Why would I be happy about moving to Utah? I don't want to move to Utah! I like it here. Why can't I just stay here? I don't want to move anymore!"

"I know you don't understand this right now, Alcatraz, but trust me. Valeo Academy was meant to be temporary. We don't keep girls here unless a family hasn't shown any interest. It is healthier to be raised with a mother, father, sisters, and brothers. I know you're attached to this place, but a home with a nurturing family is better for your growth. It will give you more stability and—"

"I don't want to move anymore!" I cried. I jumped out of my chair. "I like it here. I don't get you people! First, you put me in a home where my cousin uses me up like a soiled rag. Then you take me out of there and put me here where I am finally starting to make new friends. I like my classes and I'm finally getting used to the weather. I am finally starting to fit in, and now you're telling me I have to do this all over again? No! I don't want to go anywhere! I don't care how loving the family is. I want to stay here!"

"I know you do, and I feel bad to uproot you like this, but later on down the road you will see this is for your own good. The Robinsons have adopted with us before so I *know* you will be in good hands. They are a superb family with six children for you to befriend."

"Six kids!"

Elizabeth nodded. "Yes, they have five natural kids, three boys and two girls then they adopted a Haitian girl two years ago from the State of Illinois. Now they would like to adopt another girl for their youngest daughter. They chose you!"

"I didn't know I was up for sale!"

"Every child here can be adopted, Alcatraz. It's just that not many families work out in the child's best interest. I've known the Robinsons for the past three years now. I worked with the State of Utah to help them locate Aiyana, their Haitian daughter. I know they won't replace the Boydsteins, but I don't believe any family could get any closer."

"Who am I gonna talk to out there? Are you moving with me?"

That question seemed to bother Elizabeth, for we had finally connected on a much deeper level.

"I'm afraid not. Unfortunately this week will be our last session together," she said.

"This week?"

"Yes, this week. Your new family is flying in

from Salt Lake City on Saturday to pick you up."

"Why don't I have a say in this?" I demanded. "How can you guys just make all these life decisions for me without my permission? I didn't agree moving to Chicago. I didn't agree moving to Valeo, and I don't agree with moving to Utah. Why can't I have a say in my life?"

"Because, Alcatraz, you are only fourteen years old. No state in the U.S. allows a fourteen-year-old to make decisions on his or her own. Your rights begin at the age of eighteen. Most girls aren't fortunate enough to have such a wonderful family adopt them. They are shipped out to different families, yet return to us like your roommate, Nicole."

I calmed down with a slow, long inhale. "Why did they choose me?"

"For starters, they have a heart for displaced minorities so they requested a Hispanic teenage girl around the same age as their other daughters. The pregnancy rate for Hispanic girls under the age of sixteen is very high and that greatly concerns them. They are fully aware they can't save every girl but impacting just one is important to them." She must have noticed my tears and disappointment because she quickly added, "But you can exchange e-mails with everyone and keep in contact. This goodbye doesn't have to be forever."

My heart sank. I had become attached to Valeo Academy in the past couple of months. Nicole, Leinani, Rosa and my teachers became a close-knit family to me. I had even grown to like talking to Elizabeth every week. She helped me process a lot of pain. I drew nearer to the truth about God with my new Religious Studies instructor and the texts we read. As weird as it may sound, my life actually felt "together."

Stability had resurfaced in my world, and now it was being torn apart. Again.

* * * *

I was in such a daze during my last week at Valeo that my eyesight blurred throughout the entire week. I bumped into walls, knocked over chairs, tripped down stairs, forgot books in my room. I could not believe I was moving to Utah, of all places! Who lives in Utah? I guess I would soon find out. My good-byes to Nicole, Leinani and Rosa were pathetic. We all cried our eyes out and pretty much slept in the same room all week. We'd grown to be sisters and I really felt like I was leaving my heart behind. As much as I didn't want to come to Chicago, I didn't want to leave.

That Saturday morning I made my way towards the administrative building with only one suitcase. God knows where I'll end up. I watched Elizabeth walking nervously back and forth on the front stairs. It was obvious to me that she didn't want me to leave, either.

A blue minivan was parked in the driveway near Elizabeth. There were three bodies in the car and the kids appeared to be arguing. I paused momentarily. Witnessing this sibling rivalry from afar evoked memories of me, Henry and Natalie from right before the crash.

"We've been waiting for you," Elizabeth said. It sounded like she was trying her hardest to be pleasant but I heard the sadness in her voice. "Are you ready to meet them?"

"What choice do I have?" I snapped.

A tan, brown-haired, brown-eyed woman popped up behind Elizabeth with a cup of coffee in her hand. She peeked at me frantically while a man pulled her hand from behind, apparently to calm her down.

"Katherine!" the woman shouted, handing off the coffee to the man behind her. He was motioning for her to go back inside the building.

Elizabeth turned around and said, "Yes, Tina Robinson, this is Katherine Boydstein, better known as Alcatraz. Alcatraz, this is Tina." Elizabeth paused, then turned back to look at me. "Your new mother." Her facial expression showed a mixture of concern, joy and anxiety.

Tina beamed. "Oh my goodness. Just look at you! You are even more beautiful in person than in the pictures."

I don't remember having pictures taken, I thought.

"I'm Tina and this is my husband, Craig." Tina turned her body to point to her husband. "And we..." she started. It seemed like she was trying to hold back her emotions. She looked at her husband. "We are your new family."

Elizabeth stepped away from the door as Tina lunged toward me. She gave me a long, affectionate hug. "Wow!" she said, pulling back. "Let me take a good look at you." She turned me around and her eyes wandered all over my body. Finally her eyes caught mine. "You are perfect." She teared up. "You are just perfect!" She gave me another hug. After our embrace she stepped out of the way from blocking her husband. I could tell he wanted to hug me, but he just extended his hand.

"Katherine," Craig said, "Tina and I are privileged to be your new parents. We prayed and prayed for the perfect daughter to complete our family and we believe you are an answered prayer from the Lord. We are grateful to have you with us."

Before my mind could process another thought I dropped my things and took off running. Away from Elizabeth. Away from the Robinsons. I ran past the pond, the Math building, the running track. I had no destination other than to leave their presence. I didn't want to live with them. I didn't want to move to Utah. I didn't want to invest myself to another family.

I'd been through this before, moving to an unknown city with an unknown family. The memory jolted fear into my chest and I ran faster. I cut through the courtyard behind the student center past the mini bodega, fell to the ground and wept like a baby. Why was this happening to me? Why did I have to be moved from place to place like a piece of used furniture?

At that moment the Boydsteins crossed my mind and my heart released a flood of painful tears. None of this would be happening if I hadn't wanted to eat at Hi Life Restaurant. None of this would be taking place if I had just died in the car with the rest of my family. What was I doing here in the first place? Why did I have to be the only survivor?

"Why? Why?" poured from my soul and before I knew it I was screaming at the top of my lungs. The pain was so unbearable I couldn't breathe.

"Don't be sad. It'll be okay." I was startled at the sound of the young girl's voice and quickly jumped out of my stupor. She stood about five feet five inches with milky white skin, long, wavy brown hair and thick glasses. She spoke again, "I know you don't know me well enough to believe me, but I think you really will be okay. I'm Molly, by the way. I'm one of the Robinson kids. I'll be your new sister."

"H-how did you know where I was?" I stammered.

"I followed you. It wasn't easy, though. You are fast." She smiled. I noticed her panting. "But I have three brothers, so I'm used to chasing people."

I had no choice but to go with them. We left Chicago Saturday afternoon and arrived in Utah Sunday night. I can appreciate the beauty of Utah now, but back then I didn't value the ice-capped mountains, crystal water and clean, crisp air. None of that penetrated my heart and I honestly can't recall any details of my stay. They were a sweet family but I hardly spoke to any one of them during the drive, dinner or hotel stay. I can't even tell you any of the kids' names, my mind was so numb. I remember Molly who chased me, and Aiyana, the Haitian, but that's about it.

When we arrived at their home I was shocked by the size of their house. It looked like a mansion. Each child lived in his or her own room equipped with a private bathroom and humongous walk-in closet. I only vaguely remember details of the family or the house. I didn't stay around long enough for that.

After dinner that Sunday night I went to my room and rearranged my bag. I took some pencils, sketchbooks, journals, toiletries, underwear, and socks out of my suitcase and stuffed them in my backpack. I wasn't staying. I couldn't. I didn't know where I was going but I just wanted out. I wished I could return to

Valeo but they would probably just send me back here or punish me for running away, so I planned to return to the only place I called home: California.

After everyone fell asleep I sneaked downstairs, opened Mrs. Robinson's purse and stole all the cash she had in her wallet: one hundred fourteen dollars and eighty-seven cents. I had no clue where I was going as I made my way down the posh East Carrigan Canyon Drive and followed signs pointing towards Interstate 80. Twenty-four hours after arriving in Salt Lake City, at fourteen years of age, I did something most people have never done: I hitchhiked my first ride.

After awhile a semi pulled over. "You want a ride?" the driver asked.

Shivering out of fear on the vacant highway, I answered, "Well, where you going?"

"Where you headed?"

"Los Angeles."

"So am I," he responded. "Why don't you hop in with me and I'll drive you there, unless you want to walk seven hundred miles?"

Glancing down the long, dark, empty interstate, I knew I had few options. Unless I planned on walking in worn out tennis shoes, sleeping under bridges and eating food from the dumpsters, I pretty much had no choice but to accept his offer. Every nerve in my body cringed at the sight of this burly-looking stranger with curly black hair and stained, crooked teeth. Not knowing if I'd arrive in L.A. dead or alive I hopped in his truck. He took off west on I-80 towards Reno, Nevada.

"Where in Los Angeles does your family live?" he asked. Silence. "Here, take this." He handed me some tissue. I blew my nose and wiped the tears from my eyes and noticed he continued staring at me. "What's your name?"

"Alcatraz," I muffled, not knowing whether or not I could trust this man.

"Well, hello, Alcatraz. My name is Dan. Dan Buford." He reached out his hand for me to shake it, but I refused. "Are you ready?"

Despite his gruffly appearance his words were gentle and soothing. I turned around to look if any other cars were driving by, hoping to God Elizabeth was somehow following me to bring me back to Valeo, but there were no cars. His truck was the only vehicle on this side of the road.

Empty Coke cans, Snicker wrappers, No Doz and McDonald's bags lay chaotically on the floor. His radio crackled to life with the voice of a female operator. "Fifty-four fifty, come in. Fifty-four fifty, come in."

"Go ahead for fifty-four fifty," he said into the handset.

"What's your twenty?"

"I'm heading west on 80 in Salt Lake. Just passing the airport."

"Copy that."

Dan replaced the handset on the dashboard and accelerated to seventy five miles per hour. It was a little faster than I'd like this gigantic truck to be moving, but it beat walking seven hundred miles.

"Why you walking the streets alone?" he asked me. Silence. "You running from something? Or should I say someone?" Again, silence. Dan sighed and shook his head. "It's a shame how many young girls there are on these streets alone. Walking from one problem into another. You're not ready to tackle this life by yourself, kid. I can tell you that."

I didn't answer Dan, but was curious about how many runaway girls he'd met.

"Say, you talking to me at all or is this gonna be a silent twelve hours?" he asked. No response. "Hope you don't mind listening to some teaching 'cause that's what I listen to on the road. Keeps me sane and awake." Dan reached behind his seat to grab a couple of CDs. "We got twelve hours ahead, so if you get tired you can go in the back there and lay down."

I didn't trust him enough to be in the back of his truck. I just pushed my seat back, used my bag as a pillow and cried myself to sleep.

I awakened alone in the truck. The sound of a country hillbilly blared from the dashboard. He said, "Grace is what sets true Christianity apart from every other religion in the world. Other religions may acknowledge and worship a one true God. They may even agree that Jesus existed and that his teachings are admirable. They say that he was a good man, perhaps even a prophet but definitely not God manifest in the flesh. Religions refuse to acknowledge Jesus Christ as the only way to salvation. He is the only way to have a right relationship with God."

Are you serious? Please don't tell me that I am riding with another preacher! With all these problems staring at me in the face, right now God was the *last* person I wanted to hear about.

The voice on the radio continued, "Salvation is a gift from God to man that is appropriated by grace through faith. You can't earn it or work for it. You just have to receive it."

At that moment the truck door opened and Dan

popped his head in.

"You have to go to the bathroom? Now would be a good time to go if you do. It's also a good time to pick something up to eat if you're hungry. You must be hungry. We've been driving for three hours."

Gazing around my environment, I noticed several trucks at this particular gas station with drivers loitering by, all older, scrappy-looking men with big bellies, beards, dirty jeans, and baseball caps. Even though my bladder cried for relief I was scared for my life to walk inside by myself. Dan must have noticed my fear 'cause he offered to escort me inside.

I sat there staring at him in a daze while still tuned into the hillbilly on the radio. He was saying, "The gospel as referred to in Romans speaks of the good news of salvation independent of our performance. It's by God's grace that we are saved independent of our performance. We do not have to work for this. It is a gift."

"Oh, I see you like the teaching!" Dan grinned.

"What is this?" I asked.

"It's a message from a well-known minister from Colorado. He is a powerful teacher of the grace of God. One of my favorites. I listen to him often while driving on these long trips."

"I've never heard anything like this."

"Well, don't you worry about that. You two will have a whole eight hours to get acquainted." He laughed. "Come on. Let me walk you to the bathroom."

Something about Dan seemed safe to me. He had a peaceful aura surrounding him and a fatherly love beaming out of his eyes. I was more afraid of having no home, family, friends, or money than I was of him. After I went to the bathroom, Dan kindly paid for a number one from the McDonald's adjoined to the gas station. We got back in the truck and continued the ride. As I sat there eating my Big Mac I couldn't help but pay more attention to the man on the radio.

"The gospel is good news, not bad news. It's literally too good to be true news. Many things have been promoted as the gospel that aren't good news. For instance, quite a few people in the so-called Christian culture of the United States associate the gospel with teaching that says, 'you're a sinner. If you don't repent, you're going to hell.' Now these are true statements. There is a heaven and a hell, a God, and a devil, and you will go to hell if you don't repent and receive salvation. But even though all of that is truth, it's not good news."

"What is this?" I finally asked.

"The teaching is called 'Grace: God's Power Revealed.' One of my favorites," Dan said.

"What is he talking about?"

"Basically, he's teaching that salvation is a gift. The reason Jesus came to this earth was to give everybody an opportunity to receive the abundant life as a gift. Christians sometimes teach people that doing good deeds like attending church, tithing, never cursing or lying, or volunteering gives you brownie points with God, like God is judging us on what we are doing for him. On our performance. But the gospel of Jesus says that it is not about what *we* do for him. It's about what Jesus did for us! It's about his death, burial, and resurrection. That is the power of God that manifests his glory here on the earth. Jesus came to give us eternal life."

"Oh my God. You sound just like Mr. Lubbock," I said.

"Who?"

"Nobody. Just a teacher I had back in school. He taught Religious Studies."

"Oh well, that's great that you got a man who knows the truth about the Word of God. How did you like the class?"

"Well, I only had the one religious class, but it was interesting. He taught about different religions too, like Hinduism, Islam, and agnosticism. It was cool."

"Which one do you believe? Do you know?"

"No. I'm not sure there is something or someone worth believing yet."

"That's fair. I wasn't always a believer. Had my fair share of searching and non-belief in my day." He slurped a large Coke.

Much to my surprise I wanted to hear more of what he had to say about his beliefs. After finishing my Big Mac I asked, "What is eternal life?"

"Well, my dear, eternal life means knowing God in this Earth and beyond. You might have heard that Jesus came just to forgive your sins and that is true, but it entails so much more."

"Is eternal life the same thing as being born again?"

"Eternal life is what you receive after you're born again. It is a gift."

"What does it all entail? I mean, you said it includes more than just forgiveness of sins."

"Well. How deep do you want to go with this? You want the long answer or short answer?"

"You said we had eight hours left of driving so

you might as well give me the long version."

Dan laughed, "I guess you're right about that. Ain't no point in me mincing words here, huh?"

Dan smiled at me and turned down the radio. "The word *salvation* in Greek is the word *sozo* meaning prosperity, healing, deliverance from oppression, and forgiveness of sins. I personally translate it as abundant life. Anything good that edifies and enhances your life for the better is a part of salvation. Physical health is a part of salvation. Financial prosperity is a part of salvation. Deliverance from negative habits is included. Purpose for your life. Joy and peace. Anything good you can think of that is going to make your life better is salvation and it springs forth from eternal life. The more intimate you are with God, the more his salvation will manifest."

"So truck driving makes your life better?" I asked.

Chuckling, he said, "Right now it does because I lack for nothing. I am debt free. I own my house and cars. My wife can stay at home and raise our three children without having to worry about how the bills are getting paid every month. I get to hold Bible studies in our home on Tuesday nights. My doctor gave me a clear bill of health. I yearn for no good thing. I'd say I'm blessed, blessed, blessed."

"You teach Bible studies? Are you some kind of preacher or something?"

"No, I wouldn't say I'm a preacher, but my wife and I do lead Bible studies in our home every Tuesday night. It is my way of serving people when I'm at home during the week. I drive Friday through Monday. I usually get in early Tuesday mornings then head out again on Friday."

"What do you teach?" I asked.

"I follow a program called Discipleship Evangelism. It has forty-eight lessons to teach people about what all is included in the salvation package when they give their lives to Jesus. Kinda like the questions you're asking me now. I teach along with my wife and kids."

"How old are your kids?"

"My oldest is about your age. She's fourteen. Her name is Mary. My middle girl, Kelly, is ten and my youngest, Samuel, is eight. They are the most precious kids in the world." He reached in his back pocket for his wallet. "Here are some pics."

"I don't want to see them!"

"Oh, I'm sorry. I didn't mean to offend you, Alcatraz. I'm just a proud papa."

"Can we just drive quietly? I don't want to talk about this anymore."

Memories of Dad, Mom, Nat, and Henry flashed into my mind. I remembered my mom and dad taking family pictures to put in their wallets to showcase in front of their friends. My dad once told me when he was away on business, he used to take out the pictures and kiss them.

As the memories passed through my mind I wondered what Leinani, Rosa and Nicole were doing. All the people that made me feel loved resurfaced from my soul and I began to cry uncontrollably. Without explaining anything to Dan I turned, faced the passenger window, and once again cried myself to sleep.

A few hours passed. I woke up when I jolted forward by the slamming of brakes.

"Idiot!" Dan yelled. "I tell ya, I don't know how

some of these people pass driver's ed." After noticing how the incident startled me, he quickly apologized, "Oh, I'm sorry. I didn't mean to wake you. I just can't stand dummies who weave in and out of traffic."

I turned from Dan to find a red Porsche ahead of us driving at least ninety miles per hour.

"How was your nap?" he asked.

"Fine, I guess," I said.

"I'm sorry about earlier. I wasn't trying to freak you out."

Silence. I could tell Dan's head was loaded with questions about me and he was choosing them wisely.

"So where are you from originally?" he asked.

"San Diego."

"Oh, from America's finest city, are ya?"

I didn't smile.

"I've spent a lot of time in La Jolla. It's beautiful there. It reminds me of Italy in a sense."

"You've been to Italy?" I asked.

"Yep. A few times. That's where my grandparents are from so I used to visit every summer when school was out. They lived in Tuscany."

"That's nice. I wish I could go to Tuscany right about now."

"Do you have family or friends in San Diego or are they back in Utah?"

"Neither."

"Oh, okay. Well in that case I'm gonna drop you off at a shelter on Presidential. I've taken loads of girls there. That'll be a great place for you to get on your own two feet."

"Look man," I interrupted. "I just need you to get me to LA. I can take care of it from there."

"You think so?" he retorted. "How old are you?"

"Old enough to take care of myself."

"So you're probably fourteen or fifteen? This shelter helps girls in the same age range. They provide you with housing, food, and transportation. They can even help you get into school."

"Right until a holier than thou couple adopts you with their six kids and sends you packing to Utah. Thanks, but no thanks."

Dan sat silent for a few moments, then he finally turned up the radio. We remained quiet the rest of the trip.

When we arrived in Los Angeles he looked over at me and asked, "Do you have any money with you?"

Silence. We stopped at Harbor City Truck Stop. Before he let me out he reached into his pocket and pulled out a wad of money. He began to count the bills individually, stopped, and then sighed.

"You can come stay with me and my wife if you like?" he asked. "We have a spare bedroom in our home and it wouldn't be an inconvenience at all."

As scared as the thought was to be on my own, I refused his help.

He finally said, "You know, there is a better way to live. I know you might not believe it but you don't have to live a life of fear. God cares about every aspect of your life. Every detail. He can and will protect you and provide for you. I know you might be thinking he has done a lousy job up until this point in your life but the truth is there is also a bad side at work in the world. A lot of people don't like to acknowledge this..."

Dan's voice trailed off and he glanced out at the other truckers in the gas station. "But there is a devil out here and his work is everywhere. The sad truth is that people blame God for his work. I know you're too young to understand all this, but the point is," he hesitated for a moment, "that Jesus loves you, Alcatraz. He really does love you and he really does care about your welfare. He wants to be the father you might not have."

I wanted to tell Dan to shut up, but I couldn't. As angry as I was at God for allowing all this tragedy to happen to me, hearing someone cared about me penetrated my heart.

"Well," Dan continued, "for what all it's worth, I really do believe you're going to be okay. That's a good feeling to have because I don't sense that about a lot of runaways I pick up. But I have that feeling about you. There is a significant call on your life. Don't quite know what it is but I do believe you are somebody special with a great purpose."

Dan handed me a wad of money, opened the truck door and headed toward the gas station. He had given me two hundred and six dollars.

What am I doing? How am I gonna survive out here? Who is gonna take care of me? Where am I gonna live? These questions flooded my brain the next few moments as reality sunk in. I realized I was in Los Angeles, California with no safety net or a road map on how to get one.

A light bulb switched on in my mind. I sincerely had nobody to call, food to eat, bathroom to take a shower, or bed to sleep in. In twelve hours I matured from a fourteen-year-old girl guided by experience into a decision-making adult guided by the wind. For the first time in my life I was literally on my own.

None of these circumstances came to mind while

packing my bags in Utah. I guess you really don't know until hindsight kicks in because now I sat in Harbor City with no family, no friends and three hundred twenty dollars and eighty-seven cents to my name. I grabbed my bag, opened the truck door and strode quickly toward the main street bypassing the beer-bellied truck drivers fueling their tanks. After a few steps I picked up the pace, made a right and jogged some more. I turned to see if anyone was chasing me.

I made another right then took off running. I had no idea where I was going and I didn't care. Panicked and out of breath, I ended up falling over a bench at a random bus stop. My eyes flooded with tears because my problems were still present. I had nowhere to go!

Within a few minutes people gathered around me to wait for the bus. I figured Hollywood would be a good place for me to start because my family and I had visited often. I spoke to a heavyset African-American woman holding a baby. "Excuse me. How would I get to Hollywood from here?"

"Oh that's a long ways away. You get on this bus that's coming here, the 550, till you get to San Vincent and La Brea. Then once you get there you goin' get on the 212 heading north toward Hollywood and Highland. Make sure the bus say 'Hollywood' on the front and not Hawthorne. That bus goes in the opposite direction. Get off at Hollywood and Highland then you'll be in Hollywood."

"Thanks. Do you know how long it'll take me to get there?"

"You got a good two hours in front of you. The bus makes plenty of stops but once in Hollywood you good 'cause they have buses that run twenty-four hours."

"How much is it to ride the bus?" I asked.

"Two dollas n' ninety cents should get you to La Brea, and a dolla fifty to Hollywood if you don't have a pass."

"Thanks much for your help."

"No problem. The 550's here so you only have one bus left."

That bus ride introduced me to an entirely different world I'd only seen on television: screaming babies held by teenage mothers, Hispanic men with shaved heads covered in tattoos, students cramming for a test and black rappers working on lyrics. Elderly worn-out ladies and gentlemen carrying grocery bags stood in middle aisle. I sat paranoid in the front seat behind the handicapped section, squeezing my book bag very tight. The bus lurched forward and we were on our way. We passed bikers, prostitutes, the homeless, red and blue sirens. We passed seedy gift shops, newspaper stands, piercing parlors, youth hostels. The more I saw the more my chest tightened. This bus ride exposed me to the very brash Hollywood culture.

A sense of ease overcame me as I exited the bus at Hollywood and Highland. I strolled by bright lights, traffic jams, flashing cameras, body sleeves, spiked hair, restaurants and shopping malls. I was right in the heartbeat of Hollywood! The uneasiness I'd felt earlier vanished. It sounds weird, but in those short two hours of my arriving in L.A. I felt like I was where I belonged. I absolutely loved all the action surrounding me. I was home!

My leisurely stroll intensified in a few moments when I realized I had no bed to lay my head. I was too scared to sleep outside with all the homeless men on the street, yet I didn't know anyone in town to bunk with. I had no alternative but to keep walking. I walked by a youth hostel, Hamburger Hamlet, the Kodak Theater, Schrader Boulevard, a Scientology building, North Cahuenga Boulevard, magazine stands and night clubs until I arrived at Metamorphosis Teen Center on Vine.

Standing in front of the center I inhaled, believing this place was going to be good for me. I looked to my right at the punk rockers passing me and to my left at the dirty men standing on the corner. I could either go inside the center or muscle it out here on the streets alone. Needless to say, I chose the former.

From the outside the place looked like a hole in the wall but inside it resembled a mid-priced college dorm. The receptionist was nice and she didn't ask a lot of questions. She assigned me a room and explained the rules on the short tour. There was a reception area, lounge, dining room, computer room and three classrooms. Eight dorms housed thirty-two teens, sixteen boys and girls. The girls were in the east wing and the boys were in the west.

The regimen at Metamorphosis reminded me of Valeo: breakfast at seven, lunch at twelve and dinner at five. They offered GED programs, spiritual studies and counseling assistance. Metamorphosis also had connections with every kind of agency imaginable: health care agencies, clothing agencies, education agencies, residential agencies, substance abuse agencies. The list went on.

The mission statement plaque on the wall stated: "To help children escape the Hollywood street life and provide a home-like environment in which abused and/or neglected teenagers could live safely as they mature into productive and independent young adults." Teens here chose to get help of their own free will after running away from family situations, they were not placed here by the state like at Valeo.

I mumbled, "Thank you, God" under my breath. I had chosen the right spot.

The rooms were composed of two double bunk beds, four mini lockers and one connected bathroom for all four residents of that room. When I first entered the room I quickly noticed an empty top bunk. I threw my bag up there and locked myself in the bathroom to pout on the floor and figure out my next move. Moments later I heard cackling outside the bathroom door in my room. Two of my roommates had arrived.

Knock, knock, knock, knock. "Hey, hurry up already, why don't you?" one of them yelled.

"Who is that?" another girl asked.

"I don't know. Must be someone new."

"Well, she apparently don't know the rules around here."

Again, *knock, knock, knock,* this time with much more anticipation.

"Hurry up! I've got to use the bathroom," the first girl said.

"I'll be out in a minute," I finally responded.

"I don't care if you *justgot* in the bathroom. Hurry the hell up!"

Rage rose up in my heart and my face reddened. I swung open the door. "Look. I just got in the bathroom, okay? So if you got to go then you need to go somewhere else!"

"Who the hell are you coming up in here telling us what to do? Get out of my way!"

Her attempt to shove me out of the way triggered my very first fist fight. As she tried to push me with her right arm I grabbed it and threw her headfirst toward the mirror. Her friend dived at me, grabbed my neck with her arm and began choking me. I immediately pressed in her eyeballs with my thumbs. She let go. I turned around and punched her in the face, knocking her about five feet backward.

I turned back around to see what was going on with the first girl. She was still recouping from her head being slammed into the mirror, so I pulled her by the hair and threw her outside the bathroom.

Both girls looked severely hurt.

"Like I told you," I said, "I'll be out of the bathroom in a minute." I slammed the door and locked it. I walked over to the sink to rinse my face but noticed the broken glass surrounding the floor, sink, and toilet. Paralyzed by my first fight and its repercussions I turned on the shower so no one could hear my sobs. Later I learned that my little squabble was the norm here.

I fearfully walked to the front desk to report the broken mirror.

"What happened?" the receptionist asked.

"I kinda got into a fight. My roommates were rushing me to get out of the bathroom and tried to—"

"Let me guess: shove you out of the bathroom by your arm, right?"

"Yeah, how'd you know?"

The receptionist shook her head. "I should have known not to put you in the room with those two.

They always cause trouble with newbies. Here, give me your key. I'm moving you to another room." She grabbed my key and picked up a walkie-talkie. "Come in, engineering."

"Go ahead," said a voice through the walkie-talkie.

"I have a broken bathroom mirror in 234."

"Copy that. Two-three-four. I'll get right on it."

I could tell she had done this plenty of times before.

"Here," she said, handing me a new key. "Go get your things from 234 and move to room 330."

"I have my stuff already." I had brought my bag with me in case they asked me to leave.

"All right then. Just walk to the end of the hallway. It's the last room on the left. Don't worry about those two. We've warned them several times about their behavior and told them their next issue will be cause of eviction."

"Oh. Well, I don't want them out on the streets. I just don't want them to bother me again," I said.

"You are not the first girl they've attacked. We've had similar stories from various girls. There is a three-strike policy here and they were on their second strike. It's not your fault. Some people we just can't help. Let me know if you have any problems in your new room."

"Okay. Thank you. What's your name?"

"Tameka Jones, but people around here just call me Meka."

"Well thank you, Meka."

When I walked into room 330 I saw an Asian girl on a bottom bunk. She was reading a tattoo magazine.

"Hey. How's it going?" I said, stumbling into the

room.

"Hey." She put down her magazine and jumped up from the bed. "I'm Kuriko."

My jaw dropped. She was covered head to toe in tattoos! "Oh my God! Are all these real?" I asked her, amazed at the beauty of her body art.

"Why yeah. How could they be fake?" She laughed.

"Did they hurt?"

"Some of them did because of their location, but the majority of them didn't."

"Is your body completely covered?"

"Not yet."

"You mean, you're gonna cover your entire body with tattoos?" I asked.

"It's called a body suit. You must not be from around here 'cause they're pretty popular," she said.

"Well, I just moved from Chicago."

"Yeah, I don't know if there as many suits in Chicago. What's your name?"

"Alcatraz."

"Holy shit! Are you serious? Like the prison?"

"Yeah, I guess like the prison."

"That's rad, man. I've always loved that name. How old are you?"

"Fourteen."

"Oh, wow. You're a baby! Well, welcome aboard." She gestured to show me around the room. "As you can see there isn't much to it. I sleep down here. You'll sleep up there 'cause bimbos Donna and Stacey sleep there. Bathroom is right there and that'll be your locker. You will have the far end of the closet since we've taken up the other spaces."

"That's cool. I don't have much stuff anyway so

I don't need much space," I said.

"Well, I'm headed to work. See you tomorrow."

"What do you do?"

"I dance."

"Oh, that's cool."

"No, it's really not," she replied in a serious tone.

"Can I watch you?"

"I don't think you want to witness this live show, kid."

"Oh. Ok." I threw my bag on the top bunk and slowly looked around the room.

Kuriko threw some things in a duffel bag and headed out the door. She stopped with one foot out the door and turned back to me. "You really wanna go?"

"Yeah, actually. I've never seen live dancing before."

"I wish I was treating you to a Broadway play, so you can have a real live experience."

"Why? Where are we going?" I asked.

"Just follow me."

We traveled back down Hollywood Boulevard toward Kuriko's job. Even though she was covered head to toe in tattoos she was an extraordinarily beautiful girl with a cute round head, perfectly shaped oval eyes, button nose and small, full lips. She had changed from ripped leather pants and tank top to a fuchsia sweater dress, knee high boots and feather peacock earrings. Her tattoos really became her.

When we arrived at Hollywood and North Cherokee I saw a line around the corner to get inside of a unique club, The Geisha Room.

"Come on. Let's go around the back," she said.

"Why can't we just walk in the front?" I asked.

"No questions tonight kid. Just remember...*you* asked to come!" Kuriko yanked me by the arm down the dark alley.

I wondered what I'd gotten myself into. What kind of club was this? Why couldn't we enter through the front door like civilized human beings? Behind the dumpster there was a hidden door I would have never noticed if I'd walked this alley alone. A nicely-tanned male sumo wrestler with a fish eye opened the back door and we both jolted backwards.

"Who is this?" he asked Kuriko. He stared me up and down.

"She's with me, Samsung. Let us in," she said.

After taking one more glance at me he nodded his head and stepped out of the way for us to enter.

"Hey, Sapphire, you got any red lipstick?" an Asian lady in a delicately embroidered bikini asked as soon as we stepped inside the door.

I swung around to see who she was talking to but to my surprise, Kuriko answered, "Yeah, I got some."

"Let me use it, please. I'm about to go on."

Kuriko opened up her duffel bag and shelled out the lipstick. "Is that what you're wearing tonight?" Kuriko asked her.

"Yeah, enough with the kimono unwrapping. I end up like this anyway. Why waste anyone's precious time?" She winked. Then she looked at me. "Oh. Who's this? She's fresh."

"This is my new roommate, Peaches. Peaches this is Belle. Belle, Peaches."

"Nice to meet you, Peaches."

"Uh...nice to meet you too," I responded.

"You can keep the lipstick. I have plenty of others," Kuriko said.

Belle smiled. "Thank you, girl. You're a godsend. Nice meeting you, Peaches. Will I be seeing you around?"

"Maybe," Kuriko interjected. She grabbed my hand and headed down the hall.

What I stepped into backstage was nothing short of a three ring porn show. My mind could not wrap around all the activity I witnessed. Down the corridor were several doors, some open, some closed. Through the first open door I saw three naked Asian ladies bent over a table with a machine doing profane things with their bodies. The next couples of doors were closed but I heard moaning, slapping, whipping and screaming. In the following rooms I witnessed a young woman with her head between a man's thighs and two girls making out with an elderly man. Two girls made out with each other right by the pay phone.

"Geez, what is this place?" I finally asked in horror and disgust.

"I told you didn't want to come, but you insisted," Kuriko said.

"I didn't know it was gonna be all this!"

"Yeah. No one knows what goes on backstage. Jacob!" she yelled. A tiny Asian man appeared out of nowhere. They greeted each other cordially, speaking some Asian dialect. She spoke English again, "Yes. Can you take Peaches to the main dining room please, front and center? Make sure she gets whatever she likes."

"Yes, Sapphire-san." He bowed to her then motioned for me to follow him. I looked at Kuriko, not knowing where I was going or who I was going with.

"It's okay," she assured me. "You're safe with

him. Go to the main dining area while I get ready. I'll meet you after the show."

Dark, elegant and sophisticated, the restaurant differed drastically from the backstage brothel atmosphere. Earth-toned browns, gold trimming and modern reds colored the carpeted walls. A few inches from the floor were short square, black tables coupled with embroidered red, legless chairs and matching pillows. The table was decorated with delicate Asian dinnerware, including rectangular plates, dainty teacups and engraved chopsticks. A ceiling-to-floor sized Buddha waterfall was engraved in the wall near the entrance. Green shrubbery sat in the corners of the room. A wall-length handcrafted black marble bar with six rows of premium spirits sat adjacent to black marble dance stage. A stripper pole was front and center on the stage. The entire ensemble was designed for the Chinese emperor and it was unlike anything I had ever seen, though I had frequented some pretty fancy restaurants in San Diego.

"What would you care to drink?" Jacob asked me.

"A Coke is fine."

He lowered his chin at me. "One Coca-Cola coming up."

I sat back in my chair to observe the scenery. This place brimmed over with clientele, all enjoying the conversation, atmosphere and food. I got so inspired by the sights I broke out my pad and pencil to replicate the setting as best as I could.

"Here is your Coke," a waiter said. "What would you like to order, ma'am?"

"Uh, what's good?"

"Everything on the menu, ma'am."

Really? He couldn't just break it down for me! "Okay, um, I'll have what Sapphire normally orders."

He smiled. "Right away, ma'am."

As soon as the waiter left I got to work on duplicating the aesthetics of the place. There was so much activity going on I decided to mute the backdrop and focus more on the people. I had never sketched an Asian person before. As I outlined the faces I noticed something eerie. The clientele here was composed of older, wealthy, socially graceful businessmen nestled side by side with young Asian women. Well, not even women, more like teenagers. *Girls my age.* I put down my pencil to scan the room. Older men in their forties, fifties and sixties were wining and dining girls who looked like they could be in my geometry class!

Just as my dinner arrived, the dining room lights dimmed and a turquoise spotlight flashed on a woman center stage. I saw a painted white face with ruby red lips and over-dramatic black eyeliner. Her stringy black hair flowed to the middle of her back and she showed off a beautiful blue and white kimono with matching umbrella. A waltz-like song played in the background and this ethereal creature began to sway.

It wasn't until the beauty lifted her arms to the sky, twirling softly, that I noticed all the tattoos on her forearm. This graceful dancer onstage was Kuriko! She looked so exquisite I didn't even recognize her! She moved like a piece of art that left not one dry eye in the room. As the music intensified so did her movements. Her body flowed with the music to the point you couldn't divide them apart. She *became* the music. I was simply blown away by her performance.

At the end of her piece, Kuriko humbly took a bow and walked toward my table.

"So, what'd you think?" she asked. She helped herself to a lobster wrap.

"Unbelievable. The entire show was mesmerizing. I didn't even recognize you!" I said.

"Thanks. Glad you enjoyed it."

A few people interrupted our conversation to congratulate her.

"Where'd you learn how to become one with the music like that?" I asked.

"I've been dancing longer than I care to share. I've kinda turned it into my escape," she said.

"How did you get started?"

"My dad died when I was two years old and my mom couldn't afford to care for me and my siblings by herself so she made us dance in exchange for money."

"Oh, that sounds neat. Different."

"Actually, it wasn't. It was a nightmare. That's why I ended up here."

"How'd you get here?"

"I don't want to talk about this anymore."

"Fine. We can talk about something else."

"What is that in your notebook? Are you an artist?"

"Yeah...well...sorta. I like to play around with realistic art a bit," I said.

"Let me see." She studied my entire sketchbook from cover to cover. Her face lightened. "This doesn't look like playing around, 'Tra—I mean, Peaches. You are very good."

"Thanks. It's been a passion of mine since I

could hold a pencil."

"Ever thought about making your passion a profit?" she asked.

"Huh?"

"Artists get paid a lot of money out here for their art."

"How?"

"You could be a cartoonist for a television network. A web site designer. A graphic artist for a major magazine or book publishing company. Or you can be a tattoo artist."

"Tattoos? Are you serious? People get paid for that?" I asked.

"Oh my God, like thousands. Some even hundreds of thousands. Tattooing is very popular out here, as you can see when you walk up and down Hollywood Boulevard. It's even worse on Sunset and Melrose."

"I've never drawn on humans before, just paper."

"You can practice on me and my friends. With skills like this, girl, it's only a matter of time till you become one of the biggest tattoo artists in Hollywood. Trust me!"

9

Kuriko introduced me to several of her friends in the following months. Most of them were older businessmen, but others were accomplished artists. I never quite understood why so many older men were interested in her because she was only seventeen. She refused to explain herself to me so I stopped asking questions. I met my two other roommates who'd created their own little secret club in which they were the only members. I pretty much spent all of my time with Kuriko.

"Don't pay any attention to them," Kuriko warned me. "We got into it when I first arrived but I set them straight. No problems since then."

"Did it turn into Wrestle Mania, like my first roomies?" I asked.

"No, it wasn't that bad." Kuriko laughed.

"Seriously unnecessary. Speaking of which, I haven't seen them around lately."

"Yeah, they probably got kicked out or moved on. People don't last long here."

"Where do they go?"

"Well, some go on to school. Some get their own apartment. Some get picked up by pimps."

"Pimps? What's that?" I asked.

"Oh my lord, girl." Kuriko shook her head. "How long have you been on your own?"

"Not long, really." I realized the one year anniversary of my family's death was just a few short months away.

"Obviously. You need to stay close by me. I'll show you how this game is played."

Something about the way she said that frightened me. What all did I need to learn?

"How long have you been here?" I asked.

"A few years. I'm about to get my own pad, though, not too far from here. You can room with me if you want. I'm looking for a two bedroom."

"But I don't have much money to pay for anything."

"That won't last long. Not after you put your artwork to good use."

"You think I can make money from my art?"

"Hon, I don't think, I *know!* Let me introduce you to Blue Moon. You'll make a killing at his shop. He's the hottest shop on Hollywood."

"How do you know he'll give me a shot?"

"'Cause I know Moon. Grab your sketches. Let's go."

* * * *

Blue Moon owned a tattoo shop in Hollywood called The Human Canvas. I was awed by the Polaroids mounted on the walls. All shades of skin tones were beautifully decorated with various tattoos representing personal triumphs, losses, loved ones, affinities. I immediately fell in love with the environment. Beyond the pictures were royal blue walls, autographed paraphernalia, plush purple couches, antique tables and a collection of skateboards.

A burly man standing around six foot four with a long white beard, mustache and shoulder length white hair stood guard at the front desk, studying both of us as we approached.

"Moon!" shrieked Kuriko as she stretched out her arms to hug him. "How are ya?"

"I'm doin' fine, Ms. Sapphire. How you?" He returned the hug with a wicked smile.

Sapphire? This must be a customer from The Geisha Room.

"Fab as always. I want to introduce you to someone. Alcatraz, this is Blue Moon, Moon, this is Alcatraz."

"Hey there, little one," Moon greeted me.

"Hello." I stood there paralyzed, fearing he would reject my work because of my inexperience, age and looks. Hell!

"What you got in your hand?" he asked me.

"That's her to-die-for sketchbook," Kuriko boasted. "Check it out, Moon. I think she'd give this place a facelift."

"Is that right? Well let me see what you got, little lady."

"Okay," I said, extending the sketchbook. "These are just some of my drawings I've done in the past. I mean, right now, too."

"Relax, kid." He grabbed the book out of my

hand and began flipping through the pages. His expression changed from suspicion to impression. "You drew all this?"

"Yeah."

"Really?" He sounded unconvinced. He reached in the drawer to grab some paper and picked up a pencil from the holder by the phone. "Here," He threw the paper and pencil toward me. "Create something."

"Right now?"

"Unless you want to come back next year?" he said sarcastically. "Yeah, now." Then he faced Kuriko. "And as for you, Ms. Lady, why don't ya come and see what I got for ya in the back room?"

"I don't know, Moon. Will it be worth my time?" She flirted.

"Oh yeah, baby doll. I'll make it very worth your time." He then flung her over his shoulder and breezed his way through the beaded curtains.

I picked up my backpack from off the floor and sat in the lobby. I scanned the room for my project, noticing the people walking in and out of the shop. The waiting area quickly filled up with moms, dads, daughters, sons, lawyer-types, punk rockers, young and old. Every breed of life entered this shop with very different reasons for wanting a tattoo.

The foyer was separated from the actual studio where clients got tatted so I didn't get a feel for the employees until they walked out to greet a client. So far I noticed six guys and one girl, all with their own unique style and flair. No suits, high heels or pinned-up hairstyles. Attire included ripped jeans, rocker shirts, Converse shoes, wild hairstyles, piercings and of course, hundreds of tattoos. The more artists I saw the more I wanted to work here. It just felt right.

My eyes rested on a beautiful girl sitting beside her boyfriend across from me. She had wavy, dirty blond hair, crystal blue eyes and loads of makeup, but what made her stand out was the starfish tattoo around her right eye. Without staring at her I started on my creation. I decided to use my burnt umber, sepia and yellow ochre colored pencils for accent and exaggeration.

As I came close to completion, a sweaty Moon and Kuriko stepped from the back tickling each other and giggling.

Moon signaled me toward him. "Let me see what you got, kid," he said.

"Well, it's not all the way done but I did what I could in that short time."

"Whoa, Traz. This is awesome!" Kuriko shrieked. "Is this somebody here?"

"Shh. Yeah, the chick sitting in the corner there next to her boyfriend," I whispered.

Both glanced over apprehensively to see the real person.

"Wow! That's pretty damn close if you ask me," Kuriko said. I knew she was trying her best to pump me up to Moon.

"Well, Phire, I'm a have to agree with ya on this one. This portrait is damn near identical." He looked up at me. "You ever draw on a human before?"

"No, but I'm willing to learn," I said.

"Do you even have any tattoos, kid?" He started to look disinterested.

"Why don't you give her one right now?" Kuriko interposed.

"Yeah, I was just admiring all the final products

walking out the door," I said.

"You know they ain't free, don't ya?" he said.

"Oh come on, Moon," Kuriko puckered her lips while pinching his cheeks. "Let her get a little something."

"How old are you, kid?" he asked.

"Seventeen," Kuriko lied.

"Seventeen! What, are you trying to close me down for good?" he yelled at Kuriko. "No, I'm not losing my license over this mess. You have to be eighteen to get tattooed here. With a valid identification."

"She's not going to close you down, Moon. Come on," Kuriko said.

"Not in this shop!"

"Can't she just be like a helper or something? You know? Like somebody who takes out the trash, mops the floors, cleans the toilets and occasionally puts some ink down." Kuriko winked at me.

"She ain't gonna be puttin' no ink on anybody in this shop anytime soon. That's for damn sure!"

"That's fine. I'm willing to work my way up," I said.

"Look, kid, you got a lot to learn if you want to work here. Skin ain't paper and pencil ain't permanent ink if you catch my drift. This ain't kiddie land here. These people pay a lot of money for a lifetime memory so I only employ the best. I want you to know that right up front. If you aren't the best in your niche you will stay the maid. Got it?"

"Got it," I agreed.

"Aw, she's going to be fabulous." Kuriko kissed me on the cheek. "I just know it."

"She'd better be. I'm putting her on your tab,

Sapphire. If she don't work out then you have to pay," Moon said.

"You know I can deliver the payment." Her voice was very seductive.

"The shop opens at noon. I expect you here at 11:45 on the dot tomorrow. I'm considering this an apprenticeship. Since you know Sapphire there won't be a fee, but you also won't be getting paid. Now if one of the artists decides to give you some of their cut that's between you and them. Don't bring it to me, kid! Are you in school?"

"No," I said.

"Are you starting school soon?"

"Not right now, no."

"That's a shame, kid. You need to get an education."

"Oh who are you now, Kobayashi Issa?" Kuriko cracked.

"Anyway, you can start at twenty hours a week and we'll go from there. We got a deal?"

"Sounds great!" I replied. "This is gonna be so cool." I grabbed Kuriko and hugged her.

"We'll see, kid. We'll see," Moon said.

We walked out of the shop and Kuriko turned to me. "Girl, we have got to get you tatted. How are you gonna work in a tattoo shop and not have one tattoo on you? That's like being a sober bartender."

"Yeah, well Moon said I couldn't get one," I said.

"He's not the only rodeo I ride in town. Let's go see Josh."

"How are we getting there?"

"My car, of course. What, you think I walk everywhere? No, hon. Just on Hollywood. Anywhere past these eight blocks and I drive my Mustang."

"You have a license?"

"Sure. I'll be eighteen in November."

"So you're not old enough to get tatted either? How do you have so many tattoos?"

"'Cause I have different methods of payment you don't need to concern yourself with right now. Come on. Let's go meet Josh."

* * * *

A skinny, Harry Potter-looking guy with brown hair, glasses, braces, and an arm full of tattoos opened the door to his Sherman Oaks condo.

"Sapphire, my love!" He picked her up and twirled her around.

"How's it going?" she asked.

"Good, good. Come on in. Hi, I'm Josh."

"Alcatraz," I said.

"Al-ca-traz," he pronounced slowly. "I like it."

"Yeah, doesn't that sound like the name of a tattoo artist to you?" Kuriko promoted.

"Most def. You tat?"

"No, not yet. I just draw portraits and stuff." I stopped and gazed around his pad. "This is nice."

"Thanks. I'd like to think of myself as a part time interior designer, among other things." He shot a look at Kuriko. My curiosity about her extracurricular activities began to be insatiable. "You want something to drink?"

"Yeah, I'll take some water," I said.

"I want some green tea and Raisin Bran," Kuriko responded.

"Of course, your highness." He bowed before her.

"I'll help you get it," she offered. She turned to me and said, "Traz, just make yourself comfortable, okay? We'll be right back."

"Okay," I said, wondering why she had to help him boil water and put milk in a bowl.

While they frolicked off to the kitchen I put my book bag down and took notice of the decoration. This guy was eclectic. Bob Marley pictures hung alongside Bette Midler, Aloe Vera plants against red Amaryllis and statues. There were a bunch of statues.

I walked over to his fireplace where the bulk of his statues sat and noticed it just wasn't a regular fireplace: It was a shrine with pictures of Krishna, statues, stones, lamps, bells, trays, whistles and a compass, all neatly arranged on a beautiful, bold red cloth. As I approached the shrine a book caught my attention. It was sitting on a pillow in front of the fireplace, and I saw that it was the Bhagavad Gita. Oh my God! I flashed back to Greg Lubbock's class at Valeo and remembered him teaching about one particular group who studied this book. I couldn't think of the name.

I randomly opened the book and the page said: "I am the source of all spiritual and material worlds. Everything emanates from me. The Wise who fully realize this engage in my devotional service and worship me with all their hearts. My pure devotees are absorbed in thoughts of me, and they experience fulfillment and bliss by enlightening one another and conversing about me. To those who are continually devoted and worship me with love, I give the understanding by which they can come to me. Out of compassion for them, I, residing in their hearts, destroy with the shining lamp of knowledge the darkness born of ignorance."

I reread, "To those who are continually devoted and worship me with love, I give the understanding by which they can come to me." That sentence bothered me, but I could not figure out why.

I flipped through the pages to read more of the Gita and sensed a heaviness enter in the room. It was that same dark, evil presence I felt in the shower at the San Diego hospital and when I played light as a feather, stiff as a board with the girls at Valeo. I glanced at all the objects on the shrine and wondered where it was coming from just as Kuriko and Josh reappeared with a tray of drinks and snacks.

"Ah, I see you found my altar," Josh said.

"Yeah, I was just browsing. Hope you don't mind," I said, replacing the book.

"No, no. Not at all. Are you into Hinduism?"

"You're a Hindu?" Kuriko burst out.

"Uh, yeah. I've only been studying for about four years now."

"I thought all Hindus were Indian, not upper class white Americans," Kuriko commented.

"I heard that too, like India was the main place for Hindus," I said.

"It is, but there are quite a few of us Americans who practice Hinduism, especially if we're into yoga. And I for one am a die-hard Ashtanga fan."

"How is yoga?" I asked.

"Yoga rocks! It is an exercise connecting the mind, body and spirit to the breath and ultimately to the universal god," Josh said.

"Yeah, yoga is great," Kuriko added. "I used to practice back in Japan but don't have much time now with my busy schedule. I should try to get back into it again, though. It helped control my stress."

"Absolutely. It relieves stress and tension out of your body. Connects you to this moment, to all that matters. I didn't really care about the spiritual world before yoga but after practicing I started asking really tough questions my soul desperately needed answers to. The Gita and Sutras help me a lot."

"Buddha gives me all the guidance I need," Kuriko butted in. "Once I do my chants, I'm good."

"You're a Buddhist?" I asked.

"Sure am. I visited the temple on occasion in Japan but the rituals stuck with me. I still do my chants when time permits. When I buy my condo I'm going create an altar similar to this one so I can have my dedicated space. Spirituality is important to me."

One hundred and one questions ran through my mind. Here I was sitting in the room with a Buddhist and a Hindu. Live believers who could maybe help me on my quest to discover the *one* true God.

"What do you believe, Alcatraz?" Josh asked me while he turned on some tunes.

"I'm not sure yet. I know there is a God, I just don't know what his name is or even if he has a name. I still have a bus load of questions so I won't be making any altars in my house anytime soon."

Both Kuriko and Josh laughed.

"That's cool," Josh said. "I had no idea what I believed in when I was younger. How old are you?"

I said, "Fourteen," before Kuriko could lie about my age again.

"Wow, you're a baby!" Josh looked shocked.

"Yeah, but we're about to make her a woman," Kuriko said. "How about giving Traz her first tattoo?"

"Really? Are you ready for a life change that permanent?" Josh asked me.

"Yeah. I mean, standing in Moon's shop today really got me pumped. I feel like it's some sort of divine connection or something, like I was born to be tatted. Maybe that's why I'm having such a hard time finding answers within myself," I said.

"Divine connection? All right. You know these don't come off?"

"I know. I'm ready. It's time for some change in my life. This is gonna be the kickoff."

"All right then, let's get started." Josh smiled.

That night I said goodbye to parents, siblings and foster homes. At fourteen years old I was now my own woman ready to make life decisions for myself. I had no hesitation, doubt or fear about Josh etching my first tattoo. It was four names: Cindy, Tom, Henry and Natalie. I got my mom on my right upper arm and Dad on the right shoulder blade joined together with a rose vine. I did the same with my brother and sister on the left-hand side.

This night started a lifelong phenomenon of body art all over me; it was impossible to get just one. I let friends, family and professionals tat me. Anyone who could turn on a gun splattered ink on me. I got addicted to the ink like junkies get addicted to the pipe.

I observed the entire process of tattooing up close and personal in Josh's condo that night: stencil making via thermal-fax, sterilization, prepping the machine gun. Josh even broke down the intricacies of the gun to me. I was mesmerized by the process.

"So why are you so interested in God?" Josh asked as he sterilized my arm.

"When I first started drawing I felt an existence beyond me, flowing through me to help me replicate whatever I visualized in my mind's eye. And...I don't know...I just would like to know the truth about it."

"What is truth?" Josh asked rhetorically. "Before I became Hindi I was an atheist and heavy into drugs, sex, alcohol. You name it, I probably tried it. But then one day I, like you, started thinking about the manner in which this world is organized. I started practicing yoga, connecting my mind and body to my spirit and discovered that we are all gods. As the inner light flamed inside of me sweating in Dog Pose, I realized that I am god. You are god. We all are gods. He is everywhere and in everything. God is just a manifestation of whatever you want him to be wherever you want him to be. So that being said, there are several truths. There is no one truth. You just have to find the one that works for you."

"So you do believe in a god?" I asked.

"I don't believe in one true universal God no. We are all one big happy, cosmic family with different skin colors, hair textures, hobbies, goals. I do not believe in a god that is separate from humanity. Essentially, god created humanity so why would there be just one God? That brings division more than unity. Division isn't god. Harmony and balance is."

I chewed on Josh's words a moment and cringed as he lined my rose vine.

"I agree with you, Josh. I think we are all one great, big, ball of fire," Kuriko threw in.

"So how, or what, rather, is the point of Hindu? Like, why do you believe you are on this planet?" I inquired.

"Well, the ultimate purpose in life is to actualize

my atman, my true self or inner essence of human beings, to the likeness of Brahma, or the principle force that creates and changes things in the universe," Josh explained.

"To grow into our fullest potential is basically what he is trying to say," Kuriko clarified.

"And how did yoga help you unravel all this? Ouch!" I cried out when his needle touched my underarm.

Josh paused the tattooing for a moment while I composed myself, then he continued. "Yoga is all about connecting your spirit, soul, and body to the breath. So as I inhaled and exhaled my tri-part being became one. I experienced interconnectedness with my surroundings. Everywhere I went my heart beat for others. My psyche understood the ways of others. My spirit reflected others. I became one with all things: people, animals and objects. Then I studied out the yoga sutras by Patanjali and Brahma began to make sense to me."

"So Brahma is your god?" I asked.

"Brahma is the ultimate creator of all things and all humans. Brahma is a composition of male, female, and everything in between. He is infinite in every realm. So yeah, I guess you could say that Brahma is my god."

I remembered Mr. Lubbock's comments on Hinduism in class. "Do you guys worship animals?"

"Yes, we worship and respect everything. All is a representation of god."

"Is Brahma the god in Buddhism?" I asked Kuriko, trying not to get grossed out.

"Similar, but not the same," she said. "Buddha is more or less the invocation of god. Even though we are polytheist we pay more attention to thoughts, words and deeds. We are more into being good in our thinking, speaking and doing. Karma, if you will. What we exhale we eventually inhale someday."

"Oh, you guys are into reincarnation?" I asked, fascinated by these belief systems.

"Oh yes. We most def believe in rebirth."

"Yeah, we do too," Josh chimed in.

I sat in my chair in agony from the tattoo and thought about what these two were telling me. I tried to let it digest but for some reason it wouldn't. Why couldn't I believe this?

"You okay?" Josh lifted the needle away from my skin. He must have noticed I was in pain.

"Yeah, I guess. I don't know." I looked at the partial tattoo on my arm. "Something about what you guys are saying just doesn't feel right in me. I don't know why." Josh went back to work on the tattoo.

"Well it's okay, sugarplum," Kuriko said. "Everybody goes down this path once or twice in their lifetime. The truth will become clear and you will feel at peace when it does."

Peace. That was it. I didn't have peace about what they were describing. It didn't feel right in my spirit. I was in no way judging their beliefs, but I couldn't shake this feeling of heaviness, darkness and unease within me.

"There is nowhere to run on the yoga mat," she explained while eating a piece of fruit with cheese and crackers. "You are stuck with yourself in every pose. That's the one place where you come face to face with truth and reality, where your light meets darkness and you receive long-awaited answers to questions. It's where the journey to enlightenment begins. There is no escape in yoga. You are forced to face you and your beliefs. You define your boundaries and aspirations for your life." Kuriko stared at me momentarily while sipping green tea. "I am intrigued to know which truth you choose to believe and what you will do with it."

"What do you mean?" I asked.

"Which religion will enter you into the divine. There are many roads to God. It depends on your choice. That's all. Like mine is Buddhism, for lack of better terms. Josh practices Hinduism. Buddhism works for me, Hinduism works for him. When you find your road your frustration will cease."

"That makes life even more complicated to me. How can there be more than one truth? It's like a man who commits adultery. The truth is that he cheated on his wife and violated her trust. Even though he might try to explain away the reasons why he cheated, the truth is: he cheated. Period! There is only one truth in that situation. How can life be any different?"

"Life has all kinds of options. Like, you're a talented artist, right? That is a truth about you. That gift is unique to you. On the other hand, I can't draw a stick figure. We're all designed differently so our personal truth will be different," Kuriko clarified.

"I understand the creation is different. Yes, that is evident by variety in every natural element from humans to animals to nature itself. But how can the Creator be more than one? And if we're all gods then how did we create ourselves? How do we worship, or better yet, *who* do we worship? Ourselves? That seems pretty selfish to me. And there is no way selfishness equates to God. That thought is too human."

"For your age, your spirit is really advanced, Alcatraz," Kuriko complimented.

"Seriously, dude. I was too stoned to go that deep at fourteen," Josh said.

"You understand things people twice your age don't think about. Your thought process is not ordinary. I wouldn't be surprised if you are called to be a shaman, priestess or minister. The truth will find you. No worries. All your questions will be answered for you in good timing, when you're ready to receive," Kuriko said.

"You should come to yoga with us sometime," Josh suggested. "You'll probably get more clarity after practicing for a while. Spirituality is hard to intellectualize. It has to be believed in the heart to be real to the practitioner, otherwise it's just a head theory."

"That sounds cool. How often do you normally go?" I asked.

"Every day," Josh answered.

"Is it hard?"

"Hell, yeah, especially if you've never practiced," Kuriko said.

"Ashtanga class is ninety minutes long but maybe we can start off in a slower-paced class. There are some Iyengar classes at the studio. We can go to that one. Don't want to kill you on the first date," Josh said.

"Thanks. I appreciate that," I said.

"Voila!" Josh exclaimed pushing his chair away from me. "Have a look."

I walked to the vanity mirrors Josh set up in his studio and picked my jaw up off the floor once I saw the finished product. All four of their names were beautifully woven together with rose vines on both arms.

"Oh my gosh!" I gasped. "This is so beautiful!"

"Yeah that does look rad, girl," Kuriko added. "Welcome to the new you!"

Don't ask me why but after getting those tattoos my spirit felt alive and empowered, like I was meeting the real me for the first time.

I quickly turned to Josh. "Okay, now let me do you."

"You sure you're ready for this?" He grinned.

"I was born ready for this!"

"Whoohoo!" Kuriko exclaimed. "I'm next!"

"Okay, you know how to make a needle using a jig?" Josh asked me.

"What's a jig?" I asked.

"All right. First things first. Draw a design on me."

"Where do you want me to tat?"

He lifted up his shirt and glanced around his almost completely covered abdomen. "Right here's good."

"Oh, your oblique area? That's gonna hurt," Kuriko said.

"No, I'm a pro. I got my other side inked so it shouldn't be too bad." Josh winked at me.

"Okay, so what should I draw?" I asked.

"Anything non-girlie I'm okay with. And make it small. I don't want a huge train wreck on my belly."

"How about one of your statues?"

"Whoa. Impressive. You sure you don't want to start with a star or something simple?"

"Nah, man, she's a full blown artist, dude. Didn't you look at her sketchbook?" Kuriko said, once again bragging about my skills.

"No, I must have missed that."

"Well, let me show you." She ran in the living room to grab our bags.

Josh flipped through my sketchbook. "Holy shit, dude! This is good."

"Thanks." I said, embarrassed.

"I think you're definitely qualified to draw a statue. The question is, can you transfer the same quality on flesh? That's the tricky part, but nothing that can't be solved with a little practice, patience and elbow grease."

That night I not only received my first tattoo but delivered two of them all by myself! They weren't perfect but I was determined to practice until perfection. And that's just what I did.

10

"Hey, Yellow Bone, come over here," said Blue Moon. A Hispanic guy covered in Japanese animation raced over to meet me. Moon introduced him. "This is Yellow Bone. Yellow Bone, this is Alcatraz. She'll be following you today. Show her the ropes."

"Sure. Welcome aboard." He reached out his hand to shake mine.

Blue Moon turned to me. "You won't be putting any ink on a soul until I'm confident you know what you're doing. That might be three months or it might be three years, but either way absorb all you can here. You'll learn from nothing but the best."

"Understood," I answered.

Moon nodded at Yellow Bone and walked off.

"All right, girl, let's go," Yellow Bone said. We walked to the back of the shop. "So right now I'm tracing an image for a client."

"Already, at 11:55?" I asked.

"She walked in last night right when we were about to close and requested me. I was too tired so she told me what she wanted and I said I would get her in first thing in the morning." That made sense to me. This shop was busy. "Rosalinda wants an open door right over her heart and she asked me to fill in the details. I am tracing the image of the door on this light table right here." He motioned for me to sit down and he picked up where he left off.

"You can freestyle the image on the person or trace it on the light table. It's totally up to you. For starting out I would do the light board but like I said, it's up to you."

"What's the difference between the two?"

"Time. You pretty much get paid for your time here. The longer it takes you to do one tattoo the fewer hours you have in a day to do more, which translates into less cash. So unless you're a pro at freestyling on human flesh I would start here. The light table gives you a stable surface to sketch your stencil. It doesn't move like flesh. So you draw your design on a piece of paper here, which is what I'm finishing."

"Cool." I sat behind him to observe.

"Okay, so now we can Thermo fax. Have you used this machine before?" Yellow Bone asked.

"For the first time last night, but it never hurts to see it again."

"You want to cut out the design, leaving some room around the edges, like this. Then place the design between a pieces of carbon paper. Keeping the design in place, put the carbon paper in a plastic carrier like so, then just run it through the Thermo fax. Voila! Your stencil is complete. Now all we have to do is wait for the client, but I can show you how to prep in the meantime."

I found my home at The Human Canvas. No one taunted me, no one abused me. In fact, folks celebrated me here. I didn't get any flack from anybody at that shop. They accepted my personality, my style, my life choices and my questions about God. I know it might not be normal for other females but my apprenticeship was natural and seamless. Even though I was the shop's gopher, I ate, slept and drank there. I loved my cohorts, the atmosphere and the job.

I spent my every waking moment learning all I could about tattoos. The number one attraction to this profession was the connection and dialogue between artist and client. These tattoos were more than just art to people, they were heart-felt life stories.

The open door tattoo was one such story. Rosalinda was a single mom who suffered much loss in her life, like me. Her dad was shot in the head when she was seven, then her mother died giving birth to her breached sister when she was eight. After the father of Rosalinda's baby found out she was pregnant, he left her for another woman. She explained to Bone how, subconsciously, she had become distrustful of life. Not necessarily human beings, individually, but just life in general. She experienced so much pain that she shut her heart off from loving anybody and lived as a mental recluse. I got teary-eyed listening to her story because it hit so close to where I was at the time. Now she was in a relationship with a great guy who was teaching her how to trust again.

"He is slowly prodding open the door to my locked heart," she said. She seemed to glow as she spoke of him. "Because of him, I choose to accept the different wavelengths of life. I'm void of fear like once before, allowing love to pry me open. This relationship has been truly liberating."

As she shared bits of wisdom I reflected on my own life, knowing that right then I was where she had been.

* * * *

Kuriko hooked me up with a lot of her bohemian friends and co-workers who didn't mind my tattoo experiments. I perfected my lettering by shadowing script and Old English words. After a while, I found my niche in black and white photorealism. I had gravitated toward that style ever since I was little. I showed people the portraits of cartoon characters and celebrity figures I had drawn and they entrusted me to draw figures on them.

I drew classic beauties like Marilyn Monroe and Audrey Hepburn, as well as personal portraits of moms, dads, spouses and kids. In the beginning my work totally sucked because tattooing on skin is different than drawing on paper. Many of the frames for faces didn't come out right, but I soon started to get the hang of it.

Life in Los Angeles shaped up nicely for me. Within the next few months Kuriko and I moved out of Metamorphosis and into a two bed, two bath condo in the Rose Bowl area. I earned tips from my co-workers at the shop and Kuriko's friends gave me twenty dollars here and fifty dollars there for my dummy tattoos. I was able to rent the second room for four hundred a month, though I practically lived at Moon's shop. I sometimes arrived before Moon himself. I got the hang of the business operations as well as making a good cup of coffee.

The flow of the shop became such a second nature to me that Moon ended up putting me in charge of the front desk and paying me two hundred a week under the table. I booked all the appointments, set up the preparation area, arranged public relation events and even cut checks for the seven tattoo artists. I got along with everybody, though Josh was the only one I hung out with outside of work.

Moon still hadn't given me the opportunity to tattoo in the shop but I probably tattooed over a hundred people on the side. I borrowed equipment from Josh until I could collect my own.

Being a tattoo artist on Hollywood Boulevard exposed me to the lifestyle of the rich and famous where millionaires buy big houses, drive fast cars, snort, shoot and drink until their merry little hearts are satisfied. I didn't get as much into the drug scene as I did the bar scene, drinking with males twice my age. Kuriko was popular among her gentlemen suitors so we were both VIP all around town, from The X Spot in Melrose on Mondays to Excalibur in Santa Monica Beach on Saturdays. It was extravagance to excess. Older men treated us like L.A's royalty. Kuriko and I got whatever we wanted with no questions asked, though I still wasn't quite sure of the price.

One day I asked, "What do you do with all these men for them to wine and dine us like this? Like, I know you're kinda cute with a great personality and all, but you're not worth all this."

She looked me dead in the eye and asked, "What

do you want for?"

"Nothing."

"Then don't ask me anything!" That was the end of the conversation.

I grew up fast in the year I'd lived here, but in spite of everything I was very much naive to adult situations. As much as I loved hanging out with Kuriko, I barely knew her. She rarely opened up to me about anything personal. Knowing what I know now, I shouldn't have expected her to. It wasn't just from an Asian cultural standpoint but from shame. All I knew was she was born in Japan, somehow flew to the States and now danced at The Geisha Room with a slew of men courting her around town. I wondered how she ended up in the shelter to begin with.

* * * *

Unfulfillment, boredom, and anxiety overcame me every time I wasn't tattooing someone. While I was in creative mode I was fine but as soon as I stopped it was like life wasn't worth living anymore. My mood could change instantly. I masked my pain very well with alcohol. If it wasn't pomegranate margaritas from The Geisha Room then I drank hard liquor at the Roxy or wherever we were that night. On the outside girls envied me for my mad abilities, but on the inside I cried myself to sleep at night like a little, insecure baby.

No matter how hard I tried to party and tattoo my way out of my problems, I couldn't let go of the pain of my parent's death, my rape and being plucked from Valeo Academy into this Hollywood life on my own. All of those seeds were ever present in the soil of my heart waiting to be tended to. I didn't know how to process the pain except to pretend like it wasn't there. Alcohol allowed me to flee from my problems gracefully and to fit in with people who made me feel loved, accepted and worthwhile.

* * * *

"What are we getting done today?" I asked Ashram, one of Kuriko's friends.

"I want the moon, water, a lion and the number eight woven together on my thigh," she said.

"You want it to be in color or black and white?"

"Black and white. My hope is to resemble Rorschach where you don't really understand the dialogue unless you listen long and hard. You know what I'm saying?"

"Okay, so abstract, ethereal?"

"Exactly."

This moment made me appreciate Mrs. Tan's art class. It took me forty-five minutes to draw her design. We were at another barbecue over at Josh's house. I simply helped myself to his tools, a Guinness and highball glass full of Johnny Walker Black.

"What's up with the symbolism?" Kuriko asked.

"Eight is my life number. I was born on August 8, 1980. In eastern culture the number eight means infinity, and also prosperity. In China it is the number of luck. In the West the number eight means money and power. I liked the combination of the two, so…"

"Totally! Who wouldn't, right?" I said. I wanted to make conversation to cover up my fear of turning her thigh into a total disaster.

"The lion is my sun sign," she continued. "Since I was born in August I'm a Leo. The lions are the kings of the jungle, attention seekers, boasters, proud, with a really loud roar and a nasty bite. I can relate to those qualities in a personal way. It is just how I am naturally."

"What about the moon?" I asked.

"My moon sign is Cancer and water is the element of Cancer. The sun sign represents the part of you the world sees but the moon sign represents the inside of you that only close people see. It is the true emotional side of you. Cancer is very sensitive, motherly, moody, homebody-like, intuitive, loves to cook and is family oriented. That's me all wrapped up in one, yet few people realize it."

"I get it. On the outside you're proud, bubbly and attention-seeking, but on the inside you're quiet, sensitive and nurturing?" I asked, looking to Kuriko for confirmation.

"I've never seen that Cancer side," Kuriko commented. "I must not know the real you."

"Naw, man, you know me. I just don't show that side of me too often. I was created to show my bubbly, happy self to the world. It's funny how life preordains your qualities before time. Everything has a set purpose," Ashram said.

"Um, but couldn't you also be shaping your personality into that mold, too?" I dared.

"What do you mean?" she asked.

"I forgot to warn you of the great high priestess, guru, minister, St. Alcatraz who will be one of our generation's great religious leaders and thinkers," Kuriko joked.

"Really?" Ashram's eyes widened. "You are a

spiritual leader?"

"No, I'm not. Kuriko, stop saying that to people," I whined.

Kuriko chuckled, obviously getting pleasure from my embarrassment. After quieting down her laughter she said, "What? It's true. You're on this search to find truth so you can teach it to people, or what is the point? No quest is solely for self."

I never thought about my spiritual seeking in this fashion. "Like I was saying, Ashram, before I was so rudely interrupted, you discovered that Leos are bossy and Cancers are sensitive, right? Did you start acting that way after you found out or were you already like that?"

"No, I've been studying for a while now but the stars validated who I was before my studies. They showed me my strengths and weaknesses, my pet peeves and all that stuff. Astrology and numerology are very precise, orderly, predicable and on point. It's an exact science. The creator of this universe made no mistakes."

That comment piqued my attention. "The creator of the universe? Who is that?"

"Whoever you want him or her to be. I personally think the creator is a she. There's too much wisdom embedded on this side of life for the creator to be a man."

"So you believe God preordained you to be how you are?"

"Certainly. How else could my birthday fall on eight-eight-eighty? I couldn't have planned that and neither could my parents. I didn't place all the stars in order for me to have the energy of the sun yet the moodiness of the moon, God did. She concocted me this way. I am just aware of it now."

"So your god formed us after the stars?" I asked.

"When is your birthday?" Ashram asked me.

"February 25."

"You are a Pisces."

"What does that mean?" I stopped working on her thigh for a moment.

"Pisces is the sign of the fish swimming up and down the same stream," she explained. "You are extremely fickle, feeling one way one minute and going one-eighty the next. You're a girlie girl. Like, even though you are a tattoo artist and have many tattoos, I notice your pink nail polish, high leopard print shoes, well-managed, wavy hair and well-applied makeup. People might expect you to be butch 'cause of your profession, but I bet pink is your favorite color?"

"It is, actually." I laughed out loud because I had only worn black for months. This trip did something to me. "Okay, you're right so far. What else?"

"You are the kind of woman who will stand behind your man even if you have a career for yourself. You're super romantic. You believe in manifested fairy tales, romances and dreams. Your dream is for a man to cuddle you, protect you and fall madly in love with you to live happily ever after like Cinderella."

"That is so true!" I shouted. "I've always wanted to be swooped away like Cinderella. Oh my God, that is so scary."

"Yep, it sure is. Now, is your behavior conforming to the stars or are the stars conformed to you?"

"That's a really good question."

"It's one I asked myself for years until I dissected astrology."

"I'm a Scorpio. What does my sign say about me?" Kuriko queried.

"It means you're crazy as hell," Ashram said. We both laughed at Kuriko, then Ashram turned serious. She looked at me and said, "Oh, and one last thing about you I have to tell you."

"What?" I asked.

"Pisces is the sign of the great pretender. You guys are very deceiving. You are good at smiling on the outside but deep down you are miserable, almost to the point of death."

I slightly nodded. Who wants to admit she's miserable?

"The stars, numbers, natal charts and the universe are too organized to lie. When I know your name, birthday, time of birth and origin of birth, I can pretty much read your personality makeup. Like, when I was born my rising sign was in Aries at 1 degree, which means the sun was ascending in the house of Aries as I was pushing my way into this world. The rising sun is how you appear on the outside, how you act when you're around other people. So with the sun rising in Aries I appear very bold, confident, free spirited and must be first at everything I do."

"The stars get into all that?" Kuriko asked.

Ashram nodded. "Each star or ball of mass is unique in its makeup and signifies different qualities. The temperament I have and how I deal with my everyday situations is directly related to the personality of the star that's in my house at that moment."

"So basically, you have no control over how you act? The stars control it," I said.

"You hit it right on the head! For example, if Leo lands in the house of Mercury then I come across as being a know it all. I speak with great authority, see the big picture and I can persuade people pretty easily. That's because the planet Mercury by nature is very detached and reasonable, so my personality changes accordingly. I can't control it, it just happens naturally. I can almost predict how I will act in different situations depending on what star in my house that day."

"How do you know which star will be in your house?"

"Astrology is very predictable and orderly. The stars don't have a choice where they go and neither do we."

"So where does the brain come into all this?" I asked. "I mean, it sounds like we're born as programmed robots."

"The brain is given to use for reasoning, thinking and dreaming, but even that has its limitations. The stars can predict your thoughts as well."

I found it hard to buy what Ashram was selling. Even though I didn't have any concrete convictions of my own I sure didn't think we were just mindless robots being pulled by a ball of fire. To keep the conversation polite and light I replied, "Well, that's cool. Sounds like you stay excited about life even though you know what's gonna happen."

"Yeah, not only in everyday life but financially as well. I can't even tell you how much I have profited from readings. You should let me read your cards."

"I guess it wouldn't hurt to know about the

supernatural."

"Can you read mine as well?" Kuriko asked, excited.

I put my tattoo gun down so Ashram could grab a deck of cards out of her bag. I picked a few cards after she shuffled them.

Ashram studied the cards I selected. "Oh, Alcatraz, you are very special. You have a God-given ability to tap into the supernatural. You've used it before yet haven't honed that gift."

I sat there patiently, waiting for her finish.

"I see someone chasing you," she continued.

"Chasing me?" I asked.

"Yes, yet it doesn't look like a human being but rather a spirit or non-human force. He has you surrounded on all sides and is acting as a shield for you."

"What?"

"Imagine a fort. Pretend you are camping in Yellowstone Park and are lying down inside the tent. Can you visualize that?"

"Yeah, that's pretty easy."

"Okay, well it looks like a spiritual force is all around you. It's like a strong angel is protecting you on all sides." She looked up at me. "Maybe protecting you while you're on this spiritual journey. According to the cards this presence has made itself known to you in the past as well." After looking at another card Ashram said, "And you are called to be a teacher."

"I knew it!" Kuriko yelled.

"A teacher?" I cried. "How can I be called to teach? I don't even go to school. I dropped out of the eighth grade. What am I supposed to teach?"

"I can't see that. I just see you standing behind a

podium teaching a room full of people. They are listening to you very intensely." She shuffled the cards again.

Kuriko said, "I told you. This whole 'who is God' thing is not just for you. You are gonna do something with this."

"Hmm," Ashram mumbled under her breath.

"What?" I snapped impatiently.

"I also see a girl by your side. Brunette, heavily tatted, tanned skin, shorter than you. Voluptuous body."

"Who is that? What about her?" I asked.

"I can't really see anything other than she is a superb business woman and she's gonna help you on this spiritual journey."

"What is she doing?" I asked.

"Nothing, really. I see you two sitting at a table reading a book together. A very thick book."

"This is making no sense to me."

"Keep living. All this will make sense soon. These visions are embedded in the stars. Trust me, the cards never lie!"

* * * *

I immersed myself in the rich and cultural history of tattooing. I checked out numerous books from the library and spent hours at the bookstore studying the art. In the West, the word "tattoo" came from the South Pacific culture. Captain Cook traveled to Tahiti in 1769 and fell in love with the Polynesian art form that appeared on many tribal faces. When he returned to England he brought the word *tattoo* back with him, derived from the Tahitian word *tatau* which meant "mark" or "etch."

Tattoos are an ancient art, however. Otzi the Iceman, whose bodily remains bore fifty-seven different tattoos, was estimated to have lived around 3300 BC. While discovering many mummies and Egyptian priestesses, archaeologists also saw dots, lines and images of animals in their remains.

Japan was the first culture to create the body suit. The story behind this interested me. The Japanese government repressed the lower class and only allowed royalty and the very wealthy to wear beautifully decorated kimonos. In a creative outburst of rebellion the body suit was formed. The Japanese spent a lifetime tattooing their bodies, usually in line with their spiritual beliefs and life principles. They covered them up with their clothing and exposed the suit when they thought the timing was right.

I fell in love with the tribal work from the Polynesian Islands and the decorative work from Japan, but my favorite was Coptic art. Coptics were early Egyptian Christians who became famous for depicting the images of the Bible. I found their translations fascinating, especially with the limited resources of the time. They were a persecuted bunch who suffered multiple attacks at the hands of Islamic extremists. Art was a way to express their suppressed emotions and beliefs. My spirit really connected to them because they used their art as a means to escape—kind of like me. Even though the conditions of my life were nowhere near as dangerous as theirs I admired their need to voice pain in their circumstances, all in the name of Christianity. This made me wonder why their beliefs were worth dying for.

One day I was with Josh and Kuriko, and I was tattooing a skull on his forearm. I asked him, "Would you die for Brahma?"

"Huh?" Josh looked puzzled.

"Would you die for Brahma? Like, if the times were different and society had a problem with you worshiping Brahma, would you die for your beliefs?"

"Oh, you mean like post-Christians?"

What? He knew about Christ? "Yeah, like that?"

"Probably not. Their deaths were brutal, man. They got tarred and feathered, boiled in oil, crucified and burned alive."

"You sound like a fan," Kuriko teased.

"Well, you got to admit their courage is pretty admirable, even if it was all in vain," Josh said. "Like I said, I wouldn't die for Brahma even though I know I will return. He's not worth dying for."

"Don't Muslims die for their beliefs?" Kuriko asked.

"Yeah, but that's different. Muslims kill themselves, they are not martyred. Christians are the only religious group who were martyred in that bloodied fashion. Them and the Jews."

"Why do you think that is?" I asked.

"Who knows?" He sighed. "They claim their God is the one true God and the only way to him is through Jesus. And you're going to hell if you do not believe in Jesus and crap like that. I believe Jesus was an important man, a great prophet even, but to be the Son of God is a bunch of horseshit."

"Yet you wouldn't die for Brahma?"

"So what's your point?" he snapped.

"I'm just saying, if millions are dying for this Jesus guy it just makes me think there must be some good reason. Why would you die for a god if he wasn't worth it? And why wouldn't you die for God if he was worth it?"

Josh's face reddened. "Jesus isn't worth it! They're brainwashed. He's just like anybody else!"

"Apparently not like Brahma."

"So what are you saying?" Josh shouted, jumping out of the chair. "Look, kid, if you're going to start spouting off at the mouth about Jesus, then you can just get out of my house! Now!"

"Hey! You two calm down." Kuriko jumped in front of Josh. "It's not that serious."

"I'm not trying to be offensive, Josh," I said. "I'm desperate for understanding, that's all. I want to know the truth. What makes Jesus worth dying for?"

"Seriously, Josh. Calm down. She didn't' mean any harm." Kuriko said.

Josh backed down. "Sorry. I'm sorry. I just thought you were challenging my beliefs. You're right. It's not worth getting all worked up over. I'm sorry. Cool?"

"Yeah, man, totally. I've just had a lot of weird things happen to me. I'm in dire need of answers. I'm not challenging you at all."

"I know. I know. Sorry about that, dude. Seriously, I don't know what came over me. Here." He walked over to his bookshelf to grab a book. "Read this. It's the Bhagavad Gita. It'll give you some insight into God. It's what I read when I started practicing yoga. Speaking of which, what are you doing tonight?"

"Nothing." I said.

"Kuriko? What are you doing?"

"You know I dance tonight, but I don't have to

be there until later on. Why?" she asked.

"I planned on Ashtanga with Kelly tonight, then to temple, if you girls want to hang?"

"Yeah! I'd like to check it out," I said.

"Kill me now, why don't you?" Kuriko complained. "Ninety minutes of yoga with Kelly, then two hours of dancing?"

"Then your real job commences," Josh said. He smirked and Kuriko punched him in the arm.

"I'd like to go see what I can find out," I said.

"Class starts in two hours, so let's get going. I think tonight could really help you, Alcatraz. Just believe you will receive something transformational and you will."

After all this commotion yoga didn't sound like a bad idea. Why did Josh get so upset even if I was challenging his beliefs? They were just beliefs. It's not like I shot an arrow at his mother or stole money out of his billfold. I guess that's how one gets when they are truly on fire for what they believe…or insecure about it.

11

"Stand with your feet together at the front of your mat. Root down through the four corners of your feet. Press your thighs together and rotate them inward toward each other. Tuck your tailbone down while lifting up through your belly. Draw your shoulder blades down your back. Lift your chest and bring your hands into Namaste. Close your eyes. Now inhale...exhale...inhale...exhale. I want you to feel mountain pose. Feel your alignment. Feel the earth supporting your weight. Feel your inner balance.

"Forget about all the garbage you walked in here with and in this moment focus on your breath. And only your breath. This is all that is important right now. Close your mouth and inhale in your nose and out your nose. Try to keep your mouth closed if you can. Take your breath deep into your belly, your center. The home of all your energy."

I couldn't help but open my eyes and peek at the others. How was I supposed to feel my alignment when I was constantly thinking about rotating my thighs toward each other?

The instructor was still speaking. "Now open your eyes beginning Surya Namaskara A. Inhale, your arms overhead. Exhale, bend forward. Inhale, look up and lengthen your spine. Exhale, walk into plank. Inhale here. Build your upper body strength. Exhale, lower to the ground. Inhale, come into a slight cobra then exhale, downward facing dog pose. Stay here and breathe deeply into your center, maintaining that rhythmic breath.

"Glance between your hands and inhale. Exhale, step your feet forward and release toward your legs. Inhale, sweep up with arms overhead. Exhale, mountain pose. Perfect. We're going to do that four more times to warm up your body. Now, inhale, your arms overhead."

Four more times! Is she serious? She calls this a warm up, I call this Olympic training. I seriously felt like I was about to die after the first five minutes of class. How was I supposed to get all these answers Josh and Kuriko were talking about when I was concentrating on my breath and attempting to keep pace with all these poses?

I glanced over at Josh and Kuriko to see if I was the only one dying, and I was. They looked like they were in yogic heaven. We proceeded through a bunch of standing poses, balancing poses and backbends. I even did a baby version of a headstand against the wall.

Ninety minutes later I ended up in my favorite position of the entire class: relaxation pose.

While I lay there the instructor encouraged, "Relax your face. Relieve any tension in your body. Allow your entire body to surrender. Let go of all negative thoughts. Any blocks in your visions or in your dreams. Let it all go. Let go of any blocks of self-expression, heartbreak, and disappointment or anything disempowering you. Just let it release into the earth and receive the free-flowing energy she is giving you. It's an even exchange. Let those toxins go then receive pure energy and light flowing through every fiber of your being. Be open to the channel of love immersed in the universe. Be open to receive in this moment."

I melted into the floor like a lit candle. My body became so one with the earth I couldn't feel it underneath me. I'm not sure if I was in relaxation pose correctly or in a deep coma-like sleep. I felt like an eagle floating in the air. My stomach rippled with waves. Peace and quiet cloaked my mind and I was no longer on the earth.

I entered a sea of solitude where quiet was all I heard and light was all I saw. I was being held by a supernatural force. This presence felt safe and secure. My heart yearned for nothing more. I didn't care about tattooing. I didn't care about my questions. I didn't care about my family. I was fulfilled. Complete. At home!

I nestled into these arms of safety and heard a father's voice say, "Come to Me, child, and I will give you rest." I saw myself sitting on a cloud, fully tatted, with my favorite pair of ripped jeans, white tank top, blue patented leather heels with a custom-designed belt buckle. My hair was dreaded and my body was shaking. I was crying, but as I looked up toward the sky a white light shone down on my face.

I heard myself ask, "What do you want from me?"

"I want nothing more than to love you."

"There's no such thing as love!"

"That's because you don't know me, for I AM love. I will never leave nor forsake you. I will restore everything that has been taken from you."

"Why do you keep bothering me?"

"You are hurting. I want to take your pain and replace it with my joy. If only you'd believe."

"Believe what?"

"Believe on the name of My Son. Believe that I raised him from the dead. Believe that I AM."

"Alcatraz! Alcatraz!" I heard Josh shout. I opened my eyes to see Kuriko and Josh staring at me wildly. "Alcatraz? Are you in there?" Josh asked. "She is so in another dimension right now," he said to Kuriko, smiling. "I knew yoga would help her."

"She's probably battling demons." Kuriko pushed Josh out the way and started to shake me violently. "Alcatraz can you hear me? Are you okay?"

I slowly inhaled and my mind jumped back to earth. I turned to face Kuriko.

"Where did you go, girl?" she asked. "You've been laying here since class ended, over a half hour ago!" Kuriko looked worried but that didn't faze me. I couldn't quite come down from my high.

"Did you still want to go to temple tonight?" Josh asked.

"I guess so," I said.

"Well, I can't go," Kuriko replied. "I have to dance, but you two have fun. Are you okay?"

"I'm fine. I just got wrapped up in a dream."

"Call me if you need anything. I'll be at The Geisha Room."

"Okay. I will."

"Come on, Traz. We've got to go if we're gonna be on time," Josh said. "Night service begins at nine."

* * * *

Jo dhyave phal pave
Dhukh bin se man ka
Swami dhukh bin se man ka
Sukhasampati Gharave
Sukhasampati Gharave
Kasht mite tan ka
Om Jaya Jagadheesha Hare

"Hey, this is where we take off our shoes and wash our feet and hands," Josh informed me.

"Why do we have to do this?" I asked.

"To cleanse ourselves before we pray. We can't approach the gods unclean. Purification is the only way to get them to hear our prayers or else they're empty."

"Oh, okay." That explanation didn't make sense to me but I took it in stride. When we entered the temple I freaked out. There were animals everywhere. Stray dogs, cats and birds sat alongside the worshipers. Mr. Lubbock wasn't lying! "I thought animals were in the temples only in India. I didn't think L.A. did the same."

"They're sacred, just like we are," Josh said. "Brahma created them like he created humans, so it is only right we allow them into temple to worship alongside us. And besides, Americans don't run this temple. True Indians do."

I scanned the room and noticed Josh and I were the only non-Indian couple there. It was so strange.

Walking through the doors didn't even *feel* right. We sat in front of the same statues that Josh placed on his mantle at home. There was one guy sitting at the front of the sanctuary offering all of the sacrifices to a particular deity.

"Who are those people?" I asked, indicating the guy.

"The priest is called a Pujaris. They are the only people to enter the garbhagriha."

"The *what?*"

"The inner sanctuary where he is sitting is called the garbhargriha. It's where the gods meet with man. Not everyone is allowed to enter that place 'cause it's considered holy ground. Only chosen men can speak to the gods," Josh explained.

"So, you mean to tell me people come here to pray to Brahma but you can't have personal contact with him?"

"Well, yeah. You have to give your offerings to the Pujaris so he can offer them to the gods for you. God won't listen to you, only the holy, chosen ones. Not everyone is chosen."

We rang a bell, folded our hands in front of our chest and started praying. I didn't say anything because I didn't know what to say. These people weren't speaking English. After awhile Josh went up front. Afraid of sitting alone with complete strangers and stray dogs, I jumped up to join him. The priest took his offering and poured liquid on a statue.

"What does the liquid do?" I whispered.

"I'll explain later," he said.

I examined the room to see what others were doing. Some people bowed toward the statues up front, some were lying flat on their stomachs and others were eating a bread-like substance called Prasad. The priest rose from his seat, walked around the temple and put a red substance called tilak on people's foreheads. After this the worshipers stood to walk clockwise around the room. When they reached the other side of the room they stopped and started praying again.

I didn't know why but I did not feel comfortable there at all. It wasn't anything in particular. Nobody was offending me or mistreating me but something about the place didn't sit well with me. Was it this hard to find God? Did I have to observe all these rules and traditions just to have a relationship with him through someone else? If so, was all this worth it?

"How do you feel?" Josh asked me as we walked to the car.

"The same," I answered. "Why? How am I supposed to feel?"

"Peaceful, light and clearheaded."

"I do feel pretty light, except I think it came from holding my breath. It stunk in there!"

"Yeah, the animals do funk up the place a bit," Josh admitted. "It takes some getting used to."

"What exactly were you guys saying?"

"When we arrived they were saying 'Whoever thinks of you, gets results without any mental grief. Happiness and wealth come to his home. And his bodily woes vanish.' Then at the very end we said prayers to the different gods: Vishnu, Rama, Krishna, Shiva, Brahma, Goddess, etc. It takes some time to learn the meaning of all the prayers. No one masters them on the first visit."

"How often do you go to temple?" I asked.

"As many times as I want. Sometimes three times a day. Sometimes three times a month. There are no formal rules. You never have to go if you don't want to. If you want to make an offering then it's best to go as much as possible or build a home shrine, which is why I have one. I don't have time to come here every day, but the five daily services makes coming here much easier."

"What were all the food, liquid and objects for?"

"That is called Puja. They are offerings to the deities to bless us."

"Do they ever say it's enough?"

"Huh?" Josh sounded confused.

"Like, your offerings. Do the gods ever say it's enough? How long do you offer something until it comes to pass? Does there ever come a point where the gods are like, 'Okay, good job. You have given me more than my fair share. Thank you. Go, live in peace now.'?"

"Oh, no, you will never be good enough to stop offering, not even when you reach enlightenment or your actualized true self. You will still need to make offerings 'cause there's always further to go. One never arrives at the destination. They just leave the point where they're at. Offering is for life."

I sat quietly in the car.

"What are you thinking?" Josh gently asked me.

"This isn't for me. Like, I know this was only my first time, but Hinduism seems too complicated. And I don't believe God is complicated. Worshipers prostrate themselves and bathe the statues in who knows what. There are plates of food everywhere, meowing cats, barking dogs and chirping birds. Chanting in 'ring around the rosy' form and giving my offerings to a mediator and not being able to talk to God directly is just nonsensical to me. I'm not telling you you're wrong. I'm just saying."

"Hey, man, no worries. My goal was not to convert you. Just trying to help."

"I know, and I appreciate it. I really do. But I'll be checking Hinduism off my list for good now."

* * * *

"How was temple?" Kuriko asked me when she arrived home from work.

"Not for me."

"Why? What happened?"

I recapped my night with Josh at the Hindu temple and was comforted by the disgusted look on her face.

"Are you serious? You were worshiping with dogs?"

"Yeah, they sat right next to us. They were all barking and birds were chirping. I mean, how am I supposed to hear anything from God with all that racket going on? I didn't know if I was in church or at the San Diego Zoo."

"Seriously, dude, I would have reacted the same way. That's weird. I knew they worshiped animals but I didn't think it was literally. Were they at least in cages?"

"Hell no, that was the horrifying part. The animals walked around the place like they owned it, leaving their dung wherever. I was seriously afraid to close my eyes to pray," I said.

"I wouldn't have closed my eyes either. How uncomfortable!"

"Do you go to temple too?"

"Buddhism is less formal here in the states than it is back in Japan. In Asia, Buddhism is well-organized and well-funded so the temples are extravagant, beautiful works of art, kind of like the Catholic churches here. But that's because most people in Asia are either Buddhist or Hindu so it just makes sense. Here, not really. Westerners are still learning our beliefs. Most Buddhists here just follow yogic practice and tradition as opposed to bowing, offering, pilgrimages and chanting. Josh is really the first American I met who is tackling Hinduism in full force."

"Oh, so you pretty much do the same thing as Josh?"

"Yeah, without the dung, though."

We both cracked up laughing.

"Can I ask you a question?" I asked after settling down a bit.

"Sure. What's up?" She plopped herself down on the couch.

"What do you normally see when you meditate in relaxation pose?"

"It varies. Most of the time I see nothing 'cause I fall asleep." We both laughed, then she continued, "But when I'm not asleep I see nature, mostly. Like, I'll be lying on a beach or flying in a cloud. It's usually some aspect of me in nature of some sort. Why? What did you see?"

I was terrified at the possible rejection after revealing my lifelong struggle with the supernatural. For the first time since Valeo my life seemed good. Within one year I moved into a lavish condo in the heart of Hollywood, met a great group of people, learned how to tattoo and got paid for it under the table. I didn't want to ruin my friendship with her because of my psychotic supernatural occurrences.

"Okay, if I tell you something, will you freak out?" I asked.

"Probably," she joked.

"No seriously. Will you?"

"What is it?"

"Okay." I exhaled, took a moment and decided on which experience to share. "I went to church once with my uncle's wife, right? It was a Catholic Church. Anyway, I have no clue what the priest was talking about but somehow I understood the pictures."

"Pictures? What do you mean?"

"This church had pictures showing a man on his way to be crucified. But the story unfolded in detail within each of the twelve picture frames until finally at the end there is an empty tomb."

"So it was the story of Jesus?" Kuriko asked.

"Yeah. How'd you know?"

"Alcatraz, everybody has heard of Jesus' crucifixion. He was a pretty huge deal."

"Well, in each picture I noticed his eyes. Kuriko, I saw a love in them unknown to me, ever. He was being butchered by the people around him, yet he had so much compassion and love in his eyes. That attracted me. Then there was the voice."

"What voice?"

"When I was looking into his eyes I heard, 'Come to Me, and I will give you rest.' I heard the voice twice and I spun around to see who was talking to me but no one was near me!"

"So you think it was him? You think it was Jesus calling you?"

"Well, I don't know. That's not the only thing that has happened to me."

"So you're struggling with believing in Jesus? Is that it?" she asked.

"I don't know what I am trying to say, really. When I was meditating in yoga class tonight I heard the same thing. I was sitting with God on a cloud, crying, until the sun shone brightly on my face and my tears disappeared. The same voice spoke to me while on the cloud and told me that I would have rest if I come to him. It was the same voice I heard in the Catholic Church. The same one I heard from the eye in the astronomy book."

"The eye in the astronomy book?" Kuriko shouted.

"I keep hearing all these voices and seeing all these visions. I just want the truth to be made plain to me. You know?"

"Well have you tried asking him what he wants with you to keep pestering you like this?"

"Yeah. I asked him tonight and he said he just wanted to love me."

"Hmm." Kuriko stopped speaking for a bit while piercing a hole through me with her eyes. Finally she asked, "Would you like to pray with me tomorrow morning?"

"You pray in the mornings?"

"I told you, when I got my condo I was gonna build me an altar."

"How come I have never seen it?" I asked.

"'Cause it's in my closet. I don't want to publicize it but I pray when I get home in the mornings."

"That would be awesome."

"Why is this so important to you anyway?"

"I wish I knew, girl. Ever since I was a child I connected to the spiritual world, yearning to know the mystery surrounding it. My heart won't be completely content until I have a relationship with God. Don't ask me why I feel this way. I just do."

"That's deep. You're sure you're only fifteen years old?" Kuriko asked.

"Well, according to you, I'm seventeen."

"Your spirit is too advanced for your brain. I cannot wait to see where this all leads."

* * * *

The atmosphere in Kuriko's room represented her very mystical nature. Her walls were painted marigold and were adorned with Asian bamboo furniture. Her Japanese Zen shrine was in in the closet. There was a Tibetan brass incense burner filled with frankincense, an oil lamp, a lacquered candle holder with vanilla tea candles, tingsha's OM mantra symbols, seven unique bowls, water, tea tree oil, rice, two large bamboo flowers, a large wooden Buddha statue and the Three Baskets book.

"What do all these objects do?" I asked.

"They help me achieve enlightenment. I'm not as spiritually in tune as you are so I must spend time with the gods. The statue of Buddha is the central focus. I invoke the peace he had when walking the earth. The seven bowls represent the seven limbs of prayer——prostrating, offering, confession, rejoicing in the good qualities of oneself and others, requesting the Buddhas to remain in the world, beseeching them to teach others and dedicating the merit.

"The flowers and incense encourage me to smell the roses despite circumstance. The candle symbolizes wisdom, eliminating the darkness of ignorance. The rice is an offering to relieve people of hunger. Even though I can't do it personally I can pray for others to help the cause. The water is twofold. It is an offering to relieve human thirst and it contains cleansing power that converts anger, greed and delusion into compassion, love and wisdom.

"The purpose of the offerings is to accumulate merit and to purge myself of any stinginess, selfishness and misery. That's the whole purpose behind this altar, but for now we need to find some answers for you and a new job for me."

"A new job? You don't like The Geisha Room?"

"No. I *never* liked The Geisha Room."

"I thought you had a blast working there."

"That's because you only see half of what I do. If you saw the whole picture you'd have piggybacked me out of there. No, it's time for another job so I'll be putting that into the universe while you throw out your desire for truth."

"Okay, let's do this. Where do we start?" I asked.

"Meditation is about reaching a certain place in the mind where we transcend all the external situations and be still and happy in every situation. We invoke holy beings to come down and help us attain these goals. Daily practice at the altar gives us the opportunity to achieve this. By meditating on these objects our minds are purified and they totally absorb into the object. This keeps us detached from the external suffering and constantly attached to calm on the inside where all the answers lie. Meditation is the ultimate form of liberation from the distractions of this earth. It is the only way to true freedom."

Sometimes it was hard to believe Kuriko was only eighteen years old. She had the wisdom of a woman three times her age.

"How long do we meditate?" I asked.

"As long as time permits. I can sit here for at least an hour if not more, depends how tired I am. The more I keep my mind still and the more offerings I give the more answers I receive."

"How do you use all this stuff practically?"

"The first thing I do in the morning is wash my face and hands so I can stand clean before the altar."

"You do that, too? We did that yesterday at the temple. What is up with God that we can't just come as we are? Why does everything have to be so clean?"

"Alcatraz, God is holy. We have to be holy to stand in his presence or else he won't hear our prayers. Wash your face and hands here."

I begrudgingly obliged.

Kuriko continued, "Then pour fresh water into the seven clean bowls, placing the bowls in a straight line. Close, but not touching. Try not to breathe on the water so you don't contaminate it. It has to be pure, fresh water."

"What if I brush my teeth? Will it be safe for me to breathe on the water then?"

"This isn't funny, Traz. Be serious now," Kuriko said controlling herself from laughing. She continued, "After lighting the candles and incense I dip a piece of tree twig in the water while chanting my verse for the day. Then I sprinkle the twig with water and I visualize the offering being blessed. I invoke that blessing into my life and proceed with all the other offerings."

"Every day?" I asked.

"Yes. The more I do it the clearer my mind becomes."

"Why do you chant?"

"Chanting stills the mind even faster. You focus in on the resonating sound of your voice and it becomes a meditation. Have you ever chanted before?"

"I played with it a bit in Chicago but it isn't a ritual of mine."

"You want to try it? You can see firsthand the immediate effects."

"Sure, why not?" I outwardly agreed but inwardly it seemed too over the top for me to practice daily.

"Okay. Sit here on this pillow," she instructed. "Sit in a comfortable position, preferably lotus, like this, if you can. Now close your eyes and focus on your breath first." It wasn't hard to twine my legs like hers. After a few inhales and exhales she said, "Now repeat after me: oh ah hum, oh ah hum, oh ah hum, oh ah hum."

We both chanted for the next five minutes or so. I felt a weight lift off of my chest. Kuriko proceeded to then bang the gong and chanted more intensely and we continued a few minutes more. After we quieted down I opened my eyes to see Kuriko staring at me. "How was it?" she asked.

"What did we say?"

"Body, speech, mind."

"I felt weight lift off me," I said.

"Was it like a heaviness?"

"Yeah, like a burden or something. It lifted off my heart area."

"Yeah, that is your heart chakra. You probably

released a negative emotion holding you back."

"My what?"

"Heart chakra. Chakras are invisible wheels on the inside of our bodies aligned along the spinal cord correlating to specific developments in our life. The heart chakra is the wheel of love. You probably lifted a burden off of you that was blocking your ability to give or receive love. Maybe that is why Jesus is chasing you—to help you receive love."

As I opened my mouth to respond I choked up and started crying.

"What's wrong?" she asked.

"I guess I don't understand why God would want to love someone unlovely as me?"

"Good question. I don't have the answer to that, but when you get the answer, let me know."

I sat there sniffling, afraid I would contaminate the altar full of offerings.

"You look a lot brighter," Kuriko said. "Whatever lifted off of you allowed more light to flow into you. That was a pretty powerful release for a first time chant."

"I guess." Tears flowed down my cheeks. "I don't know about any of this."

"About what?"

"You have such a deep foundation in this stuff but I don't know if I believe it. It's just like Leinani. She had such a foundation in Aether but I couldn't get into him. My uncle's wife believed in the Catholic Church. Willie the chaplain and Dan the truck driver had a deep belief in Jesus and Anne at the hospital believed in the universe. Josh practices Hinduism and you're a Buddhist. Everyone else seems so far ahead in life.

"I have such an inner hunger for truth but there are so many options. It seems everyone has his or own way of dealing with life. Their own truth, their own relationship with the supernatural. When you explain to me that darkness was lifted and light flowed in I just don't know about any of that. This chanting only confuses me more."

"Why does it frustrate you?" Kuriko asked. "If anything, it should bring you peace. You are getting closer to your peace, Traz. The more religions you cross off your list the more narrow your options. Spirituality brings peace, not frustration. You are trying to live in too many moments. Just be here right now and listen to what your heart is telling you now, not with Leinani or Dan or whoever else. Their religions obviously didn't work or else you would have clarity. Just be here and listen now. There's no reason to be frustrated."

"I'm tired of all the variety. Having too many options can be a burden," I said.

"I totally understand you, Alcatraz. More than you realize. I have asked the same questions about my life. All I know is when you chant you give up some of the power all those questions have on you. Answers don't come in the middle of a storm. It's usually after the storm has calmed down where you hear the still small voice. You will never be able to find answers as long as you are frustrated, confused and uneasy. You have to disassociate yourself with your desire to know more. In time all you need to know will be revealed to you. I can see it."

12

Competition for a chair at The Human Canvas was fierce. There were seven artists present, all of them geniuses at their niche. Blue Moon was the grandfather of the shop. He's been a legend in Hollywood since 1980, rocking out traditional styles like no one in the business. Alex was known for his pin-up work, portraits and vibrant colors. Sang came to L.A. two years ago from Singapore and made a name for himself with his body suits, Japanese caricature artwork, Asian comic book characters and Kanji calligraphy.

Josh was the master illusionist. Ebony was our prized black baby doll. I called her "Afro Sheen" because she had the biggest hair I had ever seen. I really admired her because this industry is very white male dominant. Any woman who carved a name for herself got my instant respect. Yellow Bone was known for his graffiti-like tattoos. Thai claimed he meditated while giving a tattoo, and he had mastered many styles and techniques.

Then there was me. After a year of apprenticing and practicing tattoos on people outside the shop Josh encouraged me to speak with Moon about getting my own chair.

The conversation with Blue was short and sweet. I showed him my updated portfolio of all the people I tattooed within the past year and pretty much begged him to give me a shot. He started me in the last chair to pick up straggler clients wanting small artwork done.

I wasn't getting paid the full sixty percent commissions like the other employees in the shop due to my inexperience and lack of paperwork. Instead, he gave me a thirty percent cut. Looking back, I realize it was a raunchy deal, but I was glad he gave me a shot. I had to start somewhere, especially since no other tattoo shop in town would even allow a fifteen-year-old to use the bathroom.

"Hey, what's going on?" I asked a beautiful bohemian girl waiting in the lobby.

"Hello. I'm Kimberly," she said.

"Hey, Kimberly. Alcatraz."

"Nice to meet you."

"What are we getting today?"

"I want a small butterfly on my lower back. Here's my rendition of it, but whatever you want to do to spice it up you go right ahead."

"All right. Do you want color or black and white?"

"You know, I have enough color butterflies on my body." She showed her tattoos to me, revealing beautifully colorful butterflies on her ankle, wrist, inner thigh and back of the neck. "I kinda want to do something different, so black and white today."

"Ok, great. Give me a few minutes to draw something up and I'll be right with you."

"Sounds great. Thanks."

I returned shortly with my design. She accepted it and I led her to my workspace.

I shaved her lower back and transferred the stencil. "Why do you love butterflies so much?" I asked.

"They're beautiful in nature, but deeper than that I love the freedom they embody. I have always felt caged, like a bird trying to sing but never quite finding my notes."

"Why can't you find your note?"

"Girl, I've been through the wringer and back. I've lived a long and hard life," she said. "I had a baby at sixteen and wasn't ready to be a mom. I don't think anyone is ready, but especially not me, not then. I didn't know how to love my son the way a mom should love. My intuitive nurturer never kicked in like everyone told me it would. His very existence clipped my wings. I tried to nurture him to the best of my ability but it was a hoax. I've been way too hurt to give him the love he truly needed, you know? Nobody ever loved me."

"Yeah, I do know, actually."

Tears welled up in Kimberly's eyes unexpectedly. "Whoa. I didn't think I was gonna be doing all this," she joked as she wiped her face. "Every day with him is very mechanical. Wake up, cook breakfast while getting him ready for school, get him on the bus then I go off to work. I pick him up after school, feed him a snack and cook dinner while he works on homework. Then I run him a bath and put him to bed around nine-ish. I have to take a bath myself and study for my classes because I attend graduate school. Then it's off to sleep around 2:30 a.m., just to get back up at 6:00 a.m. to repeat the madness.

"It's a mundane routine that suffocates every bit of life out of me. So, I figured since I couldn't quite have the freedom I desperately wanted in my life I'll put it all over my body. Hopefully one day I will attain it in the natural, if that makes any sense?"

"Makes perfect sense. It's kinda like drawing your vision board on your body instead of a poster board," I said.

"Exactly! You feel me? That is precisely what I am doing."

I felt sorry for Kimberly yet at the same time I felt privileged to be a part of her personal journey to freedom.

"What are you in school for?" I asked.

"Business management, but I hate that too."

"No! You don't like business either?"

"No, can't stand it. Doesn't give me the opportunity to create, travel or give back."

"Then why did you go to school for it?"

"'Cause it seems like the practical, rational thing to do. Business is international, so if I majored in something global I could be in demand. And that's true, I am high in demand as far as my field goes, but I hate my job. I hate sitting in an office every day. I hate training these lazy people, Alcatraz. I hate driving to the same location. I hate just thinking about the place."

"Is there anything you do like about the job?" I asked.

"The check! The check is off the chain. The check is the only reason I am in the building, you hear me?"

We both cracked up.

"Seems like you have the Monday blues daily," I said.

"Welcome to my world."

"Well, if you had the vocation of your choice, what would you do?"

"I'm not quite sure. I do know I want to travel and see different continents."

"Why don't you teach English overseas, or something like that? I hear English is very in demand. You probably wouldn't have any problems finding a position for it. I know you have a kid and all, but it doesn't hurt to look."

"Mmm. I never thought about that idea. You're right. There are many opportunities abroad for English instructors! I know of several programs where the companies are willing to pay for teachers to come and teach their students. I'm gonna look into that!"

"Free of charge." I winked.

Nine months later I received a postcard from Kimberly. She had accepted a teaching position at a university in Granada, Spain. She sold everything in her apartment and enrolled her son in an international school there. Now she can travel all over Europe and northern Africa within a few hours. Her postcard thanked me so much for giving her the idea to make her dreams a reality.

Instances like that happened over and over at The Human Canvas. I often received gifts from people who told me I helped them change their lives for the better. It was icing on the cake for me.

I flourished as a tattoo artist in Los Angeles. I

soon had appointments lined up and I quickly became one of the most sought after artists at The Human Canvas. At almost sixteen years of age I tattooed Hollywood celebrities, Fortune 500 businessmen, stay-at-home moms, college kids and every Joe in between. Even with the unfair cut Blue Moon was taking I still earned around a thousand dollars a week! Not bad for a middle school drop-out. I absolutely *loved* my job. It wasn't even like a job to me, more like hanging out.

Tattoos became my voice, my medium to be heard and understood. It was a world I fit into like a glove. The longing in my heart for acceptance was gratified here. Complete strangers entrusted me with not only their physical bodies but also their emotional baggage. I connected to people on the deepest levels. Spending a couple hours together naturally creates a chemical bond between two people and I quickly began to make new friends.

I delved into people's psyche for wisdom and understanding and that had to be the number one part of the job. I absolutely worshiped the fellowship. I loved learning about people and their subconscious. Why people think they way they do, say what they say, do what they do, why they end up in certain situations and getting to the root cause of problems. It was as exhilarating as riding a roller coaster. Being a tattoo artist afforded me the opportunity to combine both my passions: art and psychology.

* * * *

"Hello, Alcatraz. My name is Candy and this is my friend, Justice." Candy handed me a picture.

"Nice to meet you." I shook both of their hands half-heartedly.

"I want to get this water lotus flower on my back. Nothing big, just something that can fit on my right shoulder blade here." Candy turned around and placed her hand directly on the spot she wanted her picture.

"Okay. Not a problem. Did you want the exact same coloring as the picture?" I asked.

"Not exactly the same. I was thinking the leaves could be more vibrant green, like Scotland green. And the flower petals should be ivory white. I also wanted it to look like it's coming out of muddy water."

"So you want the water to be muddy brown, but the flower to be vibrant and alive growing out of the mud?"

"Dead on!"

"That was right on," Justice added.

"Okay, cool. Just give me a minute to draw it out and we'll get started," I said.

"Great. Thanks."

I nearly floated to the light table. I honestly don't even remember my feet touching the ground, I was so elated.

"You ready?" I asked as I put my gloves on.

"As ready as I'll ever be." Candy looked at her friend.

"You'll be fine," Justice reassured her in a warm, calming voice.

"There's no turning back now," I teased.

"I know," Candy said. "I'm ready. Let's go!"

"So tell me about the lotus flower," I outlined the muddy water with gray ink.

"Well, to me the lotus flower represents victory.

It is the only flower that grows in muddy water and turns out untouched. It's beautiful despite the environment it grew in."

"Oh, that's cool. I didn't know that. Where do they grow?"

"Mostly swamps, ponds and streams. It starts growing at the bottom of the water and rises above the water at full bloom. It's usually pink or white and breathtakingly beautiful to see up close."

"Do you relate to that personally or do you just like the look of the flower?"

"Last year the doctor found an aggressive, malignant tumor on my fallopian tubes. By then the cancer had spread throughout my entire reproductive system and he insisted I have a complete hysterectomy."

"Whoa. That must have been hard."

"I fought the hysterectomy and told my doctors they were not taking out any of my organs. I was designed to give birth to healthy children and that is exactly what I intended to do."

"You told the doctors that? And what did they say?" I asked.

"They fought back and insisted that I either have the surgery or undergo chemotherapy and kill the cancer that way. They thought surgery would be a better option."

"So which one did you end up choosing?"

She sighed. "I eventually collapsed and had the hysterectomy along with five rounds of chemo. It was scary, but the Psalms pulled me through."

"What are Psalms?"

Candy made eye contact with Justice and said, "The Psalms of David. They are an encouraging book in God's Word."

I immediately turned off my machine. "God's Word?"

"Yes. The Bible is Jehovah's Word."

"So you guys are Christians?"

"Not quite. We're Jehovah's Witnesses, but not very good ones." Candy smirked at Justice.

"We don't follow every rule as taught," Justice chimed in.

"What all is taught?" I asked.

"A lot!" They both said simultaneously. Then Candy continued, "We don't get to Kingdom Hall as often as we should."

"Is that your church?"

"You could call it that. Our parents are really into witnessing but we aren't. I believe in Jehovah and I read the Bible, but if I were a strict disciple then I wouldn't be here right now."

"Why not?"

"'Cause Jehovah's Witnesses aren't supposed to get body piercings or body art. It's against Mosaic law. That's why I want it to be small and on my back so it's not visible to everybody. I'm not trying to fight with my parents even though I'm grown and don't live at home anymore." She rolled her eyes in disgust.

"Seriously," Justice agreed, obviously in rebellion along with Candy.

"So what do Jehovah's Witnesses believe?" I asked.

"Basically, we believe in developing a relationship with Jehovah, or God, to perfect our nature. We believe in living pure lives and helping others to do the same. We do that by faithful study of the Bible," Candy explained.

"We basically aggravate the human race by constantly knocking on their doors every week, offering Bible studies," Justice exaggerated.

"I take it that's your favorite part," I joked. We all laughed. I got the feeling that Justice had a slightly different view of Jehovah than Candy did. "Is it the same Bible that Christians read?"

"We only read the New World Translation along with our Watchtower Bible studies," Justice said. "Well, I say we, but Candy and I are more liberal in our beliefs and truly only follow the Bible. Preferably the New King James Version."

"How can different interpretations come from one book?" I asked.

"That is the century old question. I don't know how that's possible but it is. Like, even if you delve into Christianity there are many sects. It's not like the Nation of Islam or Judaism where people can memorize their entire Scripture at age ten and recite it again at age one hundred. The text is uniform and the translation is untouched by man. I think the Bible is the most misunderstood book in the earth!"

"Then why read and preach it?"

"'Cause we think we're right. All religions are self-righteous. We think we have all the answers about God and the spiritual world," Justice responded.

Finally I asked, "Do you guys really believe in Jehovah?"

"I do," Candy answered. "I do really love reading the Bible. It just does something indescribable to me. During the past year I read in the Psalms almost every day to encourage me during the chemo process and I felt uplifted after I was done. It speaks life to my soul."

"Yeah, there are some good things about the Watchtower, too. I just don't have the same convictions my parents do and don't want to bother people on Saturday mornings when they are trying to have breakfast with their families watching cartoons. Ya know? I feel people will find their own way without me shoving it in their face every week." Justice confirmed my thoughts that she had different views. "I'm more spiritual than a Witness."

After I was finished with Candy's flower she jumped up and looked in the mirror.

"Oh my goodness! This is perfect! Better than I anticipated. Thank you so much, Alcatraz. Thank you so much. This is exactly what I wanted!" she cried.

Candy walked to the front of the shop to take pictures and pay for her services, but Justice walked back toward me.

"Alcatraz, can I say something real quick?" she asked politely.

"Yeah, sure," I said.

"I just have to tell you that God will wait for you."

"Huh?" My heart felt like it fell into the pit of my stomach. "What are you talking about?"

"You have questions about God. You've always had them since you were a little girl and you want to know the truth about him. Does he really exist? If so, where is he? Why did he allow bad things to happen to me? Why did he take my parents away from me?"

I thought my heart had totally stopped. How did she know my parents were dead?

She continued, "You want to know the answer to all those questions and you have been seeking them for a while now. Well, I just feel led to tell you that God will wait for you while you search. He wants to answer all your questions and then some. He wants to give you a personal revelation of who he is. He will show himself to you in a way that is undeniable and everything you ever wanted to know will be answered in a single moment."

"How do you know all this?" I asked.

"Because he told me while we were talking about Jehovah. He told me to tell you he will wait for you to choose no matter how many paths you take. He knows you will not be fulfilled until you know the Truth. However long it takes for you to accept the Truth, he will be waiting for you with wide open arms."

Tears rolled from my eyes as I stared into very familiar eyes piercing straight through me. Barely whispering, I managed to ask, "What is the truth, Justice?"

"Now that I can't answer for you. It's like I said earlier, I don't like telling people what to believe. You have to find it for yourself, and you will. He told me you will!"

Just then I recognized her eyes! They were the same eyes in the picture at the Catholic Church I visited when I lived with my uncle, in the astronomy book at the library. They were the same eyes I saw looking at me from the truck driver on the way to L.A. They were eyes of understanding, eyes that always seemed to look straight through me, yet they didn't judge me. I felt secure every time I looked into these eyes. They were eyes of unconditional love.

I thanked her for the prophecy, ran to the bathroom, locked the door and bawled like a baby.

* * * *

"Can you bring me another pomegranate margarita?" I asked the bartender backstage at The Geisha Room.

"Great day at work, huh?" Kuriko asked as she applied her mascara.

"Fine, I guess." I slurped down the margarita like it was water.

"You work on any celebrities?"

"No, just some cancer survivor. It was a pretty cool story, actually. She had a cancer on her fallopian tubes, underwent a hysterectomy, chemotherapy and survived it by reading the Psalms."

"Oh, so she was a Christian?"

"No, a Jehovah's Witness."

"A Jehovah's Witness! Oh no! She didn't set you up for Tuesday night Bible studies and invite you to Kingdom Hall on Thursdays did she? You don't need to get caught up with those people, girl. They've all had a little too much of the punch. Trust me!"

"Ten minutes!" some lady called out to Kuriko. Well, Sapphire.

"All right, Margie, thank you," she responded. "Hurry up and tell me what happened."

"No, they were actually cool people. Both of them resented going door to door asking people if they want to set up Bible studies."

"They must be younger Witnesses because some of the people I've met who practice that religion are crazy as hell. Their belief system has too many holes in it."

Yours does too, I thought, but decided not to get into an argument.

"Are you okay?" A worried look crossed her face.

"I don't know. It was a just a weird day…Excuse me! Excuse me!" I opened the door and yelled to find one of the servers. "Can I have another pomegranate margarita? In fact, make it two!"

"Wow. Is there something you're not telling me?" she asked. I gulped down the last of my drink before two more arrived at Kuriko's door. "This is really frustrating you?"

"What?" I asked.

"This whole God thing. She talked to you about God, didn't she?"

"Yeah, but it's irrelevant. Anyway, I'm gonna finish my drinks and get out of here."

"Why are you afraid to make a decision?"

"I guess because I want *truth,* Kuriko. It's not enough for me to read all these texts, chant and follow all these leaders if I don't believe in what they're saying."

"You don't need to let this keep tormenting you. Be at peace. Just make a decision and see how it goes. The beautiful thing about life is nothing is set in stone. If you believe one way for a while and it doesn't work for you it's okay to change paths. The further you go down the path the clearer it will be. Like you visited a Hindu temple and realized in a short amount of time that belief system wasn't for you. Just make a decision and see where it leads."

As I left The Geisha Room, margarita in hand, I meandered down Hollywood Boulevard toward our condo. I felt so empty and uneasy. Despite the love I had for my job, my friends, my environment and the money, my heart needed rest *now.*

I finally decided to do something I had yet to do in my life. I sat on a bus bench, took another swig of my margarita, looked up at the sky, and whispered, "Who are You? What's Your real name? Why is there so much confusion about You? God, I am really tired of searching for You. Reveal Your true Self to me and send someone across my path to teach me more about you. I need answers now. Thank You for listening to me. Hope to hear from You real soon. Bye." I slurped down the remainder of my margarita and passed out right there on the bench.

13

The very next morning I was setting up my station and in walked this rocker-chick with long, blood-red hair, faded jeans, jewel-encrusted heels and a thigh-length, studded purple jacket. She and her friend walked over to our picture books to view previous clients. While browsing she looked up and our eyes met. She gave me a big smile and headed my way.

"Hey. I want a new tattoo on my foot. Can you do it today?" she asked.

I didn't answer her. I couldn't answer her. All I did was stare at her flashing me this huge smile. This girl was glowing! "You must have got some good sex last night," shot out of my mouth. I hadn't even thought about what I was saying.

She and her friend looked at each other puzzled. "Huh?" she asked.

"The only people who come into this shop glowing like you usually got some really good sex before they come in here, or they're on a good high."

The two cracked up laughing and it offended me. I wasn't trying to be funny but before I could go off I noticed her eyes.

"No, it's not that. I haven't had any sex in a long time and I don't drink or smoke. Sorry to disappoint you." She snickered.

"So what are you so happy about?" I pleaded, desperately needed something to cheer me up that day.

"I'm happy to be alive. Every breath I take is pure blessing."

I noticed her faded green T-shirt said "I ROCK JESUS." Her name was Sarah Kelly, lead singer and pianist of a Christian rock band called Shalom.

"What type of tattoo do you want on your foot?" I asked.

Sarah described a cross emerging from an empty grave with a rose vine draped over it. I configured the picture and showed it to her.

"Let's do it in a private room if you have one available," she said.

"It's an extra hundred fifty per hour," I warned.

"That's fine."

"Let me check if one is available."

I wondered why she wanted to be secluded; no one in the shop recognized her. One of the private rooms was available so we set up shop in there and got right to work. While imprinting the sketch onto her foot I felt power coming from her. I looked up to see if she was doing something out of the ordinary but she and her friend were just looking at pictures.

I cannot begin to describe how hard it was for me to have a conversation with this chick. Normally I had no issues connecting with people in my chair but for some reason this one was odd. I couldn't even trace my outline on her foot straight due to my shaking hand. *What was my problem?*

"Are you okay?" she asked me.

"Yeah," I lied. "I just need some music. You like Tchaikovsky?"

"I love him! He's one of my favorite composers."

I ran to my station, retrieved my boom box and turned on Tchaikovsky. As I got into my groove I eventually relaxed a bit more, but not much. My hand was still shaking.

"Are you sure you're alright?" Sarah's friend, Nori, asked me.

"No. I'm not alright, but that's not your problem. I just need to focus." I inhaled deeply and regained my composure. *What was this energy coming from her? Why was I so nervous?* "So," I tried to begin a conversation, "what does this tattoo mean to you?"

"Well, the cross represents the sacrifice Jesus paid for me. It displays the unconditional love for me that I am so grateful for. The cross creates that joy you questioned earlier."

I envied the bliss shining through her eyes.

"The rose vine around the cross is my favorite flower and it also signifies the love of God. My life is not always easy yet I can always look outside and feel God's love through his creation. I love flowers of all kinds but roses are my favorite by far. They remind me of the beauty in every situation despite the ugliness present."

"You must have had a great upbringing. Where are you from?" I don't know where that question came from.

"I grew up in foster homes, Alcatraz. Both of my parents died in a car crash when I was three and I was sent to foster care immediately after that."

"Really?" I shouted, dropping my gun.

"Yes, really. I did not have a great upbringing. I lived in very abusive households, ran away three times, slit my wrists twice, had an abortion at sixteen and got involved in prostitution where I was busted by an undercover cop. But this is where the grace of God comes in. The detective could have sent me to jail like my co-hookers, but he didn't. Officer Holms was a minister at this Christian girls' home called Wellspring. Instead of sending me to jail where I deserved to go he sent me there. It was basically a retreat for troubled girls. That's where my life did a one-eighty. I lived there from the time I was sixteen up until I turned twenty. So no, to answer your question, I haven't had an easy life by far."

Tears streamed down my face at our similarities. I hadn't opened up about my past since moving to L.A.

"Why are you crying?" Nori asked me.

"What happened to you at Wellspring?" I asked Sarah.

"I was introduced to the love of God. At first I didn't want to hear it because I blamed him for everything, but as I let my guard down and let the Word in, he healed my past wounds and restored my life.

"I didn't realize this, but I hated God. So many tragic things happened to me in foster care that I didn't even believe God existed. I blamed him for killing my parents, my foster care experience and all the other crap I experienced. Without telling the graphic truth, I didn't live with the Brady Bunch families. A lot of crazy things happened to me in that government program and I carried around a lot of self-hatred, anger, bitterness, guilt and a gnawing feeling that I didn't belong anywhere.

"I always tried to fit in with the crowd and needed acceptance in such desperate ways that I harmed myself in every form of the word. That is why I started hooking because I wanted to feel like someone cared. I'm telling you, I had a lot going on when the state enrolled me at Wellspring. Dealing with all that in this program made it difficult for me to hear that God loved me, accepted me, approved of me and valued me. I couldn't receive it. It literally took like eight or nine months to start chipping down the walls constructed around my heart."

"The patient love of God." Nori raised her arms and closed her eyes, repeating verses of praise to God. Sarah started praising God as well and I was appreciative of being in a private room.

Sarah continued her story, more for her sake than for mine. "At first it was hard to believe that God would love a dirty, worthless girl like me. I didn't believe I deserved it and wouldn't accept it, but once I found out that Jesus' love is unconditional..." She choked up and started crying. Before I knew it she belted out a song with the most amazingly raspy Janice Joplin voice,

Amazing grace,
How sweet the sound
That saved a wretch like me.
I once was lost but now am found,
Was blind, but now I see.

I literally could not move as I listened to her powerful alto voice.

"I'm sorry," Sarah apologized. "I just get so excited talking about Jesus and what he has done for me. I found my voice at Wellspring and I'm telling you, Alcatraz, my life has not been the same. God is just so glorious. I now travel the world expressing my heart through music. I have best friends for life, I walk in divine health and I have a joy that money can't buy. I am blessed, blessed, blessed."

Sarah teared up again. "Don't get me wrong. I still have problems, and my life is not perfect by far. But life couldn't be better for me compared to what it was, and it is all because of him. Putting a tattoo on my foot is the least of my appreciation for him."

I couldn't speak, swallow or breathe. I was dazed in a trance listening to this complete stranger's past that resembled mine. Confusion, rage, pain, questions, comments and flashbacks flooded my mind. I didn't know how to communicate.

Nori looked at me and asked, "Alcatraz, are you alright?"

"This moment is so weird for me" I said.

"What's weird about it?" Sarah asked. "Was it my rambling about my childhood or my testimony? I didn't mean to make you uneasy, I just get excited. Maybe a little too much."

"I have to go to the bathroom," was all I could manage to say. I jumped up. "I'll be right back."

"I think it might be better to discuss your issue with us honestly," Nori stated boldly, jumping between me and the door. "I have a feeling we can really help you."

With that invitation, I exploded. I told them

everything. My perfect life with the Boydsteins, the car crash, the hospital experience, my meeting with the chaplain, Willie, the nurse, my uncle and what happened to me in that house. I told them about the Catholic Church and what the picture said to me, Valeo Academy, the talking eye and the voodoo I practiced there. I told about running away from my adopted family, the truck driver and my life here in Hollywood. I told them about the familiar eyes I see in certain people. For the first time since the death of my family I explained my life without inhaling a single breath.

Every emotion under the sun resurfaced and I didn't know which one to identify. Both of them stood there and listened to me intensely, nodding their heads in complete unison as if they understood everything I went through.

I ended up wailing, "I just don't know. My heart feels there is a God, but then I look at my life and it just doesn't add up. This human experience doesn't make sense to me! If there is a God why would all this bad stuff happen to me? Why would I have to go through all that? Why did the Boydsteins have to die? Why was my virginity stolen? I am so torn and I'm sick of it. I am so sick of this confusion."

I fell forward to the floor bawling like a baby. Both Sarah and Nori embraced me in their arms while I cried the longest, most relieving and cleansing cry I had ever experienced in my entire life. After what seemed to be an hour of non-stop sobbing I had no more tears left. I felt like I vomited my life all over Sarah's green T-shirt. I was drained mentally, emotionally, and physically.

"Who sent you to me?" I asked Sarah. "Did

someone send you here?"

"Not a physical being" she said. "I honestly wanted to get a tattoo, but now that I'm here I know for sure who sent me."

"Yeah, it's pretty obvious," Nori chirped in looking over at Sarah and then at me. "He's chasing you, Alcatraz. God is chasing you, trying to give you the answer you have always desired to know."

"What *is* the answer? What *is* the truth?"

"Who he is!" Nori said. "His name is Jesus, Alcatraz. The missing void you're trying to fill with work, people and booze can only be filled with a relationship with Jesus."

"Trust me," Sarah interrupted. "I know exactly what you're going through. I have been there and can say with one hundred percent confidence that this life isn't fulfilling you. Your soul and spirit longs for depth. A deeper relationship."

"Let me explain." Nori adjusted the position of her chair. "Jesus is the visible image of the invisible God. If you want to know who God is you have to know who Jesus is. They are one and the same. There is no getting to God without going through Jesus."

"I've been all over the place internally," I said. I blew my nose with a Kleenex. "I've even tried to convince myself he doesn't exist, even after all his obvious attempts to rescue me."

"It's hard for you not to believe in God because that's a lie." Sarah now led the conversation. "The invisible qualities of God can be seen all around us, so to believe he doesn't exist is just lying to yourself. I did the same thing. After all the drama in my life I forced myself to believe there wasn't a God even though deep down I knew it wasn't true. My heart didn't agree with my mouth. Even as I was sitting at Wellspring listening to them preaching about the love of God, I tuned it out by trying my hardest to ignore their statements. The truth was inevitable and eventually I bowed down to it."

"Do you understand what we're saying?" Nori asked.

"I suppose," I said. "But if there is a God, why did he take my family away from me?"

"I struggled with that same question for years," Sarah responded. "And this is what gave me peace. God did not author my family dying in a car accident. In a sense my family died because they were driving drunk. That was not God's doing. He gives mankind a free will. It was the choice of my irresponsible parents to operate a vehicle under the influence of alcohol. A lot of people place fault on God when it was just a series of poor decisions. My parents were driving under the influence of alcohol. They got into a car accident and killed seven people. I was the only survivor. That decision had nothing to do with God. That reality took awhile to settle."

"Yeah, but my parents weren't drunk," I said. "We were on our way to the Hi Life Restaurant. The tire blew out and that caused the car to spin..." I paused for a moment as the experience flashed back in my mind. It seemed like the accident occurred only yesterday. I had blocked it out to cope with life, but as I sat here and shared it I could still feel raw feelings in my heart. I hadn't forgotten a single detail, nor had I forgiven myself.

"I know it's hard to understand, but sin caused us to live in a fallen world. Stuff happens that is not caused by God but by sin and Satan. He is the prince of the air. Anything that kills, steals and destroys is his handiwork, not God's. Jesus came to give us life more abundantly, not to take any good thing away from us. I am so sorry about your family passing in the car crash, but don't allow your relationship with God to suffer because of it. It is not his fault!" Sarah said.

"We're not conning you into anything," Nori quickly stated. "We're just sharing the Truth with you. You make the final decision. God will not be angry at you either way. Jesus took God's anger at the cross. He's waiting for you to accept him with open arms but will not force himself onto you. That is not love."

"How do I know *this* is the Truth?" I asked.

"Jesus is the beginning. We weren't born to worship created things but the Creator who created things. That's why you couldn't get into those other religions. All religions are man-made and they lack power because their gods are dead. Christianity isn't about religion. It's a relationship with an ever-present Father. God is alive! Jesus rose from the grave and is now sitting down at the right hand of the Father. He was not martyred. He gave his life in exchange for the good life here on earth, as well as in heaven."

I must have had a befuddled look on my face because Sarah asked, "Is this all too much for you right now? Would you rather just finish my tattoo?"

To my surprise I said, "No! This is good. I need to get clarity in this area in my life once and for all. Once I achieve understanding in this area then the missing piece of the puzzle will fit perfectly!" I couldn't believe I was sharing this with two strangers. "What do the eyes signify?" I asked them. "Why do I see the same eyes in multiple locations? I am looking into those eyes right now."

"He wants you to know how much he loves you so he is sending his people to meet with you. God is patiently making himself available to you through his people." Sarah explained.

Then Nori spoke, "You have a dynamic call on your life, one I don't think you would believe even if I told you."

"Why does everyone keep telling me that?" I asked, exasperated. "You are like the fourth or fifth person that has told me that."

"Because it's true, but don't take our word for it," she said. "Let *him* reveal your purpose to you."

"I have to believe in this Jesus guy to get it, right?"

"No, you don't *have* to do anything," Sarah said. She spoke softly. "He will never force you or coerce you. That is the sacrificial love he has for you. He loves you enough to wait on your deathbed if need be. He will never condemn you or be angry at you for not believing. He wants you to be saved more for your sake than his. You are the reason he came to earth."

For once I experienced peace about what they were saying. It was a peace like I'd never experienced.

"So you say Jesus is the only way to see God?" I asked.

Sarah reached into her oversized Coach bag and pulled out a mini Bible. "Let me show you something," she said excitedly. "It's a Scripture from the New Testament that might or might not make sense to you, but I'll read it anyway. It is in the book of John."

As Sarah flipped through the pages, I innocently asked, "Who is John?"

"My favorite disciple, ever! He wrote five books in the New Testament. John, 1 John, 2 John, 3 John and Revelation."

"He couldn't get more creative with the book titles?"

"I know, right?" They both belted out hearty laughs. Sarah continued, "Listen to the words of Jesus here,

'There was a man of the Pharisees, named Nicodemus, a ruler of the Jews: The same came to Jesus by night, and said unto him, Rabbi, we know that thou art a teacher come from God: for no man can do these miracles that thou doest, except God be with him. Jesus answered and said unto him, Verily, verily, I say unto thee, Except a man be born again, he cannot see the kingdom of God. Nicodemus saith unto him, How can a man be born when he is old? can he enter the second time into his mother's womb, and be born? Jesus answered, Verily, verily, I say unto thee, Except a man be born of water and of the Spirit, he cannot enter into the kingdom of God. That which is born of the flesh is flesh; and that which is born of the Spirit is spirit. Marvel not that I said unto thee, Ye must be born again.'

"Jesus is explaining to this man how people can know God." Sarah closed the book.

Nori explained, "Born again, or saved, means accepting Jesus into your heart, believing he died on the cross for the forgiveness of your sins, healing your spirit, soul and body, prospering you and delivering you from oppressive spirits."

"What happens after I believe in him?" I asked.

Sarah perked up. "Well, the number one thing I gained from a relationship with God is his love shed abroad in my heart. Oh my goodness, Alcatraz. It's like a waterfall. This was the most important thing for me. When I fellowship with God, my Father, I fellowship with love. I had to really adjust to this because I never felt loved before. I had to stop looking at what was wrong with me and see me the way he saw me.

"I am a child of God. He loves me despite all my faults, despite all my experiences, despite all my issues and problems. I didn't believe it at first. I couldn't believe because I live with me and see everything that's wrong with me. That is the biggest benefit: knowing his love. To me, everything else is secondary."

"Yeah, me too," Nori supplemented. "For me, it was knowing my acceptance. I always had a problem fitting in with the crowd and in essence ran with the wrong people. It wasn't until I accepted Jesus and realized he accepted me just the way he created me, I'm telling you," she paused as tears formed in her eyes, "that did it for me—knowing how much he loved me and accepted me with all my quirks, like fishing."

"Fishing?" I asked.

"When I was younger I was over at my friend's house and her family took me fishing. I fell in love with it. That was meditation for me and something I wanted to spend my free time doing. But being born and raised in the inner city, fishing is not an experience most kids enjoyed and I was often teased because of it. Naturally, I acted like I didn't like it and spent my time doing what the people in the neighborhood did. It basically included sleeping around, hitting the bong and downing shot after shot.

"After I got born again I realized Jesus implanted the desire to fish in my heart for my pleasure. There's no other reason. I'm not supposed to start a fishing ministry or fishing business. He gave me that as sheer recreation."

"Okay." I said, wiping tears from my eyes and blowing my nose.

Sarah said, "I love sharing my testimony with people and encouraging them if I can. But I just want to tell you, my testimony is not only for me. It is for anyone who chooses to believe. Jesus died on the cross for everybody, not just Nori and me, and anytime you want to receive him all you have to do is ask him to enter your heart. It's that simple."

"Receive him?"

"Just confess with your mouth that he is Lord. It is an easy prayer and not as complicated as church has made it out to be. He wants a relationship with you, not for you to follow all these man-made rules. All you got to do is ask."

I completed the tattoo on her foot and small-talked about her music, touring and the music business.

As I was about to open the door to let them out, Nori asked me, "Do you mind if we pray for you?"

"For what?" I asked.

"That God will make himself real and known to your heart. I want to pray for peace."

"I guess that's fine." I left the door closed.

Sarah and Nori both grabbed my hands to form a circle.

Sarah began praying, "Heavenly Father, I just thank You today for this precious child of yours. God, You are no respecter of persons and just like

You revealed Yourself to me, I believe You will reveal yourself to Alcatraz. Lord, she is hurting inside and Your Word says that You are the Comforter, so I just pray right now that You comfort her, God. Give her an inner peace that surpasses understanding, Father. I thank You that Your finished work of the cross heals Alcatraz of her past wounds.

"Father, I thank You that by the blood of Jesus she is healed in her spirit, soul and body. I speak restoration and divine protection over her right now. I pray that You reveal to her Your unconditional love for her. Show her how much You love her and approve of her, Lord. Unmask Your heart to hers. I ask that love floods into her heart right now, in the name of Jesus. May Your truth awaken every fiber in her being right now. Your Words do not, cannot and will not come back null or void. And I pray all this in the name of Jesus Christ. Amen."

My entire body heated up. A blazing fire overwhelmed my chest, belly, arms and legs. The air got incredibly heavy and thick like an invisible down comforter wrapped around me on a chilly day. My knees shook and I felt too weak to remain standing. I stepped forward to open the door and my right leg gave out on me. I fell toward the door.

"Are you alright?" Sarah asked me.

"I'm fine," I lied. I quickly and kindly thanked Nori and Sarah for their prayer and business and ushered them to the front door.

* * * *

I went back into the private room, locked the door behind me, grabbed a beer out of the mini fridge and sat down in the chair. I stared at myself in the mirror, then I looked up to the ceiling and twirled my hair around my finger. Finally, fifteen months after my move to Los Angeles, on October 29, 2005 at 4:34 p.m., I decided. I got down on my knees, folded my hands and prayed.

"God, I have had a lot of things happen to me that make me feel like I don't deserve to be saying this, but I really do want to know You. I can't quite understand how, but I just feel that You do exist. I don't know everything about You but I do believe that there is one truth, and I think love is that truth. So...I confess that Jesus is Lord of my life. I believe he died on the cross and rose from the grave on the third day. I believe my sins are forgiven and..." I paused, then slowly proclaimed, "I believe that You *do* love me."

Immediately a strong force poured into my heart! An undeniable angelic presence stood there with me and completely embraced me. All the heaviness weighing on my heart lifted and a quiet peace entered. This feeling reminded me of the meditation I did while in yoga class, but I was not meditating.

I was wide awake, flying in the sky, stretched in this warm wave of love. I became oblivious to where I was, who I was, what I was doing or supposed to be doing. I didn't want to leave this moment. I felt like I was walking in heaven with not a care in the world.

And then I heard, "Receive My love!"

I fell forward in happy tears. Those were the words I'd been wanting someone to say to me since my family died. I didn't know how badly I needed to hear them but he apparently did because I could not stop crying. I just laid there on the floor in what felt like a bubble being swooped up by my spiritual Prince Charming basking in a peaceful love that satisfied my heart like no other vice.

Just then the door swung open.

"What the Hell are you doing in here? We've been pounding on the door for an hour!" Moon yelled.

There's no way I've been on the floor for an hour!

"Your last appointment left at four thirty. It's now 5:37! What are you doing in here? And why are you laying on the floor?" Moon fussed. He waited for me to respond.

I glanced up to notice all my co-workers staring down at me. "I've found the best high!"

"What?" Yellow Bone asked.

"Where'd you get it from?" Ebony asked.

"Jesus is what I mean. He loves me. This is so awesome. I can't even put into words what I feel right now. I feel like I'm surfing in the Pacific. His presence carried me to another state, like not even here on this planet. Like I just kissed heaven. This is better than X!"

I didn't notice how ridiculous I sounded until I snapped back into the moment and noticed that everyone was looking at me like I needed to be admitted to a mental hospital.

"Uh, Traz," Josh started. "What are you talking about?"

"I'm talking about Jesus!" I yelled. "I just gave my life to him."

"Just right now?" Josh asked.

"Yeah, right now, and I'm telling you guys I am so high!"

"Jesus makes you high? Dude, if I'd of known

that I would have believed in him years ago," Yellow Bone cracked, though I believe he was serious.

"This isn't about *getting* high. This is about experiencing his love." I stood up and walked toward the door. "I just got saved!"

"Saved from what?" Sang asked.

"Saved from myself. Saved from sin. Saved from Hell."

"All in the last hour?" Alex asked.

"I'm serious. I am a new person now," I said.

"So you're a Christian now?" Ebony asked.

I thought for a moment. "Yeah, I guess so. I am a Christian now."

"Enough with all this Christian stuff. Let's get back to this high," Bone interjected.

"Well, you know now that we can't be friends anymore," Josh said.

"Why?" I asked.

"'Cause I hate Christians and I hate Jesus. I don't want to be around anyone professing Christ."

"How do you hate Jesus, Josh? You don't even know him." I was offended by his comment. We had become good friends and he had never sounded like that before, not even when we were talking about how he thought Jesus was just a good man or when I told him Hinduism wasn't for me.

"Oh, and you do? You've known the man for an hour, Traz. I've been studying him for years. Trust me, the guy is the biggest con artist in history. He brainwashed all his coverts to give all their money to the church so the preacher can live fat while the congregation is on welfare."

"Whatever, dude," Thai said. It was really weird because he never adds his two cents about religion or politics, or anything else for that matter. "He's no more of a con than any other man professing to see God like Buddha, Mohammed or Joseph Smith."

"No, trust me." Josh turned back to me. "Once you start studying the history of him you will notice how he brainwashed people and performed witchcraft all of his life. He was wise, I will give him that. He had great insight into life, but as far as his powers or lordship, that's all just a bunch of crap."

"The girl just met the guy, Josh. Dang! You could at least give her some time to digest what just happened before shooting off at the mouth," Ebony said.

"Just know you're in for a big disappointment, kid. A big disappointment," Josh said. He left the room.

"Don't let him destroy your moment," Sang consoled me, rolling his eyes in Josh's direction. "He's only going by his experiences. You can't let that dictate your life decision. If Jesus is the one for you then don't let anyone talk you out of it."

"Yeah, if you are high on Jesus then stay there. I'd pay big money for that kind of high," Thai jumped in.

"Thanks, guys," I said, relieved that at least not everyone thought I was crazy.

"Well, let's get back to work," Moon interrupted, sounding like a corporate professional. "That's cool to know what you're going through. Just make sure it doesn't start affecting your work. You can't afford to be locked up in the private room lying on the floor for an hour. Got it?"

"Understood. Thank you, guys," I said. Everyone left the room.

I sat back in my chair, still on cloud nine from my personal experience with God.

I smiled to myself as this thought ran through my head, "Thank You Jesus for chasing me all these years and loving me unconditionally despite my ignorance of you." I closed my eyes and breathed deeply, relishing the moment. I reached in the fridge to grab another Dos Equis, opened it and guzzled it down. I quickly cleaned up the work station in the private room and walked over to the door.

Glancing around the room I placed my hand over the light switch. "Now what am I supposed to do?" I turned off the light.

THE END

BOOK 2 EXCERPT

ALCATRAZ THE RIGHTEOUS PEARL

PRELUDE

"You did what?" Kuriko had been making a peanut butter and jelly sandwich, but she set down the knife and bread in the middle of spreading the jelly.

"I did it. I gave my life to Jesus," I said.

"When?"

"Today at work. Some rocker chick named Sarah Kelly came to get a tattoo, then next thing I know she's telling me she was a prostitute, raised in orphanages and Jesus was the first love she'd experienced. I couldn't help it. I broke down crying."

"Wait, wait, wait. Why were you crying?"

"'Cause, Rico. I felt this power coming from her. I couldn't even line her foot. Just being around her made me nervous. Then when I tried to excuse myself her friend Nori damn near tackled me in front of the door so I couldn't avoid them."

"So you're saved now?"

I thought about it. "Yeah. Yeah, I guess I am."

"Well, it's about time you made up your mind."

I told her how Josh wrote me off after my salvation.

"You're kidding me! He did not undermine you in front of everyone 'cause of Jesus," Kuriko said. She picked up her sandwich again.

"He said he studied the man for a while and is convinced I'll be deceived by Jesus' teachings and the church."

"Don't pay any attention to him. He probably didn't mean it. I bet we go over his house tomorrow and he throws some chicken on the grill, concocts his famous Mojitos and forgets all about it."

"I hope so."

"So now what? You gonna attend church every Sunday now?"

"That Jehovah's Witness did give me her card and told me to call her if I had any questions. I'm still not quite sure the differences between their beliefs and the rest of Christianity."

Kuriko threw the knife in the sink and turned to look at me. "One is sane and the other insane, that's the difference. Please tell me you won't attend Kingdom Hall?"

I belted out a laugh. "What is it with you and Jehovah's Witnesses?"

"Seriously, Traz, they are by far the most annoying religion on the planet. I'm afraid they might get you to drink the kool-aid at their meeting then you'll want to drag me door to door with you on Saturday mornings. I'm telling you now, I'll have nothing to do with any of 'em"

"They didn't seem crazy to me. I mean, they were getting tattoos against their religion's policies. Justice told me tattooing is one of the forbidden sins."

"Everything is a forbidden sin, that's the problem. Trust me. Whether they seem normal or not they are all crazy. Every single last one of them."

I settled into Kuriko's white Umarmung.

"You okay?" Kuriko asked me. She downed a glass of milk.

"I wish I could describe how I feel in words, Rico. I am totally stoked. My heart feels so full. This is gonna sound strange, but I feel like I just French kissed God."

"Is he a good kisser?"

I smiled. "The best kisser. I can't imagine a man's kiss feeling like that. His embrace was warm, soft and loving, nothing like I'd ever experienced before."

"Soft and loving? No. Men don't kiss like that, if they kiss at all. They're too busy shoving their tongues down your throat and ordering you to bend over. Nothing gentle about the ordeal. Take it from me."

I chuckled at Kuriko momentarily until her face changed from joking to serious. With great shame in her eyes she looked down on the ground. The room remained quiet for a few minutes. Finally eyeball to eyeball, she asked me, "Do you think he would French kiss me as lovingly?"

This question caught me off guard because Buddhist philosophy, meditation and prayer were very much a regular part of Kuriko's daily regime.

"Why do you ask? I thought you really loved the Buddha?" I asked.

"I do. But as I sit here and listen to your Jesus

story I realize that love is lacking in my relationship with the Buddha. In all my life I've never felt a warm, soft, gentle love from Buddha. Not back in Japan, not in the temple or even in my prayer closet. Not anywhere. So I was just wondering. Do you think he would accept me the same way you describe? Or would my lifestyle warrant harsher treatment?"

"Jesus accepts you right now, Kuriko, despite your profession. You've probably just been living like me and haven't noticed."

1

"What!" I shouted. I couldn't believe it.

"I'm sorry, kid, I have to let you go," Moon said.

"What do you mean, let me go? I have appointments booked for the next two weeks."

Blue Moon stood guard at the reception desk. He wouldn't let me go to my booth.

"Alcatraz, I believe you are a very talented and promising tattoo artist who will no doubt go far in the field, but I can't have outbursts like I had yesterday in this shop, kid. Highly unprofessional. That makes people here extremely uncomfortable, and I'm one of them. So I went ahead and packed up your station for you. All your supplies are here. I even threw in some extra materials so you can freelance. Sorry it had to end this way, kid, but I'm in a tough spot here."

I knew immediately Moon was talking about Josh. That jerk! He probably bitched to Moon, "If she continues to work here then I quit." Since he has seniority over me, and everyone else in the shop, Moon caved in. I couldn't believe it! All because I made Jesus my Savior?

"Moon, come on, surely we can work this out. I experienced a supernatural love yesterday. I didn't know that was gonna happen to me or else I would have waited until I got home. Come on, man." I threw up my hands. "You can't fire me because of that. I work too hard here and I know you see that. I'll keep it under control from now on. I promise."

Moon hesitated for a moment. "Here." He slowly reached behind the desk and handed me my stuff. I could tell he didn't want to do this. He must have felt strapped because Josh was a cash cow. Moon looked back towards the other tattoo artists then turned to me. "If you need a recommendation just have 'em call me. I'll refer you to any shop in town. You won't have a problem getting another gig. I'm sure of it." He turned around and walked towards his office in the back.

I stood there for a minute, stunned. I looked around for Josh, but as usual he wasn't at the shop yet. His day didn't begin until two p.m. I turned around to leave and almost ran over Ebony.

"What's with the box?" she asked.

"I know this is a long shot, but have you seen Josh this morning?" I asked her.

"Not since yesterday. Why?" She took another glance at the box then gasped. "Oh no."

"What? What do you know, Ebony? Tell me," I said.

She motioned me to follow her outside and we went to the corner coffee shop. I ordered a Java Chip Frappuccino double blended and she got a Mudslide Frappuccino with an extra shot of espresso. We sat at a nearby table to talk for a few minutes before her one o'clock.

"Yesterday after you left early I heard Joshi spittin' at Moon on my way to the ladies room," Ebony said.

"Yeah? What did he say?"

"It went along the lines of, 'Moon I refuse to work here with that demon worshipper.' Moon was like, 'I thought she was your friend. What's all this nonsense? 'Cause of God?' Then Joshi was like, 'I don't care, man. I don't do Christians. Either you get rid of her or I walk, and I'll take my clients with me.' Joshi stormed out of the room and I pretended to be coming out of the restroom. I saw Moon with his head down cradled in his hands. I know he didn't want to let you go but you know Joshi can convert a bum off the street into a regular, even if the bum didn't have the money. He'd kick the habit until Josh was paid in full."

"That jerk! I can't believe him. As many times as we hung out? I mean, he gave me my first tattoo. Not only that, but he showed me the ropes!"

"Exact same thing Moon said, but you know he's a businessman at heart. I'm sure he'll give you a good reference."

"He told me he would, which is cool. He technically doesn't have to do that since he fired me." I sighed.

"I'll keep my ears peeled for you, too. If I hear any gigs open I'll definitely give you a call. Do I have your number?"

Ebony and I swapped numbers while walking back to the shop. We stopped outside.

"What are you gonna do for money?" Ebony asked me. "Do you have enough to pay bills?"

"I have a few grand saved from the last year of work. I live with Rico so my expenses aren't that high but I do need to find another gig soon. I'll probably only last two or three months off my savings."

"Well, if you ever need anything just call me. I do pretty well. I can spare you a few thousand if you need it."

"Thanks, girl, but I should be okay. There is one favor I have to ask, though."

"Shoot."

"Can you text me the numbers of my clients? I had appointments booked for the next two weeks and would hate to miss out 'cause of Josh's stupidity."

"I hear you. Yeah, sure I can do that. Do you have everything you need to freelance?" she asked.

"Pretty much. I just need to consolidate everything."

"Do you drive?"

"Illegally. I'm learning to drive Rico's Mustang."

"At least you can make house calls. There's good money in house visits, girl. No overhead, booth rental fees or manager cuts. It's all yours."

"Nice," I said.

"Well, I got to get going. My one o'clock is probably waiting for me. I'll call you with your clients' numbers sometime tomorrow. My day is too hectic today."

"All right. Thank you so much, Ebony."

"No problem. See you around."

I walked slowly back to my condo with several thoughts running through my mind: What am I supposed to do for work? How am I gonna pay rent? Where am I gonna get a job at fifteen years old? Moon did Kuriko a favor by offering me an apprenticeship but there's no guarantee another shop owner will extend the same favor. I wouldn't even turn sixteen for another three and a half months! I didn't have any legal identification, social security card or birth certificate to even apply for a *real* job. I didn't even know what state to begin digging for those documents. California, where I was allegedly born? Illinois, where I was state property or Utah where the Robinsons adopted me last July?

Losing my job at the tattoo parlor turned my world completely upside down. Other fifteen year old girls loitered around in the tenth grade in their cute plaid skirts, studied for SATs, borrowed their daddy's car for driver's ed and worked at Forever 21. I was an eighth grade dropout, runaway, semi-tattoo artist rooming with a battered Japanese stripper. I didn't have a mommy or daddy to get me out of difficult situations in life. The only person I had was three years, three months and twelve days older than me, and I decided to wake up.

* * * *

"He fired you?" Kuriko croaked, half asleep.

"He said my spiritual outburst offended everybody in the shop, but I know Josh was the only one behind this."

"You can't be serious? Is that legal? Can Moon just fire employees for their beliefs?"

"Well, technically I wasn't supposed to be working there in the first place, remember? We both lied about my age so it's not like I have a case against him. Whatever. I'll figure something out."

"That totally sucks, puss." She yawned and

rubbed the sleep out of her eyes. "I can talk to him if you want."

"No, don't bother. You've done enough for me already."

"Well, it shouldn't be that hard for you to get hired by another shop. At least now you have a tattoo portfolio."

"But I'm still a minor. No boss in their right mind will hire me. Moon was doing *you* a favor."

"I can get Mamasan to get you a job at The Geisha Room."

"The Geisha Room? You mean as a dancer?" I raised my eyebrows.

"No, no, no. You can wait tables. The clients in that place are loaded. I've personally watched them leave a ninety dollar tip on a three hundred dollar tab. You could earn money there while you find another tattoo job."

The thought of working at the Geisha Room didn't excite me. Flirting with middle-aged men seated next to teenage girls was not my idea of a good time. Plus, this past year I've overheard Kuriko crying herself asleep on several occasions after work. I never dared venture into her room to ask why though I know her tears had everything to do with her job. However, I did need the money and there was no telling how long it would take me to find another full time tattoo gig.

"Let me think about it and get back to you. I want to search other options first," I said.

"Totally understandable. Let me know what you come up with. In the meantime, no worries about the rent. Just focus on finding another job while I cuss Josh out."

"No, don't even bother. I don't care about him anymore. If he's that mad about my salvation then we don't need to be friends. I have other issues to deal with."

"I'm removing him from my client list. I'll make my money elsewhere."

"How much did you make from him?"

"I could hit Josh up for an easy three to four hundred dollars for a few hours, and he wasn't even that demanding." She grabbed her phone from the nightstand and started pressing buttons. "Deleted. On to the next trick."

"I don't know how I will ever repay you for being so nice to me," I said.

"Oh, don't sweat it. What are friends for?"

"True." I lay on top of her to give her a hug.

"I don't want a hug from you, girl. I want a ham and cheese omelet with a warmed croissant, Greek yogurt and a fruit smoothie."

I smiled and hit my roommate with one of her pillows, then ran off the kitchen to prepare her breakfast.

That night I lay wide awake in my bed. Even though I'd been up for the past eighteen hours my body was not tired. Within twenty-four hours my life had done a one-eighty. I gave my life to Christ, was betrayed by a friend and fired from my job. I lost all my personal identity because being a tattoo artist wasn't just a job for me. It was who I was. Now I didn't know how to view myself. Tattooing gave me a reason to wake up in the morning.

I liked the stability of working at one central location and attracting clients to my booth instead of chasing them around Los Angeles. Plus, clients drove in from all over LA County, Orange County, Riverside County and even San Diego County to visit the infamous Human Canvass. The artists claimed zero marketing effort to reach clients but were responsible for the 100 percent retention rate. A walk-in or referral more than likely turned into a life-long customer. Now freelancing was on my shoulders and I didn't have a client roster, license or car to drive. I would have to bother Kuriko for her Mustang every night, and I knew it wasn't gonna fly for long. She made her own appointments.

Feeling frustrated and restless I got up and dug in the one container I kept from my childhood. In it I found the Bible that Greg Lubbock gave me in Religious Studies back at Valeo Academy. I randomly opened up the thick book to the Gospel according to Matthew.

I read, "Come unto Me, all ye that labour and are heavy laden, and I will give you rest." I had heard God tell me to come to Him: in the picture at the Catholic Church, in the astronomy book at the library and during my yoga meditation. All three places I heard the same thing. "Come to Me and I will give you rest." I had no idea that passage was actually in the Bible.

I closed the book and looked up at my closet ceiling.

I closed my eyes, inhaled deeply and prayed, "God, I don't know if you can hear me. I'm not quite sure how this Christian thing is supposed to go but I really need help now. I gave my life to you yesterday and got fired today because of it. Is that how living for you goes? Am I to suffer now that I believe in Jesus? I thought life would get better and right now it seems to be getting worse. I need a job. I need a car. I need a license. I need a place to worship you. You say here that your yoke is easy and burden light but I feel heavy, confused and alone. What am I to do? Why did you want me in your kingdom so bad? Where do I go from here?"

Thump. Thump. Thump. I snapped out of my prayer at the banging coming from the front door. I picked myself off the closet floor and heard Kuriko rushing to open it.

"Well hello, stranger." I heard her say.

"How are you, my beauty?" an unfamiliar male voice responded.

I cracked open my door and saw an old, fat Asian man with thick glasses dressed in a sharp grey Gucci suit.

"Would you care for some water?" Kuriko offered.

"Where's the bedroom?"

"I see you like to get right down to business. This way, my prize."

Within minutes all I could hear was groaning, huffing, puffing, bed squeaking, screaming, then silence. I heard faint small talk before her bedroom door opened.

The man walked into the living room sweaty but fully dressed. "Thank you for your kindness on such short notice. I shall return home to my family but will be in town next week. Do you have availability?" He handed Kuriko a stack of money.

"You know I always make time for you. Just call me from the airport," Kuriko said.

He kissed her on the cheek and left.

"Who was that?" I asked, scaring her as she

closed the door behind her gentleman suitor.

"That? Oh, that was Hibachi-sama. A longtime friend."

"How much money did he give you?"

"Well, let's see, shall we?" She smirked and counted the twenties and fifties in her hand. "Three hundred and seventy dollars. Not bad for three minutes."

"Why are you sleeping with all these guys, Kuriko?"

"Why does it matter to you?"

"'Cause I care about you and don't want you to get hurt."

"Ha." She laughed out loud. "Girl, these tricks can't do any more damage than what's already been done."

"Seriously, Rico." I walked towards her. "I love you and I don't want these guys to flip you the wrong way."

"Look, chica. I appreciate your concern, I really do. When I say nothing can be done to me that hasn't already been done I mean it. I've been turning tricks since I was four. I got this." With that she went in her room and closed the door.

END OF EXCERPT

ABOUT THE AUTHOR

A.R. Robinson was born in Chicago, Illinois and enjoys day spas, mission trips, yoga, fighting against sex trafficking, and writing in coffee shops.

THANK YOU for purchasing this book. I hope you enjoyed it! I would love to hear your comments and feedback. Please feel free to email me at aleshia@lovegodandtattoos.

If you have a moment to spare, I would really welcome a short review on the site where you purchased the book. Good or bad review, as I cherish honesty. Your help in spreading the word is greatly appreciated.

To listen to the Love, God & Tattoos podcast; watch inspirational videos; and buy Love, God & Tattoos merchandise, visit www.lovegodandtattoos.com

And you can find me on Facebook, Twitter, Instagram and Youtube @LoveGodandTattoos.

CPSIA information can be obtained
at www.ICGtesting.com
Printed in the USA
LVOW04s1821220416
484899LV00012B/122/P